2044

The Problem isn't Big Brother.
It's Big Brother, Inc.

2044

Eric Lotke

iUniverse, Inc.
New York Bloomington

iUniverse books may be ordered through booksellers or by contacting:

iUniverse
1663 Liberty Drive
Bloomington, IN 47403
www.iuniverse.com
1-800-Authors (1-800-288-4677)

ISBN: 978-1-4401-3471-5 (sc)
ISBN: 978-1-4401-3472-2 (ebook)

Printed in the United States of America

iUniverse rev. date: 04/23/2009

Table of Contents

Acknowledgments

I wrote this book by myself. It was long, it was hard, and it was lonely.

I wrote this book in the morning before the kids woke up and at night after they went to sleep. I wrote this book on weekends and holidays and when other people were on vacation. I owe this book to nobody but myself. My own hard work and my own solitary labor.

But no! That's a terribly cramped and stingy definition of gratitude. This book was a collective effort. I owe thanks to countless before me.

I owe deepest thanks to Amy Mortimer, whom I had the good fortune to marry and who supported her husband's desire to spend time like this. I owe thanks to my parents who raised the kind of kid who could do it. And I owe thanks to my own kids, who shared me with this quixotic adventure.

Of course, I owe professional thanks as well. To Richard Peabody for his novel seminar. To Bob Borosage and Roger Hickey of the Campaign for America's Future, and Isaiah Poole for copy editing in the endgame.

Behind them lurk so many others. I owe thanks my high school teachers, Ms. Hourihan who taught me sentences and Ms. Pertschuk who taught me paragraphs. I owe thanks to Mr. Leithem for his cynicism, to Mr. Phillips for his excellent judgment, and to my college physics professor (Was it Ralph Baierlein?) who made room for the *Voice of the Dolphins* in our semester on relativity. I owe thanks to Arlington County, Virginia, for its excellent library system, and to Temple Beth El for a quiet place to work twice a week.

The list goes on and on. I thank friends whose conversations shaped the political backstory of the novel. Drew Shepherd taught me the acronym PPW, and his lovely bride, Laura, fooled me once. I owe thanks to Patrice Gaines of *Laughing in the Dark,* Rick Perlstein of *Nixonland*, and Tyrone Parker who always greets with a hug and a smile. I even owe thanks for action at a distance. George Soros may save the world despite itself. The city of Bombay inspired Kaiserville, and the DC jail and the Sussex II prison in Virginia informed the belly chains of chapter three and Jessica's failed attempt to bang on the bars in chapter twenty-four.

I owe thanks to people who declined to publish this novel but in so doing, taught me something about the manuscript or the publishing industry. Literary agents Liz Trupin-Pulli, Timothy Wager and Manie Barron all declined with class. I even learned something from agents who couldn't be bothered to return my SASE. It all goes into the mix.

I might fancy that I sat down at a blank page to write – but hardly! The page was covered with fingerprints. People whose names I've forgotten. Bumper stickers on cars of people I never met. I owe thanks to all of them. If I like what I now see on the page, I owe thanks to everyone who left fingerprints on it.

But especially I thank my wife. Born on summer solstice, she truly is the longest, sunniest day of the year. And thanks again to my parents and my terrific children. Starting tomorrow, I won't yell at you after bedtime.

Thank you all.

Eric Lotke, January 2009

PART ONE

MARKETPLACE

Chapter One

It was a clear cold night in April and the moon was glowing gold. Across its face scrolled the words, *Microtech Corporation*.

Malcolm Moore tucked his chin into his coat to escape the chill breeze and walked as fast as he could. He was on his way home from work, and all he wanted was sleep.

He slipped past a park with all its benches empty and a hair salon filled with people getting styled. The next shop sold water filters, "Microtech pure." The message flashed brightly but didn't move or make a sound, part of the order that brought people to New Angeles, a city that started as a corporate park on the outskirts of old Los Angeles, then outgrew the unruly original.

A commuter transpo whisked past with an electric whir, the cold draft in its wake chasing him deeper into his collar. Beside him walked pedestrians on motorized rollways, heads down, hats pulled low, adding their own stride to the machine's. Malcolm walked alone on the paved, unmoving part of the sidewalk. It cost him six minutes of productivity every day and his colleagues judged him for it, but he preferred the exercise. His apartment was close enough.

Thc glass door of *Cafeteria L'Express* opened as he passed. He despised this place, but he was exhausted and famished so he stepped inside. In the blast of warmth he removed his hat, revealing brown hair cut so short it never needed brushing. His eyes were dark and his cheeks shaved clean.

He threaded through rows of people at gleaming countertops, bent low over meal cartridges, headphones on their ears, staring at their own television sets or the giant screens lining the walls. The only sound was the low buzz of private soundtracks and once, from a headphone as he passed, a gunshot. Malcolm grabbed a chicken cartridge from the rack and leaned to give a scanner a good view of his retina. It beeped, and eight Globos – Global Currency Units – disappeared from his bank account. The machine printed out a receipt:

April 7, 2044
Speedy thanks from L'Express

He slipped into a spot between a huge man eating from two dinner cartridges and an old woman dozing before an image of trees. He nodded greetings as he squeezed between, but the man was too busy racing around the channels and the woman just snoozed. Malcolm kept his headset off, but still his eyes followed the headlines on his screen. Vishnu Johnson beat Samuel Schmidt in the quarterfinals of the Singleton cup; coffee futures set a record high; water riots broke out in Karachi.

Out the window stood the Tentek building, its tapered pinnacle dominating the skyline. Malcolm worked halfway up that tower in the Family Safety Division, designing weapons for home protection. His mind pressed back to work. The motion detector needed adjustment on an alarm system and a biological disinfecting agent kept dying in transit. Malcolm found it difficult to care. He never knew what happened after he did his part, or what problem might come next. He felt like a trained monkey performing tricks for pay, and he hadn't seen the sun in weeks.

An ad reminded him of his last decent meal, a blind date with attorney Jessica Frey, more than a month ago. In theory Jessica was an excellent match – attractive, accomplished and athletic – but the evening was just proof that dating was more trouble than it was worth. She spent the evening talking about international trade agreements and an upholstery service that rotated her pillow covers every month. Neither had called the other since the date.

Suddenly, a hideous grinding screech, as of some monstrous machine running out of oil, howled through the room. Malcolm winced at the shock of sound; the sleepy woman beside him gasped and lurched upright. Lights flashed and every television displayed the words, *Action Alert.* A bass voice thundered, "Breaking news. Terror in the streets." A siren wailed. "This just in from the Counterterrorism Division."

Every screen flashed to the same image. Patrols in black body armor chasing a terrorist down a dark alley, cutting him down with bullets so powerful they ripped through his body and cratered the wall behind. The audience spiked to attention; the fat man froze with his fork in the air. The screens faded to black with the blood red letters, *Terror Alert.*

Malcolm kept eating, indifferent to the perpetual crime alerts and terrorist warnings – but the next image brought him to his feet. His father. Not just on the little screen in front of him but on the giant screens along the wall. His father's face filled the room. *Bernard Moore of Pasadena*, the screens declared. One eye was black. A bloody bruise darkened his forehead.

A newscaster with the square chin of a security guard appeared on screen. "Bernard Moore of Pasadena was arrested this evening on charges of bioterrorism." The old woman gasped. "Doctor Barry Edwards of Counterterrorism has the details."

The official face of the Counterterrorism Division appeared on the screen. "Our water is scarce but at least it's safe," he declared. "A tiny quantity of the wrong microorganism could change all that." He paused while new images filled the screen: guards patrolling the water supply, crop dusters spraying wheat fields, a baby with a face so distorted and skin so gangrenous the fat man dropped his fork and a gasp erupted from the far side of the room.

But Doctor Edwards told everyone to remain calm and that matters were under control. "An alert shopkeeper noticed suspicious activity and notified the authorities with his Tentek Safe-T-Buzzer. Thank goodness he had it. Thank goodness he was paying attention. Counterterrorism took care of the rest."

The newscaster announced that the Tentek Safe-T-Buzzer was available "at retailers near you," and the televisions returned to regular programming.

A collective sigh washed through the *L'Express* as people realized that everything was okay after all. Shoulders relaxed, people sat down. Malcolm stayed on his feet. Doctor Edwards never said what his father had done. He wanted to shout at the television. *What happened? What did he do? What did the shopkeeper see?*

He looked around for someone to talk to, signs that anybody still cared, but the *L'Express* had returned to normal, each screen carrying its own show. The old woman beside Malcolm sank back into the stand of trees and the fat man idly surfed the channels. The remaining sounds were slurps and scratches and the murmur of a baby against someone's chest. Malcolm sat down and turned to the fat man beside him. "He's not a terrorist," he declared.

The man kept skipping channels.

"He's not a terrorist," Malcolm repeated. He leaned closer, made himself impossible to ignore. "He's my father. He's a department store manager." The fat man didn't answer but Malcolm had his attention. "He's not a terrorist."

The man turned to him, unable to escape. He took another bite and worked it down slowly, then shared his conclusion before he returned to the television. "They couldn't say it if it wasn't true."

Chapter Two

Malcolm nearly tripped on the package as he entered his apartment. The size of a shoebox and professionally wrapped in brown paper, the parcel service left it just inside his door. He wasn't expecting anything.

The lights and television turned on when he stepped inside. He listened for news of his father while he hung his coat and carried the package to the shallow alcove that served as kitchen.

He grabbed a knife and sliced through a seam in the wrapping paper. Someone had paid four Globos for postage but provided no return address. He poked through loose packing material to yet another box. This one had a tab to grab, which made a ripping sound as he pulled it across the track. The box sprung open.

Inside was a glass phial and a note.

He removed the phial carefully and held it up to the light. It was simple enough – like a jelly jar with a screw-on lid, filled with a clear colorless liquid. It looked like water, but Malcolm knew it could be anything.

The note was more puzzling. On plain paper in hasty handwriting, it said:

Let's talk. Love,

Dad.

The package had been shipped yesterday. One day before the arrest.

Now he knew two things: One, his father had been arrested on charges of bioterrorism, apparently involving water. Two, he now had in his possession a quantity of water, sent by his father, under circumstances that could only be considered suspicious. He could guess that his father sent him this water because he knew the police were on his trail, and he could also guess that this water could get him in a lot of trouble.

After that, the guessing grew thin.

He turned the phial over in his hands, watching the liquid slosh around, then held it as if to unscrew the lid, testing the seal.

The lid stayed tight. The phial had been carefully wrapped to arrive intact.

He looked again through the package and all the packaging material. He was missing nothing. No further clues appeared. He kept staring at the note. "Let's talk" was an understatement the size of New Angeles.

Then he remembered that his father left a voicemail pointing the same direction. He pressed buttons at his desk until he found it. The date stamp indicated that six days had passed.

"Hello, Malcolm," the recording began. "It's been too long since we talked. There's something I want to discuss with you, though. Maybe I can buy you a cup of coffee."

He meant to call back. He'd been busy of course, pressed by deadlines, and it kept slipping his mind. He didn't realize that the next time he saw his father would be as a terrorist on TV He played the message again; it was as useless as ever, but he saved it carefully.

Only one other person might know or care. A few keystrokes later his mother appeared on the video link, sitting on a couch Malcolm recognized from childhood, an empty dinner cartridge on a tray beside her. "Hello there!" she exclaimed. "Is something wrong? My birthday isn't until next month."

"Something's wrong," he replied. "What's up with dad?"

"I don't know. I haven't heard from him lately. Maybe next month. Sometimes he sends flowers on my birthday."

Malcolm's parents had been divorced for years. What started as a marriage soon became a co-housing arrangement between people too busy to talk. When they did talk, it was usually to argue over the laundry or an unusual expense. Eventually they realized there was no point even in maintaining the co-housing arrangement. They parted amicably and Malcolm, without brothers or sisters, spent his teenage years alone with his mother.

He explained what he'd seen on TV and asked if she knew anything.

She barely seemed to be listening. "Terrorism would surprise me," she said. "But your dad did have his own way of doing things."

Malcolm thanked her and disconnected, then returned to the phial resting on the table, as innocent as a breakfast drink. But what was in it?

Malcolm needed to talk to his father. More than that, he realized, he needed to help. His father had just been arrested. Surely he was supposed to do something about it. Or at least learn what was happening.

Then he remembered the lawyer of the bad date. Jessica Frey spent too much time talking about pillows but she was the closest he had to a lawyer friend. Her number was still in the call log.

"Jessica Frey," she said after the first ring. That was lucky: they'd played phone tag for a week on the way to that bad date. She'd blanked the vidlink so it showed her face but not the scene behind. She wore a blue business shirt but her black hair was loose; Malcolm couldn't tell if she were still in the office.

Malcolm hesitated a moment, unsure what to say. "It's Malcolm Moore," he began. "We met a few weeks ago — "

She cut him off. "I remember."

Was she irate or just stating a fact? He couldn't tell, and he was kicking himself for not planning what to say. "It was a lousy date," he admitted. "But you didn't hate me. Maybe you could help me with a puzzlement." It was the best he could do.

Jessica smiled warmly. She seemed to share his assessment of the date and recognize his struggle for that final word. "What is it?"

He told her about the arrest.

She listened carefully, though she seemed less interested in bioterrorism than the fact that he hadn't seen his father in years. "Make sure he has a lawyer," she said. "And find out where he is." She pulled a keyboard into view and started typing even as she spoke.

"Bernard Moore of Pasadena?" she asked to confirm.

"Moore with an E."

She typed. "Do you know his birthday?"

Malcolm remembered his father's birthday but could only guess the year.

That was good enough. Jessica looked up as her computer chimed a hit. "Good news. He's in the jail."

"That's good news?"

"Very good news. We know where he is. And he's nearby. Go visit him."

"Right now?"

"Right now. People in the system get moved around regularly. By tomorrow he could be in Kentucky. He could get lost or hurt or worse, and the trail leading to his arrest gets colder every minute. Visit him now. And find him a lawyer."

"Can you be his lawyer?"

"Yes, if he needs transactional representation on international trade. No, if he's in jail for bioterrorism. I can look around, though. Your father might have a lawyer of his own and might have called him by now. But don't count on it."

"So I have to go to the jail."

"Do you have any other candidates?"

Malcolm looked down sheepishly.

"And say something nice. He's your father."

Malcolm straightened. "What do I need to find out?"

"Ask what happened. Ask when he was arrested. Whether he has a lawyer. Don't ask him if he's a terrorist. Assume you're being monitored."

Malcolm nodded in understanding. The gravity of a trip to jail was sinking in. "And I'll report my findings back to you."

"Okay, you can report your findings back to me – but only until he gets his own lawyer. You need to go right away. At this moment he's in the New Angeles Detention and Correction Center." She pressed a button and the address appeared on Malcolm's screen. "He could be moved at any time."

"I never really got to know him," Malcolm said. "Now it's too late." He noticed for the first time that her eyes were blue.

"It's not too late. It's never too late."

"I guess I'll see him soon. I owe him a cup of coffee."

"Treat yourself to a cup on the way." She smiled in a way that looked nothing like a lawyer. "He needs you at your best."

Chapter Three

The first taxi at the corner stand refused to take Malcolm to the Detention Center. "Too far," said the driver, an old man in a yellow uniform and yellow turban. He drove away empty in his yellow car.

"No return fare," said the driver of the second taxi, just as yellow.

Malcolm offered to pay both ways, plus a fee to wait while he went inside. The driver pulled away while he was talking, and stopped at the next stand down the street.

Malcolm pulled his lifelink computer from his pocket and told it where he wanted to go. "Are you sure?" it asked.

"Yes," he instructed.

Instead of directions the lifelink showed a man falling to the ground at a woman's touch. "Stun weapons," the screen declared. "Super cheap and all but invisible."

Malcolm pressed "Next" as fast as he could.

The next screen advertised clothing, "strong yet stylish, perfect wherever you go," and the next advertised snacks that "fit in your pockets, taste great and last forever."

Finally the map appeared. The New Angeles Detention Center was on the Pacific Ocean, in the same compound as a nuclear desalination facility, a great green rectangle on the map. The water in Malcolm's apartment probably started at that plant, sucked from the Pacific Ocean and boiled into steam, then captured and cooled back into purified liquid. It never occurred to him that the city jail might be in the same compound, but then he'd never thought about it.

Malcolm's path started on the Orange line subway nearby. He walked on the rollway and followed the navigator's instructions to a train heading west. The first stops were familiar. Stores he sometimes shopped, contractors he worked with at Tentek, a museum he'd always wanted to visit. After a while the navigator guided him onto a track he'd never used and, after a stretch, to another line that he didn't even know existed and didn't accept his transit credits. An hour later the train emerged from underground in a world utterly different from the place he started. In place of gleaming skyscrapers stood concrete warehouses and apartments so close to the track Malcolm could see inside the windows. The moon hovered over everything, wearing *Microtech Corporation* like an omnipresent deity.

The navigator told him to exit at a stop near a shopping center and buy a new ticket. He waited on a corner until a transpo arrived that was so decrepit it probably wouldn't even be legal in Malcolm's section of town.

Even at this hour the transpo was crowded, filled with people wearing uniforms of every color. Pink for Snappy Kleen, green for OmniSpan Enterprises, blue for Federated, his father's department store chain. Malcolm sat in one of the few empty seats beside a woman carrying two huge duffel bags, zippers bursting against the seams. The transpo was bursting with heat and reeked of human odors. Malcolm's navigator assured him he was going the right direction.

More people jammed on at every stop, until the seats all filled and then the aisles, but the space next to Malcolm remained empty. A woman across the aisle blew her nose into a Microtech handkerchief with such violence a child woke up three seats away. Finally a heavy man in an OmniSpan uniform fell into the seat beside Malcolm like garbage dumped from a truck. He pressed so tight against Malcolm on the bench that he could feel the heat from his body, smell him apart from the rest.

The radio blasted music so loud Malcolm couldn't begin to think. Electronic rhythms, indecipherable lyrics, a battering of sound that barely fit in the crowded cabin. The woman with the Microtech handkerchief tapped her feet and bounced in time.

The man beside Malcolm fell asleep despite the din. He leaned into Malcolm's side, his head dropping onto Malcolm's shoulder, breath in Malcolm's ear, his hand finding Malcolm's thigh for support. Malcolm considered what to do. He didn't want to disturb the man but this was too close, especially the hand. Finally he reached down and lifted it off.

The man stirred and shifted his weight in a different direction.

When Malcolm pulled the man's hand, he noticed an odd tattoo on the underside of his wrist, like an old- fashioned bar code. He wanted to decipher it but couldn't see it in the new position. When the woman across the aisle raised her handkerchief again to her nose, he noticed a similar tattoo on her wrist.

Next time he looked outside, the city was gone, replaced by a wasteland of dry, cracked earth. A white film covered everything, glittering under the *Microtech* moon. The transpo no longer stopped at corners, and nobody else got on or off. They all sat together, timeless in the overfilled cabin. Eventually they passed through a gate in a fence; Malcolm's navigator informed him they'd entered the desalination compound. Cisterns and pipes were surrounded by razor wire, and chimneys flashed red lights against the sky. He started to feel a salty grit in his teeth; dust from the factory, no doubt.

They passed through another fence and into the jail complex, a series of tan brick buildings about ten stories tall, the entrance marked "House of Correction." Everyone stood when the transpo stopped. Some people cheered. Malcolm waited his turn to unload, then walked in single file toward a concrete building bristling with artillery and surveillance. The building was the only gate in one final fence, three layers of razor wire marked "high voltage" with skull and crossbones. From his work in Tentek's security division, Malcolm could guess that the ground beneath the fences was electronically monitored and mined with explosives. Guards with large, very visible weapons stood by the door.

The passengers marched through the door one at a time, stopping first at a retina scan then pushing their luggage through a metal detector. But that was all. No scanning for drugs or bombs with equipment Malcolm designed at Tentek; no frisk, no pat search and no questions asked. The officers seemed busy watching a ballgame on their lifelinks. The officer by the back door haphazardly waved them onward, providing the barest illusion of secure control.

"I'm here to visit someone at the Detention Center," Malcolm asked him. "Which way should I go?"

The officer didn't even look. "Inside," he said.

"Where exactly for a legal visit?"

"Inside."

So Malcolm stepped inside. The moon was still in the sky, but barely visible over the surveillance lighting. The earth beside the walkway was parched and bare, too close to the desalination plant even for weeds.

Soon he reached a line of people stretching towards the jail building itself. Tents were pitched and blankets spread out; people looked like they'd been waiting for days. One girl slept soundly on an orange mat, surrounded by flowers she'd drawn on the pavement, colored chalks stacked neatly by her head. Beyond her was the woman with the huge duffel bags from the transpo, joyously greeted by people in line, the duffel bags open and explored with enthusiasm. Somewhere, a group of women sang harmonies in a language he couldn't understand.

An older woman in rags filled a bucket at a water tap that advertised "all you can drink." Malcolm was thirsty, but he kept walking when he saw the price. He passed dozens of women and children, and a few men, sleeping on mats or playing cards. Near the front of the line, people had changed from clothes for waiting into clothes that looked like their Sunday finest. The group closest to the door looked like a family, with women in matched turquoise dresses and two little boys wearing ties. Suddenly, the door opened and the family scrambled inside. Malcolm dashed forward before the door closed and shoved in behind. An armed guard blocked his path. "Wait until you're called." Other officers stepped forward with weapons drawn.

"I'm here on legal business. I need to see Bernard Moore."

"Lawyers use the South Entrance." The door closed in his face.

Malcolm had no idea which way was south and no signs offered clues. A young women in the green coveralls of OmniSpan Enterprises trotted over with a tray of coffee. "Steamy fresh, late at night."

"No thanks," he replied. "Do you know where the lawyers' entrance is?"

"Lawyers never come here." She held out a box of tobacco and candy. "Special discount. You're having a bad day."

"No thanks." He noticed the same tattoo on her wrist, stripes like an old-fashioned bar code. "Do you know which is the South Entrance?"

"Never heard of it. There's another entrance on the opposite side of the building. Staff only."

Malcolm walked around the building until, on the far side, he reached an unmarked door that opened when he pushed. Inside looked like an old high school gymnasium, with naked bricks and fluorescent lighting. A group of officers played cards around a folding table;

another watched a basketball game on a wallscreen TV. One officer sitting near the door called to Malcolm, "Visitors use the North door."

Malcolm walked up to him. "I'm here on legal business."

The guard seemed surprised but knew how to handle it. He shuffled towards a computer screen, clearing out an officer playing some kind of poker on the machine. "What's his name and PDID number?"

"His name is Bernard Moore. I don't have his PDID number handy" – he didn't even know what it was – "but here is his citizen identification number." He pulled out his lifelink and pressed some buttons; it took longer than he wanted but the officer was watching the basketball game. Eventually Malcolm read his father's personal identification number.

The officer didn't seem to hear.

Malcolm repeated it.

"I heard you," the officer said, without turning his head. A foul stopped the action. "What was it again?"

Malcolm repeated the number.

The officer manipulated the computer with one eye on the game, the clock counting down to halftime. He stopped working with seconds left and a breakaway on screen. The closing shot missed; the score was tied; and the game clock reset to fifteen minutes for halftime.

The officer looked at his watch. "You can visit for five minutes," he said. "We need to start right away."

He led Malcolm through a door where another officer screened him with a metal detector, then into an elevator. Malcolm couldn't see what floor the officer pressed the button for.

They walked down a corridor to a door labeled "Attorneys only." Inside was a row of stools before a plexiglass pane; on the opposite side of the plexiglass stood matching stools. A telephone handset on each stool was connected by wire to the base of the glass. They were the only people there.

Then Malcolm's father stepped into the other side, wearing an orange prison jumpsuit familiar from television. A chain held his feet together so he shuffled as he walked. Another chain bound his hands at the wrist and a third chain, wrapped around his torso, held his hands in place at his waist. Guards on either side directed him by his elbows to a stool in the center.

Malcolm sat down on his side and picked up the handset.

His father looked exhausted. Not desperate or frightened, just exhausted. The cut on his forehead had stopped bleeding but hadn't been cleaned. He tried to pick up the handset but he couldn't reach with his hands chained halfway down his body. He bent over the stool but it was too low. Eventually he kneeled onto his knees, which brought the handset into easy reach, but then he had to stand up again with his ankles tied together and his hands unable to assist.

Malcolm watched his father struggle. He'd picked up his own handset without thinking about it.

The officers beside his father just watched him.

Malcolm's officer said, "Five minutes. Sharp." He operated a control panel and Malcolm's handset came alive. Now through the receiver Malcolm could hear the chains rattling and his father struggling for air.

Finally his father sat down on the stool and held the handset up towards his ear, his head crooked sideways to bring it within range of his hands chained at the waist.

The officer on Malcolm's shoulder said, "Four minutes, twenty seconds."

Malcolm appreciated now how thick the plexiglas was; he couldn't hear anything through it and it was strong enough, no doubt, for any mechanical force. He also noticed that it was smeared with handprints and, in one spot, lipstick.

His hands in chains and head bent to one side, Malcolm's father opened the conversation. "Thank you for coming," he said. With a wry smile he added, "It's nice to see you."

Malcolm remembered that smile. He hadn't seen it in years but he grew up with it. "Do you want rocks in your soup?" his father used to say with that smile. "Or peas in your boots?"

The cut on his forehead started to bleed. "Are they treating you okay?" Malcolm asked. If his father had been arrested around dinner time, the wound was maybe five hours old.

"I need a lawyer."

"I know. Do you have one?"

"From the divorce. Larry Parker. It would be great if you could contact him for me. They gave me one call, but nobody answered. Parker, Ellis and Rideau. Your mom will know."

"I'll get him for you. We'll find a way to get you out of there."

"I don't even know why I'm in here."

"You don't?!"

"They didn't tell me."

"Did they ask you questions?"

"Lots of questions. They want to know where I got the water."

That matched the accusation on TV. "They think you're a bioterrorist. They think you put something dangerous in the water supply."

The handset slipped from his father's grasp.

The guard said, "Two minutes left."

His father took maybe half that time to recover the handset. He didn't even try to return to the stool, but kept speaking from a crouch on the floor. "That explains everything."

"Did you tell them? Did you tell them where you got the water? Maybe they'll let you go."

"I told them everything. Sayeh Kahn gave it to me. A plumber. He lives in Kaiserville."

Kaiserville was a poor section of town, known only for trouble. Malcolm couldn't imagine what his father would be doing there or what he did with people who lived there. "Why did he give it to you? Why did you take it?"

"Because it was a gift." His father stopped struggling to maintain his crouch. He relaxed and ended up flat on his back. The cord long enough to reach his head on the floor, he laid himself out like he was sunning on the beach. "The water is amazing. It's a miracle. It takes the salt out of seawater. You can drink it."

"How do you know? Did you try it? Why did he give it to you? Why do they think you're a terrorist?"

Malcolm couldn't see it but he could almost feel his father smiling on the other side. "Too many questions," his father used to tease when he was a child. "It will get you in trouble."

But his father was the one in trouble, and he was running out of time to answer. He said, "He came to my building for a repair. He's a nice guy. An old man." He rested and caught his breath. "He gave me the gift and told me how to use it. You should try it too."

"Ten seconds," said Malcolm's officer. He reached toward the handset; Malcolm turned so his body stood between the guard and the receiver.

His father couldn't hear and, from the floor, couldn't see what was happening. He kept talking. "Mix a cup into saltwater. After it turns fresh, take another cup out to desalinate the next batch. Drink the rest. Forever. It renews itself."

"You drank it?!"

"Drink it? I tried to get Federated to *sell* it. It's a miracle. We'd make a fortune. I have a follow-up meeting scheduled for tomorrow." Again came the sarcastic grin. "I don't think I'll make it."

The guard pulled on Malcolm's shoulder. "Time's up."

Malcolm's father rolled so Malcolm could see his face. "Goodbye, son," he said. "It's been a long time." His eyes were intense. "I love you."

The guard was pulling the receiver from Malcolm's hand. "I'll look for your lawyer."

Chapter Four

Malcolm got home about three hours before he needed to wake up, and took a pill to make sure he spent all of it sleeping. As Jessica had warned, his father needed him at his best; and this was no time to call Parker, Ellis and Rideau.

What seemed like a few minutes later a lance of electricity shot through his thigh. Malcolm jolted up straight and slapped his leg as if stung by a wasp. "*Again?!*" he shouted in the empty room. Outside was still dark except for the neon glow before sunrise.

He curled in a ball and rubbed his thigh where the implant was located. The office had promised to zap only for emergencies but they zapped all the time and it was useless to complain. The clock said it was almost time to wake up anyway. He rolled over and turned on the vidlink by the bed. "Malcolm Moore," he said to the screen.

"Tentek," replied the man in the vidlink.

That was a bad sign. The man didn't bother to identify himself by name, and Malcolm didn't recognize him. He was Tentek Corporation, that was all. Malcolm suspected that the image had been generated by a computer. "What do you want?"

"You know Gary Seltzer has been assigned to the Autochef."

"I know."

"He hasn't filed his status report. His part needs to be finished by today four o'clock."

"Gary's like that. He makes deadlines and forgets status reports. He'll probably get it done on time."

"Make sure he does."

"Okay." He slapped the disconnect button before the machine could say anything more. His thigh still hurt and his father was in jail; if there was anything he cared about less than Tentek's Autochef, it was Gary's status report. He rolled the rest of the way out of bed and stumbled for the shower.

The soap was scented with stimulant and the water preset to his preferred temperature, so he felt better almost immediately. Remembering where he spent the previous evening, he scrubbed himself hard. The radio in the shower told him that the ozone for the day was rated code yellow and that terrorist rebels in Brazzaville had boarded a bus and taken hostages. Last night, a man who lost his job had stolen a car and killed himself by driving it through his office lobby. He listened for news of his father, the bioterrorist, but the incident seemed to have passed without a trace.

Three minutes later the water chilled so he wouldn't linger. Water was too rare and precious to run down the drain, even if it would be captured and reused in its entirety. He shaved himself clean, made the bed, and pulled on blue pants and a white shirt. Today he added a tie, in case he saw a lawyer.

Entering the living room turned on the television, and his eyes followed the light. "Now for news of Microtech Corporation," the news anchor declared. "Sales this quarter have shattered expectations." She gestured to charts with figures headed for the roof, and closed with a confidential tone, "This might be a good time to buy Microtech stock."

His father's phial sat on the kitchen counter, unchanged in any way that Malcolm could see. He picked it up and swirled it around; it still looked like water.

He poured a bowl of breakfast cereal, unzipped a package of apple chunks and heated coffee formula in the microwave. The television asked him, "Need a kidney? Then Organ-ic has what you need. We grow our organs in farm fresh pigs, and don't feed them anything you wouldn't eat yourself. If you need a kidney, think Organ-ic."

Malcolm found a piece of paper and designed a simple test. He removed three large glasses from the cupboard, and filled two with clean drinking water from the kitchen sink. He paid premium prices for this water, wherever it came from; he hated to ruin even a glassful but it was a small price to pay for information.

The first glass he simply set aside. To the second glass filled from the sink he added a teaspoon of salt, and the last glass he filled with water from the bath. This water was lower in both quality and price than the water from the sink. Safe, but a little saltier. He'd just come from the shower and he couldn't tell the difference.

He lined all three glasses up on the countertop, labeling them carefully so they wouldn't be confused. They all looked alike.

Finally he picked up his father's phial. For the hundredth time he swished the clear colorless fluid around inside, and for the hundredth time he saw nothing new. It looked just like the water from his sink. He took a deep breath, and held the phial tight in both hands.

He unscrewed the lid.

He held perfectly still, ready for anything. But nothing happened. No toxic vapor emerged and he didn't drop dead on the spot. So far so good. He took a gentle breath and carried on.

He divided the fluid into equal measures, and poured one measure each into the water from the bath, the water from the sink, and the sink water with extra salt. The final measure he left in the original phial, never to be touched again. That was the control.

He wrote the time on his paper chart, then hurried for work. On his way home he would buy a purity tester at the pharmacy and start taking measurements. He wanted to trust his father, but he also wanted to know what he was dealing with.

The television stayed on until he closed the door. Its final words were, "This news broadcast was brought to you by Microtech."

* * * * *

Malcolm hurried to the office and took his place in the security line, winding silently with the sunrise crowd around a marble bust of Tentek's Chief Executive, Happenstance Jackson. People stood close in the line but were careful not to touch, a perfect parade of recent styles and flawless complexions. Nobody spoke.

When his turn came, he stepped through the weapon detector and leaned his retina towards a flickering light for his entry screening. Only now he realized that the police could be looking for him in connection with his father's arrest, or that someone might have noticed his trip to the jail. But the Tentek guards didn't even look up.

Malcolm nodded good morning to Garcia Mendez, the officer in charge, then pushed security out of his mind as he rode the elevator into routine. He steeled himself for his first task, Gary Seltzer, whose office was adjacent to his own. Malcolm had little doubt that Gary was on schedule – speed wasn't his problem – but his zeal sometimes confused people around him. Gary's door was closed and the indicator was red but Malcolm buzzed anyway; when the light turned green he stepped inside.

The room was tiny but so cluttered that Gary was invisible at first. Paper files covered his desk and half eaten food cartridges littered the floor. A dirty towel hung over a photograph of his wife. Leaning low over his computer screen, Gary himself was hidden in the junk until he moved. "How's it going?" Malcolm asked.

"Great." Gary smiled proudly. "I'm tired but on a roll. I'm cruising so hard I haven't seen my kids in two weeks." He took a long draw from an oxygen tank and kicked aside a bottle that appeared to be filled with urine, a common trick among people too busy to use the bathroom. By tradition, they wrote the letter "P" on the side and kept the pee bottle separate from the rest.

"And the Autochef?" Malcolm asked.

"The Auto2, you mean?" He was right, of course, but only Gary would bother to point it out. The Autochef was finished years ago and caused no troubles at all. A freezer-refrigerator-oven combination, the Autochef both stored and cooked meal cartridges, so customers could enjoy a meal with no personal effort whatsoever. The original Autochef had plumbing that enabled it to mix drinks and make ice, and it communicated with suppliers to stock inventory.

The Autochef's only problem was that it had a long life and a home only needed a single unit. It sold explosively when it was first introduced but now the market was stable and new sales were down, so the marketing division conceived the Autochef for Families, or Auto2 as the people on the team had come to call it. Inspired by the sensational death of an infant who drank spoiled formula, the Auto2 tested the food during preparation. Tentek hoped that purchasers of the original Autochef might upgrade, and that people concerned about the food supply might enter the market at a higher level. The design of the Auto2 was complete and a prototype was in testing, but it was having trouble detecting hazards in the freezer. Gary was supposed to adjust the settings and sensitivities until it worked.

Malcolm told him that the company was concerned about his progress and that he hadn't submitted his status reports. "The ones that keep you from getting the actual work done," he joked.

"I'll make deadline," Gary promised. "I have two different approaches. I'll send you a resolution after pledge."

Malcolm figured that was good enough and let it be. A few steps brought him to his own office. As always, he left his door open and activated his computer. Three screens flashed to life. The main screen displayed the daily maxim from Tentek Corporation, "Tentek and you – working together for the common good." The screen to the left knew that he'd eaten at *Cafeteria L'Express* last night, and offered coupons to return; the screen on the right invited him to bet on the Titans, Tentek's football team, applying wagers and winnings straight to paychecks. The displays were fixed until a mandatory scan time passed but Malcolm pressed delete as soon as he could.

He exited the Tentek network and entered Eugene, the Unified Global Network, in search of attorney Larry Parker. He turned off the voice command and searched by keyboard to keep quiet.

Quickly he learned that Parker, Ellis and Rideau was gone, swallowed up by the firm of Kirkland and Lay, which had been swallowed in turn by Lawyers, Incorporated. Larry Parker himself had retired and disappeared in the years since his father's divorce.

But there were plenty of lawyers. Lawyers, Inc. bragged of twenty thousand lawyers who spoke four hundred languages between them, and were licensed in every country. Other firms bragged of specialties in commercial instruments, consumer obligations or international admiralty. "Mine for gold among your friends," advertised a firm in the personal injury section; another simply listed its alphanumeric name, Nusense4them4tune4u.

Some firms specialized in crime, prisons and even "terrorist innuendo," whatever that meant, but Malcolm quickly perceived that this was no way to find a lawyer for his dad. He sent a message to Jessica. He needed a reference.

He checked his watch and decided he had time to study last night's arrest. He found news accounts in several locations, but all were the same and none told him anything new. The official line with the alert shopkeeper and the Tentek Safe-T-Buzzer was everywhere, typically followed by coupons or links to local retailers. He learned nothing more about the bioterrorism charge, and found no updates as of this morning.

All three of Malcolm's screens suddenly lit up. "Two minutes to pledge time," they announced. Malcolm thought about skipping the pledge but decided it was foolish. He'd probably be missed, and he couldn't use his computer anyway: one keystroke and the corporation would know exactly where he was. He quickly checked his messages and answered the most urgent, then raced for the Pledge Hall.

The daily pledge was Tentek's most sacred ritual. Every floor of the Tentek building had its own Pledge Hall, a private auditorium entered only by Tentek staff and forbidden to contractors, vendors and even family members. Rows of plush chairs faced a stage with a podium flanked by two flags. One was the American stars and stripes; the other was Tentek's logo, the ringed globe of planet Earth circled by the words, Tentek Corporation.

For Malcolm the pledge was a tolerable annoyance; for some people it was the highlight of the day, the only chance for an unscheduled chat, and the only thing all Tentek employees had in common. His Hall was nearly full by the time he arrived, and it was buzzing with excitement.

He sat down beside a woman he'd never seen. "Isn't Hap wonderful?" she asked.

She was referring of course to Tentek's chief executive, Happenstance Jackson, and Malcolm knew what the correct answer was. "He sure is. What makes you say that today?"

"Yesterday his advice line saved my life." She was referring to Jackson's promise that anyone on staff could seek his advice on any subject at any time, and he would answer them within the same business day. "Can you imagine how he does all that? He's so busy but he makes time for all of us!"

Malcolm said nothing to ruin her illusions. Let her imagine the president of a corporation with millions of employees in 24 time zones who personally responded to every employee within eight hours. Malcolm imagined cubbyholes of exhausted workers with P bottles mining the secrets of the staff and replying with platitudes from a database. "How did he save your life?"

"He told me how to dump my boyfriend."

"What did he tell you to do?"

"'To stand tall and tell him that work mattered more, and that he should get out of my way.'"

Malcolm shuddered; this was no longer idle chatter. "Did you do it?"

"I did it last night. I feel great. My boyfriend was a bit crushed, you can imagine. We've been dating three years and he thought we would get married. But I told him that was silly. I have a career to consider."

Before Malcolm could answer, the lights dimmed and the room went silent. Timpani drums pounded rhythm into the void, followed by a fanfare of trumpets. Hap Jackson stepped from the wings, arms spread wide in salutation – a holographic image transmitted simultaneously to a hundred Pledge Halls in this building alone – but he looked real and it was easy to suspend disbelief. "There he is!" whispered the woman besides Malcolm, wiggling with excitement.

The crowd jumped to its feet and started to applaud, then a chant broke out as Jackson walked to the podium, "*Hap Jack! Hap Jack! Hap Jack!*" a hundred voices cried in unison, over and over, rising in volume and definitive in rhythm-- like the stamping of footsteps or the beating of drums. "*Hap Jack! Hap Jack!*"

Jackson acknowledged the tribute then motioned for silence. When he had the room's attention he cried out, "Greetings everybody! Are you well?"

"Yes!" people shouted.

"I can't hear you. Are you well?"

"*Yes!*" The enthusiasm was almost deafening. The woman beside Malcolm leaned bodily into every yell.

"Are you happy?"

"Yes!"

"Are you ready?"

"*Yes!*" Malcolm answered loudly enough not to seem contrary; the woman who dumped her boyfriend was loud enough for both of them.

"Then let's take the pledge. Let's take it together!" Jackson turned to the flags and motioned for everyone to rise. The entire room took to its feet and, following Jackson's lead, placed their hands over their hearts. Jackson held the room in silence a moment before he began, his resonant voice leading, the crowd following in unison. "I pledge allegiance to the Tentek Corporation of America. I will serve loyally and work hard for our great goals: a safer, more productive, more prosperous world for all."

Malcolm heard only the words in his own Pledge Hall, but he knew they were combining with voices in other Pledge Halls on other floors, in other Tentek buildings and, at other times, around the world. The woman beside Malcolm sighed the final words then stood still. Everyone maintained sober silence as Jackson himself paused to savor the grace, then exited the Hall.

It was over. The lights brightened, people nodded farewell and formed orderly lines at the doors. The woman who dumped her boyfriend didn't even say goodbye. The only sound was feet shuffling towards the exits.

A whole screen of messages had arrived while Malcolm was gone – people in other time zones, no doubt – and two of them required immediate attention. He assured his supervisor, Kira Portman, that the Auto2 was on track, and opened the updates on the biological disinfecting agent that was dying in transit.

He saw the problem immediately. This aggressive bacterium, branded the Odor Eater, was designed to attack and consume odor causing life forms, and to excrete a lemony scent in return – but it was being shipped without sufficient food to sustain its own nutritional needs. Shipping obviously required more food, faster "sell by" dates or smaller quantities of the original organism.

He stated his conclusions and wondered why the other trained monkeys couldn't figure this out.

He'd set the whole morning aside to deal with the problem and it was nice, for once, to be ahead of schedule. As he closed the file, Garcia Mendez, the security officer assigned to this zone, stepped into his office. Garcia was short, strong and intensely alert; he always looked like he was about to pounce. Most people on the professional staff acted as if the security crews didn't exist, but Malcolm and Garcia chatted almost every day when Garcia came by on his rounds.

"Someone tried to break in last night," Garcia said. He looked exhausted.

Malcolm was surprised. "What happened? Did you catch him?"

"It's a little unclear. Alarms sounded and multiple backups arrived on scene, but we never really found anything. Maybe it was a dud." Garcia cared about his job and liked to do it well, but today he just looked tired.

They talked another minute about last night's alarm and the onset of spring, a mix of news and pointless chatter that had become part of their daily routine. Conversation usually focused on sports or weather – if it weren't for these exchanges, Malcolm might never know how the Red Sox were doing – though once a casual "how's your family" uncovered a grave illness in Garcia's sister. The next day Malcolm brought a small sum of cash and a reference for a physician. Garcia accepted the gesture, but his sister died a few weeks later.

Malcolm's computer chimed with Gary's solution to the Auto2, and Garcia took the cue to continue his patrol. Gary outlined one approach that increased the number of sensors in the freezer, and a second approach that changed the distribution of the existing sensors around the compartment. He'd decided to use both – more sensors in a different configuration – a typical Gary Seltzer solution. It looked sensible but Malcolm doubted it would work. Before he sent Gary's design to the rest of the team, he proposed a different approach that skipped the freezer and delayed scrutiny until the frozen cartridges were in the oven, where the heat would increase molecular activity and make taints easier to detect. Of course, Malcolm was assuming that the cartridges wouldn't be eaten while frozen because this approach did nothing to protect against that possibility – but he was willing to take that risk. He summarized his conclusions and sent them upstairs to Kira, making sure to give Gary credit for his work and point out that he'd finished before deadline.

He settled into a regular day's work, surveying designs and filling in blanks.

Around noon he received a text message from Jessica: "Attorney Alan Feige will see you tonight at 8:00. Tell him everything."

Chapter Five

Attorney Alan Feige was an older man with a white crew cut, wearing a gray business suit over a white T-shirt. He sat at a wooden desk with a statue of a cat in the corner and a map of New Angeles on the wall behind. The room was orderly and efficient, with the right furniture in the right places. Malcolm felt comfortable immediately.

"Jessica Frey says your father's in jail," Feige began. "That's ungood."

"I'm with you."

"Who's it good for?"

"Now I'm not with you any more."

"His wife? Your mom? Someone he plays poker with? Did he owe someone money? Does someone win if he loses?" He leaned back in his chair, stopping just short of the wall.

"Not that I know of. But I might not know. I haven't seen him in years."

"That's what Jessica said. Why not?"

Malcolm had been asking himself the same question. He told the truth. "No reason. I'm busy. He's busy. Next thing you know, five years have passed."

"Do you know why he's in there?"

"Bioterrorism. They said on TV."

"It says bioterrorism in his case file too." He leaned forward and pushed an envelope across the table. "Good work getting out there so fast. What did you learn?"

Malcolm told him everything his father had said, emphasizing that he hadn't done anything wrong. "All he did was receive a gift."

"Possession of contraband is a crime in itself."

"What about Sayeh Kahn?"

"That's next. What have you done with the water?"

"It's in my apartment." Malcolm described his experiment. He hadn't been home since morning.

"Your apartment's not good enough," Feige said. "If what your father says is true, we need that water to prove he's innocent."

"And to desalinate seawater."

"That's not my problem. You can save the world on your own time if you want."

"Thanks."

"Keep some water in your apartment, and keep running your experiments. Bring me some. Put some in a safe deposit box. That water could be valuable to a lot of people."

"Especially my father."

"Things will move fast. You were already an interested party and you just became a crack investigator. I want to see you every night at 8:00. Put it in your calendar until further notice."

On the way home Malcolm stopped at a bank to open a safe deposit account and a pharmacy for purity tests. In the pharmacy he saw Mrs. Pearson, the only person he knew from his apartment building. She wandered the halls at all hours, showing off her baby. Here she was, baby in her arms, as always.

"Have you met my new baby?" She wore a flowered shirt cut from the same cloth as the baby's pajamas.

Malcolm didn't know it was a new baby and he couldn't really distinguish it from the last one. Mrs. Pearson adored babies but couldn't stand toddlers, so she had hers destroyed every time he got pesky and ordered a new one cloned from the original. "Not for me, baby proofing," she once bragged.

Looking again, he noticed that the baby did seem smaller than last time. "He's very handsome."

"I'm buying purity testers too." She held up her shopping basket. "Can't be too careful with my little precious!"

"No you can't." He suppressed a wicked grin over a different way to test his father's water.

"Have you heard about the terrorists?"

Now she had his full attention. He stopped in front of a display of fingerprint kits. "Is there news?"

"They've been passing out infected water like it's a gift. In the poor parts of town it's wildly popular, of course. They just give it away for free, and people take it." She shook her head disapprovingly.

"What happens if you drink it?"

"You die, I guess. I don't really know." She looked gratefully at her purity testers. "The terrorist leader's name is Moore." She stepped suddenly back. "Is he a relative of yours?"

"Moore's a common name." He moved towards the checkout.

She followed him. "They say it looks like regular water."

"I'll keep that in mind." He indicated the testers in his bag.

"There's a reward."

That stopped him. "What for?"

"For the water. A thousand Globos to bring it in, more to name the person who gave it to you."

Malcolm moved to the exit and scanned his retinas. "Sounds like the water's dangerous. They're trying to get it all back." When he got home he would verify those rewards.

"Thank goodness for the Department of Counterterrorism." She gave her child an urgent hug. "Can't be too careful with my little precious!"

Chapter Six

It was too late. Feige was right, and it was too late.

His apartment had been burglarized. The water was gone.

His whole experiment had been taken away. The original phial, the glasses he'd measured for testing, even his notes had disappeared. The countertop where he'd worked had been scrubbed with antiseptic.

It was all very professional. The kitchen cupboards had been emptied, and the dishes stacked neatly on the countertop. His clothes had been removed from the closet and piled smartly on the bed, which itself, he could see, had been searched on top, underneath, and between mattress and box springs.

Nothing else had been taken. His television was untouched and his computer rested peacefully on the desk. The target was deliberate and precise. The apartment was not in the order he'd left it in, but it was no less neat.

He wished now he'd been smart enough to hide the water as carefully as it had been searched for – under the bed, behind the towel rack or inside the toilet tank. He was a victim of his own organization. The only containers were those being tested, all left on the countertop in plain view, handwritten notes beside them, a virtual lighthouse for anyone wondering what water received special attention.

Everything changed without the water. He couldn't explain the gift his father had received. He couldn't use it as evidence in a bioterrorism trial, couldn't take it to Federated to make up that sales meeting. For a few hours, Malcolm had in his possession water that could help not only his father, but people all over the world. Now all he had was the promise of an accused bioterrorist.

He poked around the piles of clothing as if a phial had magically been left behind, examined his glasses as if one were somehow, inexplicably, half filled with water. Then he gave up. He sat down on the floor in defeat, leaning his back against the bed. After a while, the image of his father in his mind, he lay flat on the floor.

Finally he returned to his feet and dialed Feige. Nobody in the office picked up. He left a message.

He wanted to call Jessica, but it seemed imprudent from his apartment. He could only guess what else was being monitored. The attorney he could explain, but he didn't want to lead trackers to another target.

Was he supposed to call the police? He thought that was standard procedure after a burglary– but maybe not this one. The police might have been involved. He sat down at his computer and checked Mrs. Pearson's tip about the reward. Exactly as she said, one thousand Globos had been offered for samples of water distributed by Bernard Moore of New Angeles or Sayeh Kahn of

Kaiserville. Obviously the authorities wanted this water. He couldn't complain if they took matters into their own hands.

And they guessed right, too. Malcolm wouldn't have turned over his sample voluntarily. Not with so much at stake.

Or that's how it seemed from here. He'd been spared the temptation.

There was nothing else for him to do. He didn't want to involve Jessica and didn't want to call the police. He didn't even call building management, who might well have played a role, since the door didn't appear to have been forced. So he returned to Jessica's earlier admonition, and went to sleep.

With his clothes all out it was easy to get dressed the next morning. He designated one corner for dirty laundry and started a pile. After breakfast he cleaned his dishes and left them on the counter to dry.

The bad news at the office was that the Auto2 team had selected Malcolm's idea of placing the sensors in the oven rather than the freezer, and asked him to finish it off. Now instead of being ahead of schedule on the Odor Eater he was behind schedule on the Auto2. He left messages for both Jessica and attorney Feige, and got to work.

In the middle of the morning the Counterterrorism Division amended its announcement. The reward for water samples increased to five thousand Globos. Fifty thousand were offered to anybody who could name their source.

Might Malcolm have turned over the water for five thousand Globos? Should he reveal what his father told him, even though they already knew, and try to parlay it into a reward? Or maybe he was supposed to tell them what he knew, no matter what. He had information on a matter of public concern. Did hiding it make him a terrorist collaborator? Did he need a lawyer of his own?

He dialed Feige again but nobody answered, and he didn't bother repeating his message. Head swirling, he forced himself to focus on the Auto2. Four sensors at the top of the oven seemed like plenty, one near each corner, but he had to design the wiring to make it work.

In the middle of the day, with the oven sensors nearly finished, his supervisor, Kira, vidlinked him with major news. He was being transferred off the Auto2. Malcolm had to suppress a hooray. He all but hugged the image in the vidlink.

She told him to finish the oven and plan not to return. "Leave clear tracks because if anything goes wrong someone else will need to follow in your footsteps."

He always did that anyway. "What will I be working on?

"Drinking water," she said, then softened her tone and turned almost friendly. The two of them had always gotten along well, and he knew that Kira thought highly of his work. Of course, she always placed him where it did the most good for the corporation but he often felt that she kept him close to her own projects because it made her own life easier. Now she made it explicit. She said that she'd been assigned to this new project and invited to bring one person from her department with her. She chose Malcolm instantly.

He thanked her and she moved on. "This is a major undertaking, and people from all over the company are being assigned to it. Both of us need to wrap up our other projects so we can work full time on this one." She explained that the project related to the purification and desalination of seawater. Currently, desalination took place on an industrial scale and the purified water was piped through entire jurisdictions. Tentek wanted to develop tools to process water on a household scale, so people could clean their own seawater in their own living areas.

"Plumbing will run seawater?" he asked.

"Exactly. People will clean and desalinate it to their own preferences. More for drinking, less for dishes or a bath. Pay for the purity you like."

Malcolm kept a straight face as the central facts of his life, with the exception of one mysterious phial, turned into routine conversation at the office. Suddenly, a new signal told him a call was coming in on another line: Feige.

Kira kept talking. "I'll send you a big file of background material."

He needed to hurry her off before the system told Feige he wasn't available. He didn't want to play phone tag all over again. "Great. Is that all?"

"One more thing."

Malcolm almost groaned out loud.

"Call anytime with as many questions as you like. This project's a priority."

Malcolm tried to squeeze agreement, appreciation and goodbye into a single syllable, and switched to Feige before the message system took over.

"The burglary doesn't matter," Feige declared. A neat stack of paper and glass of what looked like water rested on his desk.

"How can it not matter? I need that water to prove my father's innocent."

"Your father's dead."

For the first time in his life, Malcolm was glad he was sitting down when he heard a piece of news. He lost his balance and his stomach heaved upwards against his throat. His father was dead. The burglary no longer mattered. Neither did guilt or innocence.

"How did he die?" He seemed healthy yesterday.

"He was beaten to death by other inmates."

Malcolm groaned out loud and leaned forward, head in his hands. He couldn't imagine his father dying a violent death, the peaceful man who used to tickle him, who lay comfortably on the prison floor while he explained the water. Malcolm knew his father's failings, but *this* he didn't deserve.

But he pulled himself straight and forced himself to focus. He was talking to a lawyer; he needed to ask the right questions. "Should I sue someone? Are inmates allowed to beat him up like that? Shouldn't they run the place so murders don't happen?"

Feige took a sip of his water. "The state can't control the feelings of every inmate," he said. "Bioterrorists aren't very popular on the inside, either."

"But he wasn't a bioterrorist!" Maybe innocence mattered after all.

"Can you prove that?"

Malcolm sat still, at a loss for ideas. A new message appeared on his screen. Kira's desalination files. He couldn't prove it, and he knew it.

Feige went on. "Even if he was innocent, the other inmates wouldn't know it. They only know what he's charged with. People in jail drink water too." He took another sip. "And you talk about suing someone? Jurors don't like bioterrorists either."

Malcolm saw where this was heading. "My apartment was broken into. Isn't that illegal?"

"Somebody wanted the water. Now they have it. It might be a crime but it's not a lawsuit."

Doors were closing in every direction. He said, "For a while, I was in possession of the same water my father had. Supposing it was contraband — might I be arrested?"

"You won't be. They have the water. You don't know anything and you're not interesting to anyone. Case closed."

"Just like that?"

"Call me if something changes," Feige concluded. "Jessica asked me to give you legal counsel, and here it is. Let it go. I'm sorry about your father." He sounded sincere. "He needs a funeral, not a lawsuit."

Chapter Seven

Jessica agreed to discuss it after dinner. She said something about somebody being out anyway, so she was flexible. They agreed to a coffee shop just a few steps away from Jessica's office.

Malcolm arrived first and chose a table far from the windows. He wanted privacy and didn't need to watch blimps, fireworks or advice about buying shoes. He pulled out his lifelink and started reading about industrial desalination and municipal sewerage systems. A boy in green OmniSpan coveralls, maybe twelve years old, walked the floor trying to sell costume jewelry. He didn't even attempt Malcolm's table.

Jessica arrived fully half an hour late. "Sorry," she said. "Something came up." She wore a blue blazer with a badge on the lapel, and not the smallest hint of the smile Malcolm had seen the night of the arrest.

"No problem," he said, lifting his lifelink to show that the time wasn't wasted. He wanted to change her mood but he didn't know how. He kept quiet and said nothing.

Jessica sat down, leaned deep back into her chair and ordered hot cocoa. She kicked off her shoes and sipped slowly as if Malcolm didn't exist. He kept his own thoughts and she kept hers, and he gave her as much time as she wanted. He even chased away the OmniSpan boy who seemed to think the odds shifted when company arrived. The silence lasted until the couple at the next table had ordered coffee and left. Finally, Jessica said, "Thanks for the minute."

"Thank *you*," he replied. He'd set aside his lifelink out of courtesy, and been forced to relax himself.

"Who was the guy who said, 'Whatever can go wrong will?'"

"Murphy's law."

"Murphy was an optimist."

Malcolm laughed, then turned serious. "I saw Feige. I don't need a lawyer after all."

Jessica gulped down the last of her cocoa. "Tell me everything."

He told her everything. He told her about the package of water, and his trip to the jail, Sayeh Kahn and the break-in. He ended with Feige's conclusion that he didn't need a lawyer after all.

"You win," she said. "Your day was worse than mine."

"Thanks. I feel better now."

She pulled out her lifelink and started working the keyboard. After a moment she reached across the table to rest her hand on his own, warm and soft and unexpected. She lingered as an electric thrill reminded him why they met in the first place, then tugged him gently towards her side of the table. She guided him toward the computer screen and released his hand to press a button.

"That's Sayeh Kahn," she said.

On screen was an older man. He looked nothing but inconspicuous, just a working man near the bottom of the economy. The bio said he was sixty-three years old and he looked every minute of it, but his eyes were intelligent and kind. He worked for DynCorps as a plumbers' assistant. Nothing in his biography suggested what he would have in common with Malcolm's father, but nothing indicated terrorism either.

Jessica pressed a button and the screen changed to a map of Kaiserville. "He lives here." She pointed to a red exclamation point in a maze of streets. "That's your next stop."

"Kaiserville?! I can't go to Kaiserville."

"Why not?"

"Too dangerous." He shook his head. "Kaiserville is one big crime scene."

"You've been watching the news?" she arched a sarcastic eye. "You'll be fine. I used to go when I was a kid, and worse places too. Sometimes my father brought me for work."

"It was different back then."

"You need information. The trail leads to that apartment." She pointed to the red exclamation point.

"He's wanted by the police."

"So was your father."

"He could be in jail already. You want me to go all that way for someone who isn't there anymore?"

He had a point. She took back her lifelink and started pressing buttons. "He's not in the jail," she said at last.

"Not today, anyway. He's nowhere in the correctional system."

"Then he's on the run. He's not at that apartment." He pointed to her lifelink, though the exclamation point was gone.

"Stop making excuses. People there know all about it. You're going." She cocked her head as if struck by an idea. "I'll come with you. Tomorrow."

That changed everything. Kaiserville wasn't someplace Malcolm ever expected to go, and certainly not on a date; but then, he'd never been asked. "Agreed," he declared. He'd been planning a full work day, but tomorrow was Sunday and he could get away with it. The adventure with Jessica had more than practical appeal.

"Good. I'll bring David. I don't want you to be surprised."

"Who?"

"David," Jessica repeated. "My son."

Malcolm looked up abruptly; Jessica matched his surprise.

"I thought you knew," she said. "I would have warned you the first time we met, but I thought Gloria told you when she arranged the date. Last time David never happened to come up."

"No, he didn't." Malcolm tried to cover his alarm. This whole adventure started as a date, and he hadn't abandoned that possibility. "How old is he?"

"Six."

"Six years old! That's crazy. Can't someone else watch him while you're gone? How about his father?" He blurted out and looked embarrassed almost immediately.

Jessica skipped past his embarrassment. "David doesn't have a father. He never did. And he's coming with us. I don't get to spend enough time with him, and it will be good for him to see Kaiserville. We'll probably be safer with a kid along, anyway. People treat you better."

He saw no point in arguing.

The OmniSpan boy headed back their way. He extended his box with a bright red bead exposed on top. Jessica waved him away. "If I wanted new jewelry, I would subscribe."

Malcolm looked up quizzically. He couldn't guess what subscription she was referring to.

"Like the pillow covers," she explained.

Malcolm was astonished. On their first date she had talked on and on about a subscription that changed her pillow covers once a month. Could she still be talking about it?

She put the pieces together for him. "If I liked new jewelry I would subscribe, and new choices would come every month. But I don't want new jewelry. I want to make a mess. More precisely, David wants to make a mess. He paints with colors, draws with crayons and sprinkles with glow dye. I don't worry about it. At the end of the month, *whisk!* New pillow covers! It's a small price for a lot of fun."

Suddenly, much became clear to Malcolm. They had talked about David on the last date after all; he just didn't realize it. With different assumptions, they had talked right past each other and reached different conclusions. He would need to be more careful.

She pulled out her lifelink and indicated that it was getting late. She pressed a few buttons, then turned the screen his direction. "The line to Kaiserville starts here at Highland Junction. Meet me there in time for the 9:05 train."

He echoed, "Highland Junction at 9:05. You and your son David."

"Wear old clothes and comfortable shoes."

Chapter Eight

The station at Highland Junction was a three-sided shack with a machine that sold tickets. The walls were filthy and the floors were stamped with mud; music played from speakers so old and tinny it was barely distinguishable from the static. Malcolm arrived first, and watched dogs and rats scavenge along the track. By the time Jessica and David arrived he had a headache.

David had light brown hair and bright blue eyes, and he looked every bit like a six-year old on an outing. He grumped through the necessary introductions but cheered up when Malcolm said, "I brought something for everyone." He got even happier when Malcolm unpacked a cookie for him, and crackers to feed the rats on the track. Jessica smiled like Malcolm had hit a home run.

Once David was busy throwing crackers, Malcolm showed off the rest of his supplies – a small arsenal of tear gas, pepper spray, and a child-sized impact vest he bought with his Tentek employee discount. If he couldn't stop Jessica from bringing a child, he could at least help keep him safe.

Jessica stared at the pile in dismay. "I hope it's returnable." She said, then offered a compromise. "Good work with the treats."

"He caught it!" David cried from the end of the platform. "The rat caught it in the air. Try it again! Go long!" He threw a cracker in a long arc, and they all spent the next few minutes busy with crackers and rats until the train chased the creatures away. It was a battered old relic with a thumping engine and grinding breaks, but it arrived at precisely 9:05. Jessica gathered David, and gestured them both on board.

Plenty of seats were empty. David settled himself on a bench near a window, and the grown ups joined him. "Can I play Super Beta Brothers?" he asked.

"Sure," Jessica said.

Malcolm watched him engage his video game, then turned to Jessica. "Tentek got a lot of mileage out of my father's arrest."

"How's that?"

"Every newscast mentioned the Safe-T-Buzzer."

"Tentek probably owns the broadcaster. Did they offer coupons too?"

"Every time."

"Probably the stores too."

"You're kidding."

"Only a little."

A girl David's age walked up and started watching him play the video game. After a while he held it out to her. "Want a turn?"

She tucked her chin into her chest, said nothing.

"I just finished a game. I lost. Want a turn?"

"I'm going to visit my aunt," the girl said quietly. "I'll stay there for a while. She's my favorite aunt. She lets me drink ketchup straight from the bottle."

"Yuck!" David exclaimed. He put the game back in its pouch, then confessed that he liked to dip his sleeves in juice, and suck the fluid from the fabric.

"*Yuck! Yuck! Double Yuck!*" She explained that her mom would never let her do that because it was too dirty. She said her mom polished banisters and door knobs in a hotel downtown, and she liked keeping things clean. The girl said she wanted to be a polisher when she grew up too. "I like it when things sparkle."

David said his mother "went to meetings" and that he wanted to be a marine biologist when he grew up. The little girl had never heard of that.

Malcolm began to feel more comfortable. He wasn't worried about the train, and stopped worrying about traveling with a mother and small child. He asked Jessica, "Have you been here before?" It seemed so familiar to her.

"Not to Kaiserville, but to places like it. When I was a kid my father used to travel to unusual places for work – or when he was looking for work. Sometimes he would haul me around with him. His friends thought he was crazy for bringing me to dangerous places, but I always thought it was fun."

"I thought you were crazy too. So far it's fun."

She accepted his concession, even with the 'so far' limitation, and conversation soon turned to sports and the weather. It was just chatter to pass the time, but they were both enjoying themselves. Malcolm learned that

Jessica hated wearing suits to work, but it wasn't worth fighting with her boss. They discovered that Jessica once helped settle a trade dispute over a product Malcolm had developed. "Trivial nonsense," Jessica called it – and they laughed when they realized that Jessica meant the dispute while Malcolm thought she meant the product.

He felt no regret as the train left behind a green and white corporate park, surely one of the last along this stretch of track. He imagined that they were fitting in, and that an outsider might mistake them for a family from an outlying district. Nobody need suspect him of being on Tentek's design team or Jessica of being an attorney for the government.

A man walked up to them. "Did you mean to get off?" He broke Malcolm's spell with a gesture towards the receding corporate park, concerned that they'd missed their station.

"We're okay." Jessica thanked him with her warm and wonderful smile, then leaned against the wall and closed her eyes.

* * * * *

Kaiserville assaulted them the instant they stepped off the train. The stench of urine rose from the tracks and a swirl of grit swept their faces. The platform swarmed with people, mostly children, running around with few clothes on. A boy almost knocked Jessica down as he chased an electric ball, leaving a smear of mucous and dirt across her leg.

Two men walked by speaking of alcohol and sports. A woman leaned against a wall, picking at a sore on her leg. Dogs at the end of the platform growled and snapped over scraps of food. Billboards covered every surface, showing naked women, beauty lotions and red cars with fire breathing engines. The biggest display in the station showed a circle of people dancing around a bottle of Carnival Rum.

Flies swarmed their heads, and no arm waving or head shaking could keep them away. David screamed as a fly flew into his mouth, then jumped for Jessica and smothered against her leg. She held him close and took a few hard breaths herself, struggling for a compass in the confusion. The train whistled then pulled away slowly, grinding and thumping on ancient wheels. They watched it pick up speed until the last car left the station. On the other side of the platform, visible now that the train was gone, a heap of garbage festered in the sun. Home base for the flies.

"Can we get back?" David asked.

"Later," Jessica replied. She coaxed him off her leg and led him forward, swatting a fly that landed on his arm. She led them off the platform and past the ticket booths to a broad plaza of cracked asphalt. People of every race and nationality swarmed past, speaking languages Malcolm had never heard. One man carried a singing child on his shoulders, and led crying children with both his hands. An older woman wrapped in what looked like a bed sheet walked with an older man wearing nothing at all. In the first minute, Malcolm saw more disabilities – a one-legged man hobbling on improvised crutches, a one-armed boy playing catch – than he could remember seeing his whole life at home.

Amidst the confusion Malcolm gradually noticed the familiar. Stores whose names he recognized lined the streets. On one corner stood a *Cafeteria L'Express.* At the next stood a video shop run by Federated, his father's department store chain. Tentek's logo of the ringed Earth was visible in every direction, and people wore uniforms from familiar industries or T-shirts from past marketing campaigns. Jessica seemed to enjoy the hurly-burly, taking it all in with wide open eyes; David's discomfort had worn off and he looked thrilled to be someplace new, though he still grabbed his mother's hand. Malcolm wanted to share his confidence but he wasn't sure she knew what she was doing. His electronic navigator proved to be useless.

A young woman, perhaps eighteen years old, approached them. She was stunningly beautiful and her green eyes complimented the green of her OmniSpan uniform. Her arms were streaked with grime and a tangle of dirty hair draped across her face, hiding a delicate nose and fine chin. "Is everything okay? You look lost."

"We are lost," Jessica replied. She pulled out a photograph of Kahn and his street address. "We're looking for him and we don't know where to go."

The woman didn't even bother looking at the photograph; she studied the address and glanced around to establish their current location. "It's that way," she said, waving her hand vaguely through the row of buildings on their right. "It's not far. I'll show you."

"If you give us directions we can find it ourselves," Jessica offered.

She shook her head. "Too many twists and turns. No landmarks. It's not a problem." She took a few steps back in the direction they just came from, pausing only to brush the hair from her eyes and tie it in a knot behind her head. In the motion, Malcolm noticed a tattoo like the fat man on the jail transpo – two parallel bar codes on the underside of her wrist.

"What's the tattoo?" he asked.

"OmniSpan," she replied proudly. "I'm coded for service at OmniSpan Enterprises." She made it sound like an accomplishment. "But right now I'm only working two days a week."

"What do you do?"

"They have me changing filters in air ducts these days. The jobs change all the time. The more things you can do, the more hours you get."

"What if you want to quit? What happens to the tattoo?"

She looked at him like he'd asked what happens when people rise from the dead. "Nobody ever quits OmniSpan. I'm not even sure it's possible. Besides, the money's good and OmniSpan always starts with tagged people when they need workers. It's guaranteed." She spat on her hand and rubbed some grime off her upper arm, exposing a different tattoo. "This one lets me handle merchandise at Effexor. They used to use surgical implants but they were too easy to swap."

"How many tattoos do you have?" Malcolm asked.

"Just those two," she replied. "But I'm still young. I heard OmniSpan might merge so my wrist tag will go even further."

Jessica had been listening and now she intervened. "What do people call you when you're more than a tattoo?" she asked.

"Brij," the woman replied. "It's in the tattoo."

"I'm sure it is."

The train station came back into view but Brij led them down a narrow alley that jutted off at an angle. She suggested that they look carefully at the intersection so they could remember their way back if she wasn't with them. Turning to David she remarked, "He'll remember anyway." He swelled with pride. The alley narrowed until they had to walk single file, and under an arch; then it opened back into a street. An old man handed them leaflets as they emerged.

"That's an OmniSpan job," Brij observed. "OmniSpan assigns him a location and tracks his performance."

"He gets paid more if the location does well?" Jessica asked.

"Of course. Let's see what he's selling." They opened their leaflets, which advertised wall sized video screens at a local outlet, financing available.

"If you're planning to buy a wallscreen, you could do it from that shop," suggested Brij. "You'd do that guy a favor."

Malcolm intervened. "Wallscreens? People around here can afford wallscreens?"

Brij looked surprised. "Six people live in my apartment and four of us earn decent incomes," she declared. "My mother lost her job about a month ago and hasn't found a new one yet, but both my brothers log ninety hours a week at Federated and one hasn't missed a day in years. I bet we could buy a wallscreen if we set our minds to it." Malcolm heard more than a little longing in her voice.

She detoured them toward a Casa Fiesta, one of a national chain of convenience stores, then excused herself. "I want to check a result while I'm here." She stepped to the back while the three travelers walked the aisles. The Casa Fiesta inventory looked the same – and was priced the same – as in Malcolm's neighborhood. The shelves were filled with toys and pre-packaged meals that he knew all too well.

In the rear of the store a group of men argued over a betting counter. They wore the uniforms of various industries and waved yellow slips at each other as they watched sports results pour in over Monitor Television. "The Yankees will win in extra innings," one man shouted.

"The Yankees haven't beaten Effexor in three years," another man replied. "The Yankees are pitching Brett Strom, a lefty. He's got an EHA of .270 against left handed power batters. Gutierrez and Downey will hit him full of holes." The man caught Malcolm's eye and smiled. He was roughly Malcolm's age and a little taller; his face and arms were intanglioed with bleeding scrapes and tiny scars, as if he worked in a stream of sharp particles that nicked him continuously.

The attention people paid to sports suddenly struck Malcolm as odd. Where sports were concerned, people who had no time for friends or family could find a few minutes to check scores or watch an entire game. Students who barely passed exams spent hours poring over player statistics. Malcolm had always considered such attention as natural as work or weather, but now it seemed strange.

The group grew silent as new results appeared on the monitor. They studied the screen and some men made marks on their yellow slips. A few took slips to the uniformed clerk behind the betting counter and spoke to him softly. The shouting started again and the visitors found the door.

Brij was waiting outside. She had a yellow betting slip in her hand and she was leaning against the wall looking at her feet; she had kicked a small hole in the dirt. "How'd it go?" Malcolm asked.

"Fine," she said, but didn't smile and didn't move from her spot on the wall. She crumpled the yellow paper and shoved it in her pocket with a heavy sigh. Meanwhile, David peeked around the corner and now he came running back in excitement.

"Betas!" he yelled, and starting tugging his mom in the direction he'd come from. Brij said she needed another minute inside and that she'd catch up in a moment. Malcolm and Jessica followed David around the corner, where Casa Fiesta had mounted a large television for anyone to watch. A crowd of children huddled around the television watching an action cartoon that Malcolm figured was the Ultra Super Beta Brothers. They all stopped to watch the muscular Beta Brothers try to thwart the evil plans of an ugly midget.

At the commercial break, several kids went into the store and Jessica gave David permission to join them; a moment later he returned with a Beta Bar to his place in the middle of the crowd. Malcolm gestured his direction and asked politely, "So what's his story?"

Jessica didn't skip a beat. "I wanted a kid more than I wanted a man. There were no decent men in view anyway." She assumed he would know what she meant by this. "So I went ahead on my own. I spermbanked. The big decision was whether to go random or custom.

I decided to go random so I'd be surprised. Turns out I like him."

Malcolm hadn't given any serious thought to David's history and he had no preconceptions, but he found Jessica's story surprisingly unsurprising. It just made sense. "I noticed he's left-handed," he offered. "You're not."

"Nobody in my family is left-handed. It's all his."

On screen, the Beta Brothers were in terrible trouble. The evil genius held them bound and gagged in the cellar of his stronghold; resistance was useless and help was far away. The program stopped for a commercial break and children again migrated into the store, but Jessica indicated to David that one was enough. He stayed put.

After the break, the Beta Brothers were free from their bonds and wreaking terrible vengeance within the stronghold. They overpowered the guards and closed in on the evil genius himself. The children cheered as they snapped his neck and squashed his head underfoot; the cheers climaxed when they tossed his body into the crocodile moat where his own pets ripped it to pieces.

"What happened?" Malcolm asked David as they returned to the Casa Fiesta.

"The Betas won."

"But how? One minute they were locked in the cellar and the next they were free. What happened in between?"

"They're the Beta Brothers. They always win. The other guy was no match for their ultra super Beta powers."

Brij started walking as soon as they returned. At the end of the block they passed a line of dusty women standing with empty containers for water at a public water tap. Some women stepped slowly away with enormous jugs balanced on their heads while others held them suspended by yokes on their shoulders. One woman looked frail enough to crumble under her load, but she stepped slowly and surely over ruts and up a steep staircase with the confidence of long experience. Jessica looked like she wanted to help, but she knew the need was endless and she had other work to do. Malcolm thought of his new project at Tentek, designing equipment to desalinate water in the home, and wondered how it might affect these women's lives. He detoured past the tap where they scanned their retinas for payment but he couldn't find the price.

Soon Malcolm found himself actually enjoying the crowds, the constant ducking and weaving to avoid obstacles. This neighborhood had energy and exuberance that his own lacked. He estimated that Kaiserville had no more people than his own district, but they were easier to see. Where he lived the buildings were taller and people had their own cubicles separated by soundproof walls and a regulated climate. Here life happened on the street.

Garcia lives in a place like this, Malcolm realized. Malcolm tried to picture him on a weekend – shirt off, sweaty, playing with the kids. Garcia had an exceptional job. Few people from these districts could land a position at Tentek; they lacked the education to contribute professionally, and Tentek had no need to recruit from these ranks. The man with the bloody nicks and yellow betting slip might be as smart as Gary Seltzer and work as hard – but neither he nor his kids would ever get close to Gary's office.

The chief exceptions were the cleaning crews, diplomats who were welcome in both communities. Every night a horde of people from the ghettos and satellite townships descended upon the Tentek building and scrubbed it to perfection from top to bottom, departing at daybreak like the stars at dawn. Malcolm saw them occasionally when he stayed late or arrived early, but he hardly paid them any attention and he never tried to talk. It was like two universes occupying the same space at different times.

Suddenly, Malcolm was bumped from behind, then bumped again as a rush of children darted past; behind them came a larger crowd, running and shouting in excitement. An old man looked from a window on a second floor, and a young man in the street shouted up to him. The old man closed the shutter then appeared downstairs, charging forward with the rest.

Something was happening up ahead. The visitors were already walking in the right direction, and they started to rush faster with the crowd. David slipped away from Jessica's hand and dashed through an opening too small for his mother. "David!" she yelled but he disappeared in the stream of bodies. "Come back!" Her shouts disappeared in the tumult.

Malcolm and Jessica ran after him so now they too were part of the speeding chaos. They leaped mounds of loose dirt and toppled a tower of empty paint cans, caught sight of David then lost him behind a cart piled high with tires.

He appeared again even farther away, entirely beyond reach, then Brij flew in from nowhere and tackled him from behind. She dragged him to a stop and held him until Jessica arrived, panting and upset – but said nothing because of what they could see happening ahead. They pushed together through the crowd for a closer look.

At the center of the excitement stood three police officers. The crowd kept its distance from them, obeying a perimeter as if they wore an invisible fence. The men were dressed like battleships. Helmets with visors sealed their heads, fused to an impenetrable shell of body armor. But this outfit was designed for more than just protection. Bristling with menace and authority, it was designed to intimidate. Equipment swung from their belts – bludgeons and stunners for the disorderly, firearms for the dangerous, cuffs and nets for the elusive. Each officer was an army of his own.

In the thick of the crowd, David firmly now in Jessica's grip, they could smell people's sweat, feel their clothing and bodies press hotly against each other. Something sharp jabbed into Malcolm's thigh.

The police officers surrounded two men and a table. On the table sat boxes of cookies, an assortment of toys and a sign advertising "Grand Opening." Malcolm saw in a flash what was happening. These men had baked their own cookies and bent wire into toys, and they were starting a store of their own. Just as quickly he realized that this store made sense. These people could satisfy neighborhood needs at lower prices, and keep the earnings in the community. Another sign lay trampled in the dirt, "Fresh Bread Coming Soon." Of course.

With the crowd watching, intense but silent, the police officers handcuffed the men and prodded them with electric stun wands towards a van. They walked docilely, heads down, compliant but confused. "Daddy!"

cried a little girl, breaking from the crowd and hurtling herself towards the nearest man.

The closest officer shocked the man so he crumpled to the ground, then reached for his belt and spun towards the girl – but in that instant a woman leaped from the crowd and tackled her hard into the dirt, then pulled her kicking and screaming back into the throng.

The man rolled over on the ground and looked helplessly towards the girl. The officer hauled him to his feet and shoved him into the van. "*Daddy! No, No! Daddy!!*" the girl cried. Her voice was piercing at first, then muffled by somebody's hand.

One of the officers stepped towards the crowd, equipment swinging from his belt. His amplified voice blasted over the crowd. "In accordance with regulation Forty-One Part B you are hereby notified of the grounds for this arrest." The crowd silenced in expectation.

The officer pulled a document from his pouch and held it up for all to see, then recited a long bill of state and municipal violations. The men had handled food without culinary accreditation, processed it in kitchens without health inspections and sold it without a license; they had set up a commercial property intended for profit at a location less than 100 feet from a sign clearly stating that Casa Fiesta intended to open a convenience store. Jessica whispered that that violation alone could land them ten years behind bars, while the officer recited a list that seemed to go on forever.

At the edge of the crowd, the little girl continued to wail.

Chapter Nine

"We should go," said Brij.

Malcolm looked at her doubtfully. He wanted to see what would happen next, maybe even help the girl.

"The cleanup crew will come soon," she declared. "To disperse the crowd."

Already people were starting to move, hurrying away as if noxious gas had leaked from the center of the square. They pushed past the visitors while they talked, backing up at narrow alleys and adjoining streets. The armored van with the men inside crept through the throngs, bumping aside anyone who didn't clear the path. A second van approached from a different direction.

"Let's stay a minute more," Jessica said.

Brij was inflexible. "You'll get hurt. After that, you'll get arrested. We're already too slow." She pointed to the sky where a helicopter appeared, and now they heard its engine throb filling the air. "Come with me." She started to run and the travelers had no choice but to follow. She heaved open a door to a cellar and waved them ahead of her. "Hurry."

Jessica went first down a steep staircase illuminated only by the sunlight of the open hatch. She'd reached the bottom with David close behind, but Malcolm was only halfway down when Brij entered and closed the door behind her. Instantly the space went black. David let out a scream that filled the tiny space with terror. In the darkness, Malcolm heard Jessica scramble for her son, find him and pull him in. Malcolm froze so he wouldn't run them over, and Brij bumped him from behind. He heard something clatter to the ground and roll down the stairs.

"That was my light," said Brij. At the bottom of the stairs, they heard David whimpering and Jessica trying to soothe him.

"Jessica?" Malcolm said.

"Yes?" A voice in blackness.

"Pull David away from the stairs and stand flat against a wall. Brij and I will look for the light."

Brij had already started. Malcolm could feel her moving past him, groping her way down the staircase where she last heard the clatter. Malcolm started probing the other side, running his hands over sharp stones and bare metal beams. He followed the contour of the stairs to be sure he checked every one. He felt Brij moving beside him; several times their bodies bumped or hands touched in the darkness. Her long hair brushed across his face once as she turned. In a minute, she stood up with the light. David quieted the instant she turned it on.

They were in a simple basement. Pipes and ducts ran overhead, and boxes lay scattered across the floor. "It's a shortcut," Brij said. She guided them down a short corridor and through several rooms; in some spots they had to duck under plumbing or help each other over collapsed beams. At one point the air turned rancid and the floor turned to mud that grabbed their shoes and made an ugly slurping sound as they pulled out. "Sewerage," Brij explained and started walking faster, cautious only that David not lose his balance. A minute later she found solid ground and instructed them to wipe their shoes thoroughly in the dirt. After another long corridor they reached a staircase and Brij led them up; she manipulated a latch, then opened a door into daylight.

Outside looked like the same Kaiserville they started in. They emerged into a busy street filled with people going about their business and shops doing their best to lure people inside. The incident with the police might have been in another city in another time. People here were doing their laundry, carrying their loads and playing with their children. An old woman beside them ironed pink Snappy Kleen uniforms on a table top. Behind her, another long line of people waited their turn at the water tap.

"Is everyone all right?" Brij asked.

"When's lunch?" David replied. They all had a good long laugh while he begged to find out what was so funny, his desperation making it even more amusing. Malcolm rummaged through his pockets for crackers leftover from the rats.

All of a sudden Brij swatted her leg like she'd been stung by a wasp, and started hopping and spinning in agitation. The travelers turned in alarm. "That's OmniSpan," she announced.

Malcolm smiled in full appreciation. This was something they had in common. He pointed to his own implant. "Is it right here?"

She smiled back, and there the commonality ended. "I love it. It's always with me and they can alert me at any time. They have a job for me right now."

"Do you have to go?"

"I do if we're going to pay the rent."

Jessica interrupted. "Can we hire you instead? We'll pay you what OmniSpan would for your time. Maybe more." She didn't want to lose their guide.

"I can't reject jobs if I want them to keep calling me." Her tone was absolute.

"But we can pay for the time you've already given us," Jessica suggested.

That seemed to catch Brij by surprise. "Sure," she replied, sounding less mercenary than pleased by a bonus.

"How do we access your bank account?"

"It's better not to. OmniSpan direct deposits and other people direct withdraw. Unscheduled transactions look bad."

Malcolm was already reaching for his wallet. His own bank had doublechecked his intentions and identification when he withdrew a lump of cash before the trip. He handed Brij four 20 Globo notes.

She tried to keep a poker face but Malcolm could see he'd been generous – as he intended. She smiled in gratitude. "This is Rockefeller Boulevard. Kahn's place will be in the next block on your left. Good luck!" Without waiting for a reply, she started trotting back in the direction they'd come. David waved goodbye to her receding back.

Jessica pulled out Kahn's address to confirm it once more. They were looking for 2219 Rockefeller Boulevard. She didn't see a sign naming this street but she trusted their guide. She looked for numbers on the buildings as they walked.

The buildings in this neighborhood were short – just three or four stories high. The construction was solid but battered, red brick or concrete slab with patches of mud and grout. Rope ladders hung from upper windows, some dangling all the way to the street, others stretching only to the next floor and anchored to the window beneath. Many windows and doors were propped open or missing. David pointed as a boy his age climbed out a second floor window, scaled a ladder and reentered on the fourth floor. Moments later a man ran out the front door chased by a woman with a hammer, screaming like a hurricane; he escaped around the corner and she returned, steaming through the door. The travelers walked on.

None of the buildings displayed numbers on the street, and Jessica had no idea which one was 2219. Halfway down the block she stopped a man to ask for the Kahn residence. He had no idea. She knocked at random on a door. No answer. She knocked at the next door and someone inside pointed her two doors down.

Kahn's building looked like the rest. It was three floors tall with rope ladders connecting each floor to the one above. The front door was open. Jessica knocked to give warning, paused for response, then led them inside. They entered an empty corridor with an immaculately swept dirt floor, the texture of the broom still visible on its surface. Each side of the hall had two closed, unmarked doors; one side also had an elevator that looked like it hadn't worked in years.

"Which door?" Jessica said to David. There were four choices with no clues; he might as well be the one to make the guess.

He looked thoughtful for a moment, then pointed to the farther door on the left. "That one."

Jessica knocked. Nobody answered so she knocked again, then they heard a light shuffling inside, someone walking towards the door.

A tiny, ancient woman opened the door. She was barely taller than David and she stooped so low she strained her face upwards to look at Jessica and Malcolm. Her skin was withered with age, and a black veil reached almost to her feet. "Asalam alechu," she said.

Jessica stepped forward. "We're looking for Sayeh Kahn." She held out the photograph.

The old woman took the photo in her tiny, shriveled hand and held it close to her face, straining to focus. She stared at it, breathing hoarsely until David started to fidget. "Sayeh," she said at last, looking up at Jessica.

"Yes, Sayeh," Jessica replied.

The woman gestured them inside and led them down a corridor so narrow they had to walk single file and so low Malcolm and Jessica had to stoop. The floor was the same swept dirt as the exterior hall, and the broom was propped in a corner. "Bobeck!" the woman called. "Te'ala Bobeck." Presently they emerged in a room that seemed large after the narrow corridor. A threadbare carpet covered most of the dirt floor and a round table squatted knee high in the center. Small chairs were scattered about, and faded pillows lay propped against the far wall. Light filtered in from two small windows and a single bulb hung from a wire in the ceiling. The room smelled of eternity and dust.

Shelves filled with food cartridges covered one wall in orderly rows. The cartridges were packed so close they formed a solid mass two layers deep. This type of cartridge could last years without refrigeration, and some of them looked like they had. This shelf held enough to feed a small family for months.

The woman gestured for everyone to be seated, but when David reached for a chair she hissed urgently and wagged a finger like he'd done something wrong.

He looked up in alarm but she continued pointing and wagging until he eventually looked to the chair. It was missing a leg. She took it from him and brought him another. When everyone was seated she asked, "Tashreb chai?" and repeated it when they didn't reply. "Tashreb chai?"

"Yes, please," Jessica answered. The old woman disappeared into the next room. They heard her bustling about and clattering dishes.

A cat entered the room, black with a white heart on its chest, and rubbed against Jessica's legs. She reached down to scratch behind its ears and soon found herself with a devoted friend. The cat jumped into her lap and started to purr. Jessica leaned back in her chair, then pulled forward when it wobbled. The three visitors sat quietly, waiting. Malcolm thought of his father, tried to imagine him stooping and waiting. Had he been here? Which chair did he sit in?

A boy about fourteen years old entered the room. "I am Bobeck," he said. "Welcome to our home." He bowed deeply before the visitors.

"Thank you for having us," Jessica replied. "We have come on a mission. Bernard Moore sent us in search of Sayeh Kahn." She showed him the photo.

Bobeck looked troubled. He smoothed the photo gently where it had been folded, then sat down and studied his new companions. He spoke to Jessica but pointed to Malcolm. "That one looks like Mr. Moore."

"His son," Jessica said.

"Congratulations, sir. Mr. Moore was a gentleman."

"Thank you." His father had been here after all, and left a smooth path behind.

But Bobeck still looked uneasy. "I understand that Mr. Moore has fallen on hard times lately." He was still staring at the photo of Sayeh Kahn.

"It's true," she confessed. And Counterterrorism wanted Kahn too. "How about Sayeh Kahn? Is he okay?"

"No, Madam." Bobeck kept his eyes on the photo. "Mr. Kahn is dead."

Malcolm groaned out loud. That explained why Kahn wasn't in the system when Jessica checked on him. The police wanted him, and they got him. Malcolm had no doubt that Kahn's death had been violent.

Bobeck stepped quietly to a shelf in the corner and removed the top sheet from a small pile of papers. He handed Jessica a letter from the City of New Angeles, and she read it out loud. "We regret to inform you," it began. In one short page, with few details and no explanations, it reported that Sayeh Kahn had died in the New Angeles Detention Center on April 7.

"We knew he'd been arrested," said Bobeck. "We saw the news and heard the word. We expected he would be released within a few days." He returned the letter to the shelf, straightened the papers and tidied the stack. Bobeck was bright and friendly, but still he darkened when he finished his thought. "Mr. Kahn was in good health and he obeyed the law. He was not a terrorist."

Jessica rose from her chair and stepped lightly across to him. "I'm sorry." She took his hand in her own. "I'm certain he was a good man."

"Thank you, madam," Bobeck said with a gentle bow.

The room was silent for a long time, even the clattering in the kitchen came to a rest. Malcolm spoke up. "My father gave me some water."

Bobeck's mood brightened immediately. "You are fortunate," he declared. "Our water is gone. The police took it."

"When they took Sayeh Kahn."

"That is correct. You need to be careful."

"Too late."

Bobeck's pleasure disappeared. "Then you cannot grow any more."

Grow more, Malcolm thought. Grow. His father had talked about water that renews itself. A guess started to form about the mystery water. It contained some kind of microorganism that consumed the salt and purified the water. Like the Odor Eater did for garbage. Added to seawater, it would eat until the salt was gone. Tentek would pay a lot for an organism like that. "Who else has it?" he asked.

"Mr. Kahn gave it away freely to family and friends. People he liked. He must have met your father on one of his expeditions, or perhaps your father was kind to him at work."

"Perhaps someone can give some back."

Jessica intervened. "The reward."

Bobeck nodded agreement.

She continued to the next step. "Where did he get it?"

"I don't know. Mr. Kahn worked hard to obtain small amounts."

"Who does know?"

"Mr. Kahn."

"Who else?"

Bobeck shrugged. "Nobody." The secret might have died with Sayeh Kahn.

The old woman reentered the chamber, walking slowly, balancing a large silver tray arrayed with cups, saucers and a pot of tea. She set it all on the table then walked carefully around the room, passing each individual, including David, an empty cup and saucer. Bobeck made no effort to help, and the visitors perceived that their role was to accept, not to assist. Slowly, arthritically the aged hostess circled the room again, filling each empty cup with steaming hot tea. Her hand shook on the pot but she didn't spill a drop. When she'd served herself and sat in the last empty seat, they all started to drink.

Malcolm said aloud what he could see in Jessica's eyes and David was too young to appreciate. "Wow." The tea was fabulous, like nothing else in the world. It eased its way down, sweet and minty, nutty and smooth, dissolving tension on its way. His shoulders relaxed and he leaned back in his chair. The tea was a liquid holiday.

Bobeck could see what they were thinking. "My grandmother makes a special tea. She uses honey and mint, and she grinds pistachios, I think. Sometimes cardamom. She's made it this way her whole life."

"You can't buy tea like this," Malcolm said.

"No," Bobeck agreed. "It is not possible. The ingredients are available, however, if you look. Honey is hardest to find. Grandmother insists on real honey, which is quite costly, but she doesn't use much."

Jessica walked across the room and touched the old woman on the shoulder. "The tea is wonderful."

The woman smiled back and patted her hand. They lingered a moment before Jessica returned to her seat.

Bobeck said something to his grandmother in her own language, and she responded the same way. The two of them spoke back and forth a while, the visitors unable to understand even the gist of their conversation. Bobeck passed her the photo of Sayeh Kahn, which she unfolded and held close to her chest.

Bobeck said to Jessica. "She wants to know why you have come."

"Did you tell her about the water?"

Bobeck returned to his grandmother and they conversed a while longer, with indecipherable gestures of pouring and drinking.

Jessica interrupted the exchange to catch Bobeck's attention. "Tell her we want to help," she said. Then she changed her mind and waved him off.

She put down her tea and walked gravely to the older woman. She bent to her knees before her, like a penitent offering prayer, and touched the photo of Sayeh Kahn. Jessica looked intensely at David, her eyes filling with tears, then turned to the ancient matron. "No woman should ever outlive her child." Her voice broke over the words. "No mother should outlive her son."

Bobeck translated. The old woman let out a long sigh, like a machine running out of fuel, then closed her eyes and touched her chin to her chest. Jessica stayed on her knees and they rested together for a long time, sharing a bond across language and generation. Finally, Jessica looked up and asked softly, "Where did he get the water?" It was a plea to let them help.

The older woman shook her head slowly. "Nobody knows," she said. Bobeck translated. She pointed one finger towards heaven; no translation was needed.

Jessica returned to her seat and the room stayed still for a long time. David finished his tea and asked his mother if he could play with the cat, curled now on a pillow nearby. He stroked it gently without waiting for a reply. Jessica watched him with eyes like a mother but started talking like a lawyer.

"Did Sayeh have any special friends? Was there someone he knew forever or trusted more than anyone else?"

The old woman turned to Bobeck. They spoke a while, back and forth, asking and answering, slowly increasing in concentration. Finally the woman turned to Jessica. "Amjat," she declared. "They have been friends since the sandbox."

Jessica nodded her appreciation and said to Bobeck. "Do you think Amjat might know?"

He shook his head. "I doubt it. I don't think Mr. Kahn told anyone. But Amjat was his one special friend."

"Where is he?"

Bobeck shrugged.

"Have you seen him lately?"

"No. I haven't seen him lately. Nobody has. I was looking for him only yesterday and couldn't find him anywhere. It's odd. Amjat is usually easy to find."

Malcolm and Jessica exchanged a glance indicating exactly the same thought: Amjat knew.

"Will you tell us if you find him?" Jessica asked.

"Of course," Bobeck replied. They exchanged contact information and the visitors rose to leave.

Jessica gathered the cups and saucers and placed them carefully on the tray in the center of the table, then turned for farewell with their aging host. Her last gesture was a bow like she had seen Bobeck use, and the woman inclined her head in return.

Bobeck led them all through the door and down the streets to the train station, swiftly and more directly than they had come, hurrying because the next train was soon to arrive.

The last thing they saw in Kaiserville was the body of an old man, dead from hunger or disease, stretched beside the railway platform. His skin was gray and slack, and swollen like a lumpy cauliflower under his chin. Someone had positioned bags of ice around his body and under his head to keep it preserved, and placed a saucer for donations alongside. The bowl was filled with small coins and a few single Globo notes. Jessica led David as far around the body as possible, while Malcolm emptied his wallet into the saucer.

PART TWO

DISCOVERY

Chapter Ten

The streets of New Angeles had never looked as clean as they did when he walked to work the next day. The air was clear and cool, with a fresh breeze from the ocean. Malcolm saw everything differently, from the toilet that whisked away his sewerage to the vehicles that stayed on their own part of the street. Some things he had taken for granted; others he knew to be luxuries but he'd never imagined a world without them. Now he'd been there; it changed everything.

The change wasn't altogether positive. New Angeles' sparkle seemed artificial to him now, like a model apartment designed to show prospective tenants, not to be lived in. The advertising still flashed and danced, but now it seemed sterile and empty in comparison to muddy feet, foul odors and swinging cargo that barely missed your head. He passed a commercial for computer simulated tourist attractions like the Grand Canyon and the Taj Mahal. "Have you seen the world yet?" the promoters wanted to know. Malcolm realized he'd seen more world a short train ride away than in a whole library of computer tours.

Garcia wasn't working the front door but he stopped by Malcolm's office on his morning rounds. Today Malcolm wanted to say something different but he didn't know how to begin. Finally he asked, "How was your trip in?" He'd never before wondered about Garcia's commute – but yesterday's transit to Kaiserville had taken hours.

Garcia cocked his head strangely. "I got a seat."

Malcolm paused, uncertain on the new terrain. "Does it help your legs get through the day?"

Now it was Garcia's turn to hesitate. "Yes," he said. "It's a long ride and a long day. I log a lot of mileage in a week."

"But you're not complaining."

"No, not complaining." He moved the conversation to familiar ground. "Did you fill out the basketball pool?"

Malcolm followed. "I couldn't get to it. Who'd you pick?"

"Texaco will be eliminated by Maryland in the quarterfinals. With Smithson injured, their offense goes nowhere." He rattled off statistics. "Casa Fiesta will win it all."

Malcolm whistled appreciatively. Garcia had been tested in the betting halls of the outlying districts. "If I pay you a percentage will you pick for me next season?"

"Against the rules," said Garcia, and continued his rounds.

The day's corporate greeting was, "The world rewards the entrepreneur and the entrepreneur rewards the world." As usual, the auxiliary screens held advertisements and Malcolm waited to clear them, then the real work began. A whole raft of messages had arrived on the water project, dubbed *Operation Many Drops to Drink* in honor of a long dead poet, although Malcolm didn't understand the reference. He learned that the *Many Drops* staff had been divided into teams devoted to the three major components of the water problem – delivery, desalination and disposal. He was thrilled to see that he'd been assigned to desalination, the heart of the problem. He scanned his own assignments and checked to see how they fit into his team's and the other teams' too. Deadlines were tight, he noticed; the schedule was incredibly ambitious.

Yesterday's deadlines had already been met by others because background material had been prepared for every team. The "Delivery" team focused on getting water to the households, the "Disposal" team on piping away waste. Malcolm's job was to get the salt out, and he plunged himself into the research. He learned that the most common means of desalination was nuclear fission. Gigantic nuclear power plants like the one by the jail boiled seawater and the resulting steam was captured and condensed. Other water resources included recycled wastewater and traditional freshwater runoff, which were consolidated in municipal systems. Tentek's goal was to create a single unified municipal plumbing system for both salt and fresh, and to let households purify their water to the level they chose.

But none of Tentek's designs looked like Sayeh Kahn's. Tentek was desalinating water the old fashioned way, boiling water and collecting steam. Lots of creative energy was being applied to heat transfer systems and

Malcolm had no doubt that many teams, including his own, would develop clever new ways to bring water to a boil – but it was still the same old concept, requiring large quantities of heat and energy.

Kahn's water seemed to host some kind of microorganism that consumed salt the way the Odor Eater consumed bacteria in trashcans. Such an organism could be released into tanks of seawater to multiply and feed until the salt was all gone. Details of containment and distribution needed to be worked out – and impurities other than salt needed to be removed – but he was sure those could be solved. Sayeh Kahn seemed to have done it already.

Tentek was flirting with solutions that could change the world. Cheap, easy desalinated seawater could revolutionize agriculture, turn wasteland into rice paddies and satisfy cravings from Africa to Australia, starting at home in southern California. This was better than one strange man's bottle, or even a sample in his own apartment – especially one that authorities considered dangerous contraband. This solution would come from the mighty Tentek Corporation. Nobody would question it, and Malcolm would make it happen. He raced to the Pledge Hall for the daily pledge – *a safer, more productive, more prosperous world for all* – and returned to his desk with vigor he hadn't felt in years.

* * * * *

He paid the court to dispose of the body in a dignified way, and considered his next steps. Bernard Moore might never be vindicated in court but his death lit the path ahead, and that path led through Tentek's research laboratory. Vindication was yet another reason to move forward. He buried himself in water desalination. Organic if he could; *Many Drops* no matter what.

His mother couldn't care less about the death. "At least the water is safe," she said, taking a bite of a sandwich at her desk.

At midnight he called Jessica. He expected just to leave a message but the system found her at her desk.

"Can we meet?" he asked. "I need to talk." He was too tired for a full explanation; he just wanted to schedule something.

"Maybe next year."

"That bad?"

"Worse."

"I'll fit your schedule."

"I won't have a single free minute for at least a week."

"I was planning to hit the office at six tomorrow morning. I could stop by your place at five."

"I'll still be here at five," She gestured to her desk. She wouldn't budge an inch.

"But you'll call me as soon as things get better," Malcolm insisted. "It's pretty important."

"I'll call you. I promise." She switched off.

* * * * *

The next day he had almost the same conversation with his supervisor, Kira Portman, who'd drafted him for *Many Drops to Drink*. Often in the past Kira had given him flexibility to pursue tangents of his own, and he always returned good results. Now he tried repeatedly to reach her by vidlink, then finally cornered her in the hall.

"I have an idea about desalination," he said.

"No new ideas," she replied. "Nothing but deadlines."

"This idea might save time later."

"Great. Tell me about it later." She kept walking.

The next few days were a blur. Malcolm's office, like Jessica's, had accelerated to meet deadlines, and even the deadlines were moving up. Four days was already tight for his next deliverable but now he had two; three days was a hurry for the deadline after that, but now he had one. His entire team gunned forward as a unit, tightly controlled and highly interdependent. To do his own work, Malcolm needed conclusions or information provided by people upstream; people downstream needed conclusions or information provided by him. Malcolm appreciated the productivity of people before him, and he owed no less to the next people in line.

The team accelerated into ultratime, as this pace had come to be called. Malcolm had done it many times before and he'd mastered the routine. He came into the office around six in the morning and worked until midnight. Minus a little time on either end for physical maintenance like showering and changing clothes, that left five hours for sleep – the minimum he'd learned he needed to function for more than a few days, and sometimes ultratime lasted for weeks. He couldn't afford to miss a minute of sleep, though, and his mind kept working after he lay down, so he kept a bottle of sedatives by the door. He took a pill as soon as he got home and by the time he hit the pillow he was out. The next morning he took a stimulant so he wouldn't be groggy, and he drank loads of coffee during the day.

He was tempted to work from home so he wouldn't lose the few minutes to the commute, but that never seemed to work. If he needed to consult with just one person who was screening out vidlinks he lost more time waiting for that person to call back than if he just walked down the corridor and knocked on the door. The person might be crabby, but at least he'd get an answer.

After a few days he lost track of time. It could have been five days or fifteen, he couldn't tell. Ultratime always felt like that, with the days running together. Malcolm only got unhappy if he missed his five hours of sleep. After a long stretch of ultratime, the ordinary sixty to eighty hour work week seemed like a holiday.

In the middle of the second week a department psychologist dropped by his office. "Got a minute?" she asked.

"Sure," Malcolm checked his watch. He was used to these visits too. Central Records notified Psychology whenever someone logged more than 100 hours in a single week.

"Are you feeling okay?" she said. "I noticed the long hours. You must feel stressed." She was an affable, middle-aged woman with an engaging smile and extremely blonde hair.

"I'm holding up."

"Do you need any stimulants? I have a new one that's much stronger than you can buy without a prescription. People have been telling me it's fabulous. It might help you finish on time, maybe even ahead of schedule."

"I think I'm okay. Coffee plus the pills I got last time seem to be enough. I make sure to get enough sleep."

"Good for you. That's wonderful. Some people get stressed in ultratime and don't take care of themselves. But I want you to be more than okay. I want you to be happy. Would you like an antidepressant? Lots of people are using Methabenzeprene these days."

"No thanks," said Malcolm. The psychologist was now becoming a source of stress herself. She was taking too long and she wouldn't take No for an answer.

"All our medications are free, you know."

"Thanks, I know." Free drugs were one of the benefits of the department psychologists. In theory the psychologists could help people dodge ultratime because they had authority to recommend reducing workloads on grounds of mental health, but few people exercised that option. The waiver forms were complicated and permission had to be granted by several layers of command. People felt like they were abandoning their teammates, and their teammates usually felt that way too.

The psychologist wasn't finished. "I'll tell Operations to add more sunlight to the mix in your room. I insist on it. You'll feel better immediately!" She was referring to the interior lighting. Imitating the sun's radiation gave some people more energy.

"Sunlight would be nice," Malcolm replied.

"Let me know if you start to burn."

* * * * *

While Malcolm worked to desalinate seawater Jessica worked with an international investment consortium that looked to her like bickering kindergartners. The consortium had dissolved and now the partners were arguing over the spoils in tones that Jessica wouldn't have tolerated from a six-year-old. She spent her days and her nights in legal libraries seeking complicated solutions to simple problems.

Once she checked the court directly for updates on Bernard Moore. She saw that Counterterrorism had withdrawn its claim against him and that Malcolm had made arrangements for the funeral. "You're a good son," she wrote in a text message, not expecting a reply. She didn't tell him about the coroner's report documenting his father's injuries. His death was brutal and had taken a long time; no weapons were involved.

Some hours later Malcolm responded to her funeral message. "Thank you. Good will come." She was curious what he meant but she had to return her attention to the bickering kindergartners. She was falling behind on international jurisdiction, and she had work to do.

Chapter Eleven

By the end of the second week Malcolm's schedule started to ease. Days still began at six but they finished before midnight; last night he walked home to a fabulous sunset and went immediately to sleep. Now he indulged a leisurely breakfast, and read the milk cube while he ate. One side told the story of a young man who beat up an attacker with a stick. "Milk is security," the package declared. Television news in the background told of a woman who lost her job and went violently mad.

Malcolm muted the television and pushed aside the milk. He didn't need input like that. He needed to slow down and think hard about what had happened and what needed to happen next. He realized that weeks had passed and that young Bobeck hadn't contacted him about the missing Amjat. If there were news to report, the burden was on him to find out.

His television burst up in volume, defying his earlier mute. He spun in annoyance as the announcer bragged, "This merger is all about service. Together we can serve the consumer better than each of us individually." Malcolm was numb to exaggeration and heard about big mergers all the time, but this one already had his attention so he kept listening.

The newscaster said that Microtech had acquired Dawkins, one of the world's largest publishing houses. Dawkins owned the copyright on libraries full of movies and books, and subsidiaries in radio and television. Control of Dawkins gave Microtech access to the content as well as the vehicles of mass communication. The announcer explained that Microtech now owned not only televisions, but also television stations and television programs. "Households will use Microtech three times every time they turn on the TV," he crowed. "Only Tentek provides a similar scale of service."

That brought Malcolm to a full stop. He knew that Tentek meant more than appliances but he didn't really know what else. Television had never entered his mind until Jessica's remarks in the train, and he certainly didn't realize that Tentek already possessed the kind of reach described by Microtech's merger. He flashed back to the possibility that the broadcasts on Sayeh Kahn were just advertising for the Safe-T-Buzzer. Could it be?

The doorbell rang and he was almost grateful to see only Mrs. Pearson, baby in her arms, asking to borrow some milk. He barely listened to what she said, but his cube of security milk satisfied her completely. The last thing he heard as he left for work was the name of the new multimedia conglomerate. The company's new name was Brother.

* * * * *

He couldn't help himself. As soon as the daily greeting and the mandatory advertising had passed, he detoured to examine Tentek's ownership structure. Did it really own television stations? Dcpartment stores? He explored the network until he found Tentek's organizational chart.

Even as he studied it he realized it couldn't be right. The official schematic specified only the divisions that Malcolm already considered Tentek. The chart showed how his own Family Safety Division was a subset of the Security Division, and how the Security Division linked to units for marketing, legal, genetics and so forth – but that was all it showed. It didn't indicate relationships with any other parts of the world, and certainly not television stations. But in Malcolm's years at Tentek he had often reached beyond the list on his screen. A project last quarter involved Rickshaw, a transit company in Hong Kong that was introduced as a wholly owned subsidiary. But Rickshaw wasn't listed.

And only a few minutes ago, Malcolm had watched an advertisement for the Titans football team, dubbed "Tentek's finest." The chart was either incomplete or wrong.

He decided to run his inquiries from the other direction. Instead of examining what Tentek owned, he looked to see what might be owned by Tentek. He exited the Tentek network and, on an impulse, started with Federated, his father's department store chain. It took a few minutes to locate an organizational chart and sort out the baffling web of affiliations and mergers, but eventually it made sense. He learned that Federated was part of Quonset Corporation, which owed a dozen other department stores and specialty shops. Quonset, in turn, was part of a conglomerate called Stateside, which raised the chain out of the retail sector and into industries including trucking companies, commercial banks and six different real estate corporations.

StateSide appeared at first to be the top of the ownership chain, but doublechecking revealed a different path that first escaped his attention. A few keystrokes brought him an answer: StateSide was a wholly owned subsidiary of Tentek Corporation. A few more clicks made it certain. Tentek was absolutely at the top of the foodchain. Malcolm and his father had both worked for the same boss. He'd have to discuss that with Jessica.

He did a little of his real work so he wouldn't fall behind while his subconscious mind continued to whir, then he checked some broadcasts following his father's arrest. The first one he found mentioned sales on the Safe-T-Buzzer, so he checked the station and traced its ownership structure. By now he was learning the tricks and within minutes he had an answer. But it didn't make any sense. The station was owned by Microtech, which sold its own personal alarm system that competed directly with Tentek's Safe-T-Buzzer. Why would a Microtech station promote its competitor's product? Another question for Jessica.

One last piece before digging into a day's work on water desalination. He pulled up Microtech's corporate information to compare its ownership span. With the merger fresh in the news, the Microtech corporate hierarchy was easy to find. It was as impressive as the broadcasts made it sound.

A message came across his screen as he typed. He didn't even glance at it, eager to finish this distraction and return to his *Many Drops* assignments. Then his computer froze. Then his thigh shocked so hard he jumped out of his chair. This message couldn't wait.

The computer freeze was peculiar, though; the message function worked fine but nothing else did. Even as he figured that out he received a second shock, then the incoming message took over all three of his screens.

It was the office of Internal Affairs, Tentek's corporate police. Internal Affairs was different from Garcia's security, which simply kept out burglars and maintained order. Internal Affairs guarded against espionage and sabotage, corruption and acts of disloyalty. Its purpose was to defend the Corporation against threats from within. Malcolm had never before been contacted by Internal Affairs, but the message was simple. *Report here now.* He didn't know if they were always so urgent but he didn't want to test their patience. As lights flashed and trumpets sounded, he decided to skip the pledge.

* * * * *

The elevator buzzed with people rushing to pledge but nobody got off with Malcolm on the 99th floor. Internal Affairs had this space all to itself. Exiting the elevator he noticed scan plates built into the wall. Styled to look decorative and unobtrusive, the scan plates searched him for weapons with sensors so finely calibrated they alerted to pens with excessive metal, inert objects heavy enough to injure on impact, and chemicals that were harmless individually but could create incendiaries or poisons when mixed. During their development he'd joked with Kira that these plates could detect mere thoughts of physical nastiness.

A burly man in the brown uniform of Internal Affairs gestured for Malcolm to follow him down the hallway. The uniform was a brown business suit with a Tentek logo on the breast. The carpet and walls were the same brown as the escort's suit, and devoid of furniture or decoration. As they started to walk, a second man joined them from behind. Malcolm turned to look at him but the man snapped his fingers and pointed for Malcolm to keep his eyes forward. The sharp snap reverberated down the empty hall. The first guard led him to a room with a single straight backed chair and pointed for him to sit.

Malcolm sat.

The first guard disappeared but the second stood by the door, watching.

Malcolm knew he'd done nothing wrong. All the information he'd requested was available to the general public or internally to Tentek researchers. He hadn't even brushed the boundaries of confidentiality and he knew he was performing at least adequately in his assigned tasks.— But he also knew that he had been skirting boundaries lately, sneaking off to the jail and borrowing time to explore subjects other than his assigned tasks. He would have to wait to see what this was all about. Perhaps it was a routine affair on an unrelated matter. Perhaps something had gone wrong in the transition from his past projects, and clarification was needed. He sat patiently and succeeded at remaining composed. His thoughts strayed to his father. Is this how he felt during his first hour at the jail? Was he patient and trusting, waiting for the problem to sort itself out? Had he lost confidence and panicked? He knew how his father's story ended. He didn't like that.

The chamber was utterly silent. There was no foot traffic or video monitors, nobody whispering into computer microphones or tapping away on keyboards. On the wall a single bronze plaque carried the inscription: *Lie is the eternal sin.* Malcolm read the plaque over and over. He had no idea what sin was, other than a quaint old term meaning bad, but he knew what lying was and he'd never been a liar. On the other hand, he understood that honesty, like everything else, required moderation. He took the message under advisement, looked at his watch and thought about water desalination. He wasn't at his desk but he could still make some progress.

After a while, he grew impatient. He stood cautiously, then walked around the chamber. The officer at the door did nothing to prevent him, just watched his every move. Malcolm looked down the corridor towards the elevator, but there was nothing to see. He sat down again, closed his eyes and tried to get comfortable.

Two new officers in brown suits appeared and told him to follow them. They led him down a different hallway to a small brown room with one piece of furniture, a table tall enough to stand behind. On top of the table rested a computer, a notebook and a pen. The room was a perfect cube, exactly as tall as it was on each side, with the table positioned precisely in the center. The two men stood behind the table and Malcolm stood on the other side. Brown uniforms, brown room, brown desk.

They wasted no more time. "You have been databasing in unusual places," one officer stated. "What were you doing?"

Malcolm felt his whole body sag. So this *was* a response to his morning's activities. And perhaps last week's searches from home. He'd been caught; Tentek must have been monitoring his search functions. He thought about the sinners' plaque but decided to give the safest possible answer, even if he had to smooth the edges of accuracy. "The *Many* Drops team is big. Lots of different parties are involved." He listed some internal Tentek divisions and external affiliates like research contractors. "I just wanted to learn about my new team." He hoped they wouldn't ask what that had to do with department stores or why he thought he had time to spare.

The officers watched him, expressionless. "And Microtech? Where do they fit in?"

Malcolm swallowed hard and did his best. "They are our competitors," he acknowledged. "I wanted to see if they were organized similarly." He guessed that he was being recorded and knew that his creative blather could someday be used against him.

The two officers looked at each other, then back at Malcolm. The first officer declared, "Microtech is not your job. Your job is desalinating seawater." He stepped forward and leaned across the table, staring into Malcolm's eyes until Malcolm lowered his gaze and stepped back. "Tentek pays you to desalinate seawater. That's your job, and your entire job. Our job is to keep you on track. This is your warning."

"I'll do my job."

"Your first slip cost you a financial penalty. Future slips will cost you more. If you're not doing your job, you might not keep it. Do you understand?"

"I understand."

The escort arrived to bring Malcolm back to the elevator. As he left, the officer reiterated, "Remember, *your* job is to desalinate seawater. *Our* job is to keep you on track. And we are very, very good at our job." He signaled for the escort to take Malcolm away.

When Malcolm returned to his office he saw that the work on his computer had been replaced by a uniform display of Internal Affairs brown. The brown lifted when he hit a key, and the main screen in the center displayed the words, "Thank you for your compliance." That seemed like a sick joke but the other screens told him it was serious. The left screen notified him that his first slip cost his next paycheck plus a full week of vacation. The right screen stated that his bank account had been reduced by 25% of its overall value, and explained that fining people in proportion to their assets treated rich and poor alike – "in keeping with Tentek's philosophy of fairness." Malcolm sat down and shook his head in disbelief, then hit another key. The screens faded to brown followed by assurance that compliance would return him to normal payroll status, "in keeping with Tentek's philosophy of rewards as well as punishments."

At the bottom of the right screen were the words, "Good Luck."

* * * * *

"Can they do that?" Malcolm exploded to Jessica later that evening. Her own stretch of ultratime was winding down and he caught her on the first attempt. "Can they just take it away? Don't I get due process or something?"

He'd spent the rest of the day on water desalination but he took no joy in the work. He closed and locked the door to his office, seeking security but instead he felt trapped. All he wanted was to get out of the building as soon as possible and to see Jessica the minute he did – but first he finished his current assignments and got a leap on his next, making it clear that he was "doing his job." It was long past dark when he called Jessica from a public vidlink on the street outside Tentek. She was still at her desk but agreed to meet at the front door to her office. He arrived before she did and spent the time pacing back and forth, hoping he wouldn't be arrested for loitering.

Jessica greeted him with a smile and started for the rollway that took her home, but didn't protest when Malcolm steered her towards the stationary pavement. They walked in relative privacy while he told her what happened.

"You don't get due process," she began. "It's called 'implied consent.' You impliedly consented to this type of punishment when you signed your employment contract and were found to be in violation of that contract."

"Found by whom?"

"Found by Tentek. They determine the facts of the case, and probably hear the appeal as well. You need to watch your step." She paused as a commuter transpo pulled over in front of them. Malcolm could see that it was hers and that she was eager to get home, but she let it go. "Your biggest problem isn't the money anyway." She looked at him to be sure.

He nodded that he would be all right. He could afford the financial hit. Even the lost vacation didn't hurt because he rarely took time off; he lost vacation every year when the books rolled over.

She continued her original thought. "Then your problem isn't the punishment. Your problem is how closely they monitored your activities."

"Go on."

"I'm guessing this search of yours didn't take long. Not more than half an hour."

He nodded to indicate that it was faster than that.

"Whatever trip mechanism they use, it's pretty sensitive."

Malcolm saw where she was headed. "I confess to a boring personal life," he admitted, "but I do sometimes check movie schedules or make personal calls from the office."

She smiled. "Boring is nice, but don't forget whose office you're in. It's Tentek's vidlink and you are Tentek's employee. Everything you do is their business."

"Even if it has nothing to do with Tentek?"

"The boundaries aren't that clear. Vidlinks can be used to talk to anybody, whether or not related to business. Sometimes you discuss more than one thing in a single conversation; sometimes a single thought has multiple meanings. Tentek resolves the ambiguity in its favor. It's the same reason all your work-product belongs to Tentek."

"What do you mean?"

"If you invent something while working for Tentek, you don't own it. They do. You're working for them. Even after you leave you can't give your ideas to someone else. You signed a no-compete, right?"

"A what?"

"A no-compete agreement," she repeated, "a clause in your employment contract stating that if you left Tentek you couldn't work for a competitive firm for some period of time. Tentek doesn't want to compete against ideas developed in its own shop. Even if the ideas are your own, they may have had seeds in Tentek."

"I vaguely remember signing something like that," he said. "It was a form contract Tentek prepared for me when I started – years ago. I didn't pay much attention to it. I'm not a lawyer."

"Your mistake," she grinned, and gestured towards a transpo pulling up ahead of them. Malcolm had more questions but they could wait. He nodded goodbye, freeing her to dash for the transpo, her footsteps ringing out in the silence of the street.

* * * * *

Malcolm turned around and walked the opposite direction towards the nearest transpo line headed his way. Home was much too far to walk. He rested on the transpo, relaxing to the low hum of electric motors. The other passengers concentrated on their lifelinks, nodded drowsily or stared at video monitors mounted in the seats ahead of them. Sometimes Malcolm absentmindedly glanced at the video in his seat, still tuned to the station of the previous passenger. Without turning on the audio he recognized a discussion of the Microtech merger.

Between stops in the middle of the street the transpo slowed to a crawl. That was odd. Passengers who sat passively a minute ago started to peer tensely out the windows as other transpos sped past and even pedestrians on rollways left them behind. The man beside Malcolm checked his watch, checked it again and groaned out loud. Then the lights dimmed to emergency power and the transpo coasted to a halt. The videos went off.

At first people accepted it. They sat quietly and waited for something to happen. When nothing did they started to fidget. Some people stood and paced the cabin, others leaned to look out the windows, but still nobody said a word. One person tested the door. "Locked," he announced.

The word took a finger out of the dyke. Bedlam erupted. Everybody started yelling at once, and others rushed the door to test it. One woman climbed on top of her seat. "It's terrorists!" she shouted. She waved her arms like a prophet of doom in the dim flicker of emergency power. "It's sabotage! We're hostages!"

The woman behind Malcolm screamed so loudly it made him duck. She started arguing with the person beside her about what the demands might be, and whether to give in. Two young women near the door began to shove each other; one woman was carrying a baby, who started to cry.

Malcolm didn't move. For the second time in the same day he sat still and waited. He didn't know what had happened, but terrorism seemed unlikely. His first instinct was mechanical failure: transpos were so reliable people that forgot they could malfunction, but not so reliable that they never did. The door was probably sealed because the transpo was in the middle of the street. His best contribution, he decided, was simply not to participate. He tuned out the talk of terrorism, which was sounding sillier and sillier, and waited for the machine to move.

It took less than a minute. The lights brightened and the transpo surged to full speed. The intercom announced that an electrical failure had caused the delay and that nobody would be charged for the ride. The rest of the trip occurred without incident, and by the time the transpo pulled into Malcolm's stop the passengers had returned to their seats and resumed their business, all talk of terrorism left behind. But the two women by the door still eyed each other with hostility and suspicion.

* * * * *

Mrs. Pearson accosted Malcolm in the apartment lobby to tell him this morning's milk made her baby feel much better. "Feel his skin," she continued. "It's as soft as skylon."

Malcom gave the baby the tiniest caress imaginable, wiped his hand on his pants and kept walking. When he entered his apartment the television and lights turned on automatically as usual. He half listened for news of the transpo failure while he hung up his coat and poured a glass of water. If his father made the news, maybe the breakdown would too. There was nothing about it, though he did catch a brief update on the guerillas who had taken the bus in Brazzaville. He turned the television off and settled at his computer for a serious stretch of work.

First he checked his bank balance. Sure enough, his savings had been reduced by precisely 25%. The entry simply stated "business withdrawal" and it was authorized by the same code that permitted direct deposit of his paycheck. In the list of scheduled transactions, he saw that his next paycheck had been cancelled. Malcolm let out a long, slow breath, deflating like a balloon. He'd acted casual about this with Jessica. Yes, he had enough money and, yes, he could afford the loss. But he wasn't rich and he felt a private sense of security as he watched his balance grow. He didn't realize its importance until now, when the money disappeared.

He thought about ways to make up the loss but realized that his budget could be squeezed no further. He already lived like a monk, avoiding the cycle of earning and spending that kept his colleagues on the brink. He couldn't cut back until he'd saved the difference; it was simply gone. He had to accept it. Malcolm took a deep breath, poured a glass of water and hunted his archives for his employment contract. It was almost impossible to understand – twenty pages of compressed print and obscure legal terminology – but he was determined to find the terms Jessica mentioned without troubling her for help. He zoomed up the view and leaned forward. The print was so tight and the words so unfamiliar he traced them across the screen, one by one, with his finger as he read them.

Long after he should have been asleep he found what he was looking for. In the middle of page twelve, without any heading or indentation, he located paragraph 14(b):

> *Any or all products or processes and the proceeds of any or all products or processes developed by Employee during the time of employment, whether or not in the course of employment and however related to the subject of employment, are the sole and exclusive property of Tentek Corporation.*

Malcolm understood this to mean that anything he worked on belonged to Tentek. Jessica was right that Tentek didn't want ideas developed in, or even near, its practice to extend beyond its sphere.

A few pages later was paragraph 22:

> *Employee shall not directly or indirectly engage in work for any business that directly or indirectly designs, produces or sells any product or service offered by Tentek Corporation for a period of twenty years after leaving employment of Tentek Corporation.*

In other words, if he left Tentek he couldn't work in his own field for twenty years, most of his professional life. That meant he would be working for Tentek for a long, long time. Assuming it let him.

Chapter Twelve

Malcolm's team met at six the next morning but he started at five. He passed the great bronze statue of Hap Jackson in the entry hall while the cleaning crews were still at work, running a bit late this morning. Workers in the pink uniforms of Snappy Kleen scurried back and forth, vacuuming carpets and polishing banisters. Malcolm noticed for the first time how tired they looked. One of them dropped something, then tripped when she bent to pick it up. For all Malcolm knew, this team was finishing its own stretch of ultratime. One particularly exhausted girl – not more than fourteen years old – was struggling to load a waxing machine onto a cart. The machine weighed more than she did, and it was awkward to hold. Malcolm grabbed an edge to help her lift.

"It's poorly designed," he remarked.

The girl looked at him without understanding.

"It should have a handle right here." He pointed to the cover of the waxing rotor – but the girl wasn't even looking. She stared straight at the floor and edged away as he muscled the machine fully onto the cart.

"Gracias," she muttered as she fled back to her duties.

Malcolm had scheduled an appointment with Kira before the team meeting. She was eating breakfast at her desk, surrounded by medicine bottles that suggested how she maintained equilibrium. He explained the idea of organic desalination and his desire to start a new team.

"I have no flexibility," she replied. She guessed that they were rushing against competition or worried about security, and she observed that big projects tended to bureaucratize and that big egos at the top liked to dominate. "I can't do anything about it."

"Would it help if I already had a sample? If I could prove that it can be done?" He no longer had one anyway, but he wanted to know. Amjat was out there somewhere.

She looked at him quizzically, like she knew he had something in mind, but the door stayed closed. "It wouldn't help if you drank it for breakfast and had the genetic design in your briefcase. You'd still need a team to solve storage, distribution and all the rest. *Many Drops* isn't built that way. I can't rebuild it."

"Will you suggest it to someone upstairs?"

All she could promise was to look for an opportunity. "Keep your head down for now," she advised as they walked to the team meeting together. "Your idea is promising. But it's also very big. It doesn't matter if we start now or in a few months."

But it did matter, he realized as he sat alone in the cafeteria at lunch time. It mattered a lot. Certainly it mattered more than the team meeting he'd trudged through, trying to appear interested in boiling water with limited kilowatts while thinking about Kaiserville women standing in line at the water tap. While he ate he did stupid math in his head: how many people waited in line for water, multiplied by how long they waited each time. He calculated how much time was wasted in water lines and speculated what else people could do during that time. Every day Tentek waited translated into large chunks of other people's lives – and it was all happening within a few miles of an ocean with infinite gallons of water they couldn't drink.— Suddenly he understood what the project's title, *Many Drops to Drink*, must be referring to. He didn't want to wait.

A fanfare of trumpets interrupted his reveries. The television's hourly business bulletin declared the nation on a path to another quarter of record-breaking productivity. All the key indicators were up. Construction was up, stock averages were up and consumer activity was up. The announcer, a spirited young woman in a bright blue suit, said the economy was entering a period of unrivaled prosperity.

A man sat down at the next table and shoveled food into his mouth while whispering into a microphone and typing on his keyboard. Within a minute he had devoured lunch, then packed his keyboard and moved on. Immediately he was replaced by a man dressed in black who was asking his companion whether to take a day off for his mother's funeral. His face sagged and grey circles lined his eyes. He explained that he'd already taken a day off for her illness.

"I don't think my mother missed a full week of work in her entire life," he boasted loudly enough for Malcolm to hear. "Maybe the way to honor her is to stick to my job, stick to what matters. I have so much to do …."

Malcolm didn't wait to hear the reply. He left his lunch half eaten on the table and dashed for his office. Scarcity was everywhere. He wanted to bring some relief, and he didn't want to wait for orders. Malcolm Moore swore to bring this product to market. He'd find a way. Tentek could join him whenever it chose.

* * * * *

Jessica was bored at work. The case of the bickering kindergartners had been solved, and her schedule returned to routine. She suppressed a yawn as she reported progress to her supervisor, a large man who thought more of himself than Jessica thought he should. He'd filled his office with pictures of himself. Phil Barnes on the courthouse steps, Phil Barnes receiving the departmental Medal of Service, Phil Barnes at a black tie dinner with people who looked important but Jessica couldn't begin to identify …. The only thing Jessica liked about his office was the window to the outside.

A table held a printed list of cases to be assigned. Every week new cases entered the department and sat in Phil's inbox for distribution. Sometimes cases sat on that list, waiting unassigned, until deadlines had passed and the person on the case started with problems that could have been avoided.

Jessica idly turned pages in the list. Often it was possible to request cases of personal interest. One case had an addendum printed in red ink:

> *Brother, Incorporated, has replaced Microtech, Incorporated, as the named plaintiff in this action. All references to Microtech in the attached material are now references to Brother. Future communications will refer solely to Brother.*

She was curious to learn more about the new conglomerate, so she asked Phil to assign the case to her.

"It's all yours."

As soon as she returned to her office she examined the case. She started with the addendum on the party names. No problem there, she thought. The new company wants to use its new name and is updating its business.

She read the background. A small company in Indonesia had started to build adapters for wall sockets. Indonesia had recently converted to international standards in its electrical connectors, but many buildings still had wall sockets of the old specifications. Microtech manufactured most of the sockets in Indonesia and it had lobbied the Indonesian government to legislate a conversion to international standards. Big companies like Microtech (*Brother!* Jessica reminded herself) benefited most from standardization because it facilitated selling the same products in different markets. It was easier to make one socket for sale all over the world than different sockets for every country.

After a region switched to standard dimensions there was a high temporary demand for adapters that permitted the old and new units to fit together. Brother instantly moved to fill the Indonesian adapter market but soon discovered it wasn't alone. The new company had taken advantage of its proximity to consumers and its knowledge of local trade to carve into Microtech's (Brother's) business in adapter plugs.

The entire market for Indonesian adapter plugs was microscopic by international standards and the new company held only a fraction of the market, but it had succeeded at asserting a presence. At one point it was worth nearly eight million Globos. So far this looked to Jessica like a success story of international competition.

But then Brother had noticed the upstart and defended itself. Brother cut its adapter prices in half – far below the actual manufacturing costs – and financed the losses with profits elsewhere in the firm. The start-up had no such resources. It cut prices as low as it could, but consumers preferred to buy the Brother brand at a lower price.

At the same time, Brother applied pressure to Indonesian retailers. It warned them to stop selling the new company's adapters or it wouldn't renew their orders for other Brother products. Brother merchandise constituted such a large portion of most retailers' sales that they couldn't stay in business without it. Retailers made the obvious choice and stopped selling adapters made by the start-up.

Tentek Corporation also figured in the incident. Tentek had a small presence in the Indonesian adapter market, and when Brother cut its prices Tentek followed suit. Probably it was defending its own market share against Brother's price wars, but the impact on the newcomer was devastating. In the span of a few days, the newcomer changed from a successful competitor to an overpriced outlier. A few months later it was out of business. The company lost all its equity and ended up a million Globos in debt.

So Brother won, Jessica thought to herself. What's the case about? She read on.

After the new company closed its doors Brother smacked it with a lawsuit. Brother claimed to have lost six million Globos as a result of the trade war and it sought to recover damages from the newcomer.

Now that was mean. Legal, but mean. Jessica knew that if the start-up had any resources left, they would all go toward defending the lawsuit. The company could forget about getting back into business, or even redirecting existing relationships to new uses.

She leaned forward at her desk and started to review Brother's complaint.

* * * * *

Malcolm and Jessica had dinner that evening in Jessica's apartment. It seemed strange to Malcolm to meet in her private space, but that's because he was unaccustomed to the rhythm of small children. Going out meant either a kid alongside or additional childcare. Dinner in her home meant lots of toys and easy supervision – not an invitation to additional intimacy. After dinner she set David up with a game and turned her attention to Malcolm.

"We're doing it all wrong," he began.

"The water?"

He explained the difference between Kahn's organic approach, and Tentek's high energy steam pots. He shared his new resolution and Tentek's intransigence.

"That's great. So what's the problem?"

He looked at her like she was being dense. "It's like turning a supertanker. It doesn't budge."

"Exactly. Like a supertanker. It will take some time. Just wait patiently and do your job. Start working on organics yourself. They won't say no to a finished plan."

"Or I'll sell it myself."

She looked up in alarm. "Remember that no-compete clause. You might as well stay on Tentek's side as long as possible." The case of the Indonesian start-up skipped across her mind. "You'd rather be indispensable than adversarial. Overperform on *Many Drops* but raise as many questions as you answer. Make sure they need you."

As Malcolm agreed David walked over and put himself in the middle of the conversation. "Can I have dessert?"

"You already had dessert."

"Oh, right. I forgot. Can I have another dessert?" He grinned like he might get away with something.

"Absolutely. You can have another dessert. Tomorrow. After you eat another dinner." She smiled broadly.

"Can we play a game?"

"Malcolm and I are talking. Can we play a game later?"

"Okay." He shuffled away and started rooting through a shelf of toys.

Jessica turned back to Malcolm. "Today's not the best day to talk about new ventures." She left the water hanging and described Brother's lawsuit in Indonesia. "It's a tiny marketplace," she said. "And it will disappear completely in a few years when sockets all convert to international standards. That start-up presented zero threat to Brother, but Brother obliterated it."

"That was back in the days of Microtech alone," Malcolm added. "Now Brother includes Dawkins."

"Tentek piled on too. They didn't want to lose the price war so they underbid and left the start-up on the outside."

David rejoined them with a videogame he'd pulled off the shelf. Looking straight at Malcolm he said, "Do you want to play?"

"How does it work?"

David showed him the screen and told a story about evil enemies and galactic warriors, but the essence of the game was shooting things down and making them explode.

"Let me see it," Malcolm said. He flipped the game over and read the trademark. "It's made by Ascot," he said to Jessica. "At least Brother doesn't own the toy industry."

"Wrong," she replied. "Ascot is just a brand name. The company that makes it is Hermes, and Hermes is owned by Microtech, now Brother."

"You're kidding."

"I worked on a Hermes case once and I had to learn some of its organizational structure. At least five brand names of toys that appear to compete against each other are actually Hermes subsidiaries. The markets are more consolidated than people think."

"Hermes also manufactures security systems that I compete against in my office. Or at least I thought we were competing against Hermes. Turns out we're competing against Brother." Malcolm set the game aside. "Doesn't the government monitor for antitrust violations?"

"The definitions are pretty loose," Jessica replied.

"And the inspectors are busy watching football games in the Hermes Arena."

Jessica chuckled, then walked over to David who had grown impatient. She hoisted him high above her head, then kissed him and spun him around in circles. "Flying boy!" she cried. "Fly boy! Malcolm can't play right now, but you go get those evil spacefighters."

David whooped in delight and kicked his legs in the air. She put him down and tussled his hair. Malcolm gave him back his game. "Go beat your high score," he said.

After David had settled in, Jessica turned to Malcolm and rubbed her lower back. "I can't handle that anymore. I'm too old and he's too heavy."

"He'll miss it when you quit."

She nodded agreement. "There will be new games, though." She sat back down and changed to a more serious tone. "All this relates to your father, you know."

"Go on."

"Those broadcasts all looked the same because the stations all had the same interest. Sensational headlines over low-cost research. If they all do it the same way, they all win."

"Same for water desalination. If everyone boils water, nobody needs to change."

"Exactly. But new competition makes things different. That's what the organics are. Ask Sayeh Kahn. Ask your dad."

"And don't play with boiling water."

"Exactly."

Chapter Thirteen

Bobeck called the next morning. "Amjat is found," he stated politely.

Malcolm was already in the office, caught in the frenzy of an ordinary workday, with different texts on each screen, struggling to apply a formula on electrical phase lags and to stay indispensable on *Many Drops to Drink*. He stopped what he was doing but he couldn't take this link in the office. "Can I call you back in ten minutes?"

"Yes, sir."

"Thank you." Malcolm dashed out of his office to the nearest public vidlink. He looked around for anyone watching him and, seeing nothing, stepped into the booth.

"Greetings, sir," Bobeck said. "I hope you are well." He was standing in the room where they'd first met. Malcolm recognized the broken chair and the shelves lined with food cartridges; one shelf was half empty, a sign that Sayeh's income hadn't been replaced.

Malcolm followed Bobeck's lead through the formality of introduction. He said he was fine and that Jessica was fine too. He asked about Bobeck and his family and learned that they, too, were fine. Finally, Bobeck brought conversation to the matter at hand.

"He appeared yesterday. He looked like a new man. He had new clothes and a new haircut, and I have never seen him so clean." Bobeck recounted that Amjat had simply disappeared like Mr. Kahn, but without even the publicity of an arrest or the formality of a death notice. He'd simply vanished. His family had no idea where he could be and their inquiries led them nowhere. Last week they were starting to mourn. But yesterday, from nowhere, Amjat suddenly appeared, saying he had moved to a new home in Carillo Hills. Bobeck had never heard of the place but Malcolm recognized it as an upscale suburb on the coast north of New Angeles.

"He came into some sudden money," said Malcolm, barely hiding his sarcasm.

"Fortune has smiled on him."

"Do you know where he got it?"

"That question is not mine to ask."

"Do you know where he was while he was gone?"

Amjat bobbed his head noncommittally. If that question were his to ask, he seemed not to have asked it. "We are simply happy to have him back."

"Bobeck, I need to see him."

"I understand. I will make an arrangement." He bowed into the screen. "May peace be with you."

* * * * *

"Sunrise tomorrow," Malcolm said to Jessica. He wanted to go as soon as possible, and arriving late to work was less conspicuous than a midday break. His schedule was tight but he was sure he could find a way to make up the lost time. Bobeck had wasted no time making the arrangement, and for Amjat early morning was best.

Jessica was not free that morning, or for several days. Malcolm would go alone.

"My rich aunt lives in Carillo Hills," Jessica said. "This Amjat negotiated well. Don't drink his water unless he drinks from the same container." She felt the same way as Malcolm about a man who cashed in so quickly on the death and disappearance of his childhood friend.

For the rest of the day Malcolm amazed himself with his own effectiveness. The electrical mathematics he'd struggled with earlier now snapped quickly into place. He read new texts, digested new information and reached conclusions at a pace he wouldn't have thought possible. He stayed focused on his assigned work, not knowing how closely he was being monitored and utterly committed to staying on top of his obligations – especially if he were planning to disappear for half of the next day. By the time he logged off he was confident that he'd done more than a day's work, and he felt good about his place on the *Many Drops* team. An evaluation of his performance could only be positive.

He got his five hours of sleep and rented a car for the trip to Carillo Hills. Most of the drive was dark but he could still appreciate how the scenery changed as the urban center gradually transformed into a hilly shoreline. The sun was rising as he approached Amjat's home, nestled into a hill overlooking the ocean. The landscape was a kaleidoscope of color, with hardy green plants and little yellow flowers flourishing in a desert soil of silver mica and reddish rust, all coming to life in the morning sun. Amjat's compact white house was in a setting from a dream.

There was only one blight in view. Immediately adjacent to Amjat's home was a single stretch of wreck and ruin, as if a fire had consumed everything precisely to the property line, or a toxic chemical had rained down on the homestead of some unfortunate Job. No plants survived and the soil was lifeless brown, separated from Amjat's property by yellow tape and orange signs. "Toxic," they warned. "Keep off." Malcolm was happy to leave it behind when he turned into Amjat's long driveway lined by yucca trees and prickly pears.

A man stepped from the home as Malcolm parked his car. He was older than Malcolm, though not as old as the ancient grandmother, roughly Sayeh Kahn's age. He had an air of kindness, and he looked nothing like the scheming villain Malcolm imagined.

With a gentle bow he declared, "My name is Amjat Jinn. Welcome to my home. Will you drink some tea?"

Malcolm missed Jessica and her personal intuition. He wasn't sure what to say or how to respond to this ordinary courtesy. "Good morning," was all he managed. "Thank you for having me."

Amjat invited Malcolm inside and showed him around as they walked to the porch overlooking the ocean. The house was modest in scale but far larger than the needs of a man alone. Most of the rooms were unfurnished and undecorated, indicating how recently he had arrived and with how little, but the view from the porch made up for the empty space.

"It must be stunning at sunset," Malcolm offered.

He felt almost embarrassed as he followed Amjat into the kitchen and watched him fill the kettle from the tap and put it on the stove, remembering Jessica's sarcasm as he made sure they were drinking from the same pot. The cupboards were bare except for some teamaking essentials and generic food cartridges. Soon they were sitting on the porch drinking ginger tea and nibbling on crackers.

"You are wondering how I came to be here," Amjat said.

Malcolm shook his head in the negative. "I am wondering what happened to Sayeh Kahn."

Amjat let out a long sigh and looked as forlorn as an old man who'd lost a lifelong friend. "I don't know."

"But you know where he got his water from." Malcolm succeeded at making it sound less like an accusation than an observation by a guest who is enjoying his host's tea.

"That's too fast," Amjat replied, and said nothing more. He turned from Malcolm and looked out over the ocean, slowly sipping his tea.

Malcolm had no choice but to do the same. The sky was a stunning aquamarine, unbroken to the horizon, while the Pacific was a wild mix of green and brown highlighted by the white of breaking waves. A crescent moon hovered midway through the sky to the north.

Eventually Amjat continued. "I have asked them to join me. My children, with their children; and perhaps my sister with her children as well. We will fill up this house and make it our own."

He turned towards Malcolm, eyes filling with the tears of a lifelong dream. "There are limits, of course." He described zoning limitations and density rules, sounding like someone who was learning new rules for a new place in life, but who had long experience at working within rules. Soon he returned to what really mattered: "In this place, there are better schools. In this place, the trucks don't wake you up at night and it is possible to get ahead. In this place, my family will have new opportunity." He gestured toward other homes in view, and it was clear what kind of opportunity he meant.

This time Malcolm waited a long time before speaking again. "How did this move become possible?"

"There was the reward, you know." Amjat glanced at Malcolm to make sure he knew what he was talking about. Satisfied, he continued. "I asked for more money than they were willing to offer. Eventually we reached an agreement – a smaller offer of cash and this parcel of land."

"And you told them where Sayeh got his water."

"The knowledge was useless to him after he died, and useless to the rest of us too. I was not going to travel for water the way Sayeh did. There was no reason for the knowledge to die with him. Or with me, for that matter." He shrugged like someone who had thought long and painfully, but who had reached a decision that made sense. "This way the knowledge does some good. Maybe even more good than it was doing before."

"How did Sayeh Kahn come by this knowledge?"

"Ah, Mr. Kahn was a mystery. He always has been. He goes his own ways and he does his own things. When we were children, he found things in places that nobody else thought to look. He was always exploring, and he had a special fascination with water.

"He built a contraption on the roof of his house...." Amjat smiled at a memory he hadn't invoked in years. "He turned the whole roof into a funnel to catch rainwater and piped the water through spinning wheels and rolling balls – in every color you can imagine – down level after level. In the basement it filled a giant tub shaped like a tortoise.

"Many people developed catchments for the spring rain but only Sayeh made a world of it. Kids from all around came to watch his water when it rained, and to climb on the tortoise as it filled. Sayeh had no children of his own so he gave much of the water away."

With memories of his father in the background, Malcolm had a sudden wish that Sayeh Kahn hadn't died a violent death. "And the water that purifies?" he asked at last. "Where is it now?"

Amjat shook his head in opposition.

Malcolm guessed, "You can't say?" He feared another rejection or deferral, and only now realized that secrecy could be part of the agreement that bought him the house.

But Amjat kept shaking his head; Malcolm was heading in the wrong direction. "It doesn't matter anymore. It is no longer there." He gestured towards a window whose blind was closed, but Malcolm knew what was on that side of the house – the blighted landscape guarded by toxic warnings.

"The water used to be over there, in a small natural spring. Sayeh discovered it, I don't know how. And he discovered its properties, I don't know how. The spring trickles into a small marsh, then disappears. Sayeh, from time to time, journeyed here to bring a few bottles back to his community. He always gave it away for free.

"But nothing lives there now," he continued. "The spring is absolutely dead. Beyond any hope of redemption. That's why they gave me this particular piece of land. Recently, the value has dropped considerably." He shared an ironic grin at a positive consequence of devastation.

"But to me the land has value. Not just as a place to live and to bring my family, but because the land next door isn't as ugly to me as it is to other people. To me, it is not a place of death. To me it is a place of memory and a place of spirit. Maybe someday I will tell my grandchildren about Mr. Kahn's spring. And maybe someday, if heaven smiles, we will purchase that parcel of land."

The tea was drained and they both knew that the visit was over. They parted with pleasantries, and Malcolm wished Amjat the world of fortune in completing his move. Traffic was favorable so Malcolm reached the office by mid-morning and logged another day of stunning productivity.

Chapter Fourteen

Malcolm worked like he had two guns to his head. The first gun was his *Many Drops* obligations, which were moving fast on their own and he was determined to finish even faster. Malcolm was working with a pair of metallurgists to design fins that radiated heat as the steam cooled, and redirected the energy back into the heaters for water that had not yet boiled. He started the instant he arrived in the morning and blasted ahead without interruption, inspired by pressure, finishing every step ahead of schedule, pointing out the steps ahead.

The second gun was biotech research. He wasn't a geneticist but he wanted to present Tentek a clear outline, to prove that organic desalination could be done if they invested the effort. So far his access privileges hadn't been revoked and his activity was unobstructed.

His research quickly confirmed his original intuitions. Most organisms consumed – indeed, required – salt in small quantities. He thought that this characteristic could be used to develop a creature that processed salt through its diet. Modest engineering would be needed to increase the intake and more significant engineering would be needed to ensure that the excess wasn't simply passed on via excretions, but his preliminary investigation made him think it was possible.

Other leads looked promising as well. He learned that Tentek once designed algae to decontaminate tanks in salmon farms. These small plants considered fish feces an irritant, and they protected themselves by breaking it down into constituent parts that were independently less irritating. He also uncovered a freshwater protist that attracted attention by flourishing when tides shifted and the water turned brackish. Most of the freshwater fauna expired as the environment changed, but this species went the other direction. Unfortunately, the natural experiment ended when increased local acidity brought the whole lifecycle to a standstill. Some scientists suspected that this particular species had played more than a passive role in the environmental shifts and started additional research, but inquiries led nowhere and were soon discontinued.

The exploration was difficult but also exciting. He didn't know how Kahn's water operated but that didn't really matter; nor did it matter if Tentek did it the same way. What mattered was that he could present the idea and prove that it was worth pursuing. The biotech staff would take it from there. He raced ahead on his own private ultratime, committed to continuing for as long as it took, or until somebody stopped him.

* * * * *

Jessica had worked on the Brother case long enough to know there was no merit to its claims. The tiny

Indonesian company had done nothing improper or illegal; it had tried in good faith to start a business and struggled to make a competitive product until it lost the competition. The company had offered no bribes, planted no spies in Brother's operations, and done nothing to offend the order of international markets. It just spotted an opportunity and moved to take advantage.

If anybody's conduct skated the edge of illegality, it was Brother's. Brother had engaged in predatory pricing and leveraged favors from distributors. Jessica was close to recommending that Brother be disciplined for filing a frivolous lawsuit.

Phil, her boss, stopped in for an update but midway through her briefing he changed the subject. "My cousin won season tickets to the Tentek Titans in his office football pool," he said.

"That's nice."

"Have you been watching the Singleton tennis cup? Last night's game was amazing."

He wasn't usually this chatty and Jessica wasn't interested. "What's on your mind?" she asked before she learned what he'd had for breakfast.

"Did you know that Peter Von Hirsch is running for Governor?"

Von Hirsch was at the top of the office hierarchy. Jessica had seen him a few times at department functions but they'd never exchanged a word. She'd heard rumors that he was running for public office but she paid little attention. She nodded.

"It will be a tough race," Phil continued. "The other candidates have a lot more money than Von Hirsch. One is a billionaire financing his own campaign. The other spent two years fundraising among petrochemical corporations and he promises to stop enforcing regulations that require them to filter their waste. And this is only the party primary. If Von Hirsch beats them, he still faces the incumbent governor."

"What's Von Hirsch's platform? Why do we want him to win?"

"Because he's our man."

"Oh."

Phil started pacing around the office. "Von Hirsch's connections were with Dawkins which, as you know, is now part of Brother. Dawkins is the media part of the partnership. Von Hirsch's trouble is that when Dawkins joined Microtech to create Brother, his own connections tumbled from the top of Dawkins ladder down to subordinate positions in Brother. Some of them became irrelevant entirely."

Jessica waited for the punchline. She didn't know exactly where Phil was going, but she was already getting uncomfortable.

"Campaigns aren't only about money," he said. "Access to the media is almost as important. If your campaign is deemed 'newsworthy' you get free interviews, invitations to debate, personal stories about your kids – all kinds of positive publicity. An interview on the evening news is better than your own commercial, and cheaper to produce."

Phil paused, as if Jessica might fill in the conclusion. By now she knew exactly what he wanted but she forced him to finish the story himself.

"Von Hirsch is trying to strengthen his alliance with the people at Brother," he declared. "Without them he doesn't stand a chance in this election."

Jessica remained stonily silent.

"A victory in the Indonesia case would make things easier for Von Hirsch."

* * * * *

Malcolm hadn't cleaned his apartment since the burglary. He stepped over the dirty laundry pile and picked his day's clothing from the piles in view. For breakfast he examined the choices visible on the counter and poured cereal into a bowl without pausing to open cupboards or find a spoon in a drawer. Everything was wide open. He was starting to like it.

The changes at the office weren't so easy. Instead of advertisements or updates on the Tentek Titans, his computer started his day with dire warnings: Tentek was restructuring to confront the new Brother consolidation, and jobs were being lost in the process. Tentek expressed "sympathy to those affected" and "advance sympathy" to those who might be affected in the future.

The gravity of his risk struck Malcolm full in the face. He thought about his no-compete agreement and his unauthorized research. He didn't want "sympathy," afterwards or in advance. He wanted to stay right where he was with the full Tentek archives at his disposal, in a position to drive the corporation where he wanted it to go. But he couldn't affect personnel decisions and he refused to stop his own project. He deleted the warning screens and got to work.

The hallways were quiet and still; the only person who walked past Malcolm's office was weeping into her handkerchief. He looked up in alarm at the sound, but he didn't know her and didn't know what to do anyway. He returned to his computer. Even the morning pledge felt like a funeral. Malcolm arrived a minute early and sat with his colleagues in silence. Was he imagining it, or did the lights seem dimmer than usual? Certainly there was nothing to see but the twin flags and backs of the heads of people ahead of him, staring straight at the empty platform where Jackson would soon appear. Malcolm parked himself and shared the tension in the room. Jackson seemed to be a few minutes late, which was unprecedented; the audience held its breath in anticipation.

Eventually Jackson appeared. He walked sadly to center stage, skipped the greetings and launched into a sober recitation of performance statistics. Sales were down and longstanding government contracts had been discontinued; Brother had gained a tactical advantage in several key markets and was exploiting them ruthlessly. Malcolm recognized few of the specifics but the negative trends were obvious. Jackson hoped that everyone would stand beside him during this time of trouble, and he reassured them that Tentek would emerge stronger from the struggle.

He asked people to rise as he spread his arms in benediction. "Usually during the pledge we hold a hand over our hearts, the pump of our lives. Today I ask each of you to hold the hand of the person beside you. For these are your partners in the life that binds us all."

The audience murmured in surprise. People in this world never touched each other. No matter how crowded the transpo or small the elevator, people never touched and they said "excuse me" at the smallest contact. Jackson's suggestion violated this unspoken rule. Malcolm reached for the hands of his colleagues beside him while they were still ruminating. On his left, the woman's hand was cold and tentative; on his right, the man's was warm and moist. It felt strange, holding the naked hand of a stranger, but soon everyone responded and the room rustled with clothing as people reached for one another. Jackson held them together in silence until grips started to tighten. Finally he started the pledge. Hand in hand, they pledged allegiance to the Tentek Corporation of America, and promised to work together for "a safer, more productive, more prosperous world for all."

When the pledge ended, hands stayed clasped for one gratuitous moment more; then it was over and people started to talk. Malcolm introduced himself to the people on either side, Seneca from the Security Division and Christopher from Accounting; by the time people reached the exits the mood was normal and people were chatting, careful not to touch as they crowded through the doors. Seneca and Christopher walked the other direction, still talking.

Back at his desk Malcolm learned that *Many Drops* was in trouble. A message declared that major reorganization was needed, and that some people were being transferred off the project. He was relieved to see that he wasn't on the transfer list – though the metallurgists on his team were, so the knife had come close. Other changes affected his duties and new deadlines left him with little room for his own research.

The transfer of the metallurgists made no sense, though. He needed them. Nobody else on the team understood the heat capacities of different alloys or their susceptibility to corrosion in water. The team couldn't function without the knowledge that was taken away, and no replacement was provided.

Other changes were similarly troubling. He saw that Angela Martus, a genius at high voltage circuits, was transferred to plumbing; design master Joseph Singh was transferred from engineering to administration. Malcolm didn't know everyone but he knew enough to see trouble in the new configuration.

The whining in the next room made it worse. A neighboring team was using the crying of babies and whining of young children as a weapon in the war against terror. They had developed soundtracks to frazzle nerves where terrorists were hiding under siege, and devices to be placed in pockets or left in remote locations where the cry of an infant or childish request for water could distract at a crucial moment.

Research had already determined which cries worked best and what kind of whining raised blood pressure the fastest, but snippets of sound were still unavoidable in the work. New deadlines increased both the frequency and the carelessness of these tests. Whining filled the corridors like a flu in a daycare center.

Gary Seltzer startled him by walking in unannounced. "I got transferred to the whine team," he said.

"Lucky you."

"My kids are older now, and I don't miss that part a bit." He leaned against the wall like he might stay a while.

"We still have our jobs, at least."

"Still have them for now. The whine team's a setback for me. I took a paycut too."

Malcolm looked up in surprise. It never occurred to him that salaries went anywhere but up, even if only in annual increments. "I'm sorry." He didn't know what else to say.

"What's this I hear about a no-compete agreement? I resisted the move at first. I told Kira I could find other options – and she said 'no-compete' as if that settled it. Do you know what she's talking about?"

About this, at least, Malcolm had something to add. It was more bad news and he felt like he was piling on, but he owed his colleague what knowledge he had. Gary listened without saying anything but Malcolm could see him sinking. They both knew that it wasn't supposed to turn out like this. They worked hard and they did everything right. They should be rising to the top, not whining and boiling. Gary shook his head as he stepped toward the door. "How's the water?" he asked on his way out.

"Tastes bad," Malcolm replied.

* * * * *

Jessica missed her personal deadline. She wanted to finish her day's work before 8 o'clock, when Kid Kare closed its door for the night. Any child who hadn't been picked up by then was required to stay overnight. Jessica worked her fastest and did her best because tonight wasn't scheduled for overnight and David would be disappointed, but finally she gave up. She didn't even bother sprinting for Kid Kare's door for a near miss at five past eight. She exhausted another distasteful piece of research, then walked lamely out of her office at half past the hour, suddenly alone for the evening.

She hadn't been prepared for this part of parenting. Impetuous and headstrong, she thought she could handle the tradeoffs of work and family – and indeed she could – but it was harder on David. Right now he was changing into his emergency pajamas, not the special new ones he loved at home, and being tucked into a cot by a paid professional, not his bed by his mother. She felt the emptiness on both ends – how she missed him and how he missed her.

Still, the empty time had some advantages. Her mind scrolled through lists of chores she could do or people she could see. She called Malcolm to see if he was free, but he didn't answer and she didn't bother with a message. Then she remembered that her old friend Gloria was having a birthday party tonight. Jessica had declined the invitation, expecting to spend the evening with David, but now a party of old friends sounded perfect. After all, Gloria had arranged that first date with Malcolm; Jessica owed her an update.

"You found a babysitter for David! That's great." Gloria rushed at Jessica with open arms, but stopped because she had a drink in her hands. "I'm so happy you could come."

"I'm happy to be here."

Gloria's apartment was large for one person, and stocked with decorations and novelties.

A shelf filled with talking clocks interrupted their conversation to announce nine o'clock; another shelf was filled by neon candlesticks that lit the apartment when Gloria loved them, but now sat in a pile dark and unused. After the clocks stopped talking, Gloria jumped straight to her favorite subject: "How's your love life?" This was all she ever seemed to want to talk about. She hadn't had a successful relationship in years, and she satisfied her romantic fancies through her friends.

At this moment Jessica's most important relationship was sleeping in a row of cots under video surveillance, but Gloria didn't want to hear about that. Jessica simply thanked her for introducing Malcolm and said she'd been spending a lot of time with him.

Gloria seized the opening. "Has David met him? Does he like him?"

"They get along great." She didn't mention that Malcolm bought David an impact vest for the trip to Kaiserville, or gave him crackers for the rats on the tracks. She pushed towards simpler subjects. "How's work?"

"Work is great. They just repainted the office. The walls used to be blue and gray, but now they're pink and tan."

"And how's your love life?"

"I have a great new boyfriend. He wears nice ties and always likes my shoes. I think he may be the one for me. Do you think I should get a new haircut?"

Other friends stepped around them, and people drifted in and out of the room. Jessica eavesdropped on other conversations while Gloria discussed the virtues of curls. Most of the talk was about entertainment or sports. She overheard one fragment about the upcoming election for governor.

"I wonder if I should change colors too. It's been brown for so long. . . ." Gloria ran her fingers through her hair and pulled a lock before her eyes. "Yeck! Brown is for carpets." She giggled at her joke then talked about her new boyfriend's hair. It was blonde and completely straight; he parted it on the left and grew it a little long in the back. She was thinking about growing her own hair out too, because people kept saying she looked like Helen on *Paradise Square* and she thought maybe she should play up the resemblance.

"Do you think I look like Helen?" Gloria's direct question brought Jessica back. She answered without thinking and suddenly realized her old friend bored her. She couldn't care less about Gloria's hair, or even her love life. She'd never seen *Paradise Square* and she didn't know Helen from a mole rat. Jessica wondered if Gloria had always been like this – obsessed with ties and haircuts, and excited when the office walls changed from blue to pink. Had Gloria changed, or had Jessica? When?

She excused herself and walked around the room. One wall was filled with the poster from the Viacom classic, *Love, Beware!* The poster featured two figures running naked down a beach while jet fighters zoomed across the sky and explosions tore up the sand. The frame was a frieze of scenes and characters from other Viacom attractions. Jessica recognized the film she and Gloria had seen as consolation when one of Gloria's other boyfriends broke up with her. Suddenly, she wished Malcolm were here.

At the punch bowl she bumped into her friends Fiona and Zeke, both attorneys. The two of them were discussing the job market from very different points of view. Zeke had lost his position at a big law firm several years ago when computer software developed the ability to perform many tasks that he, a young associate, had previously performed. Since that time, Zeke had been employed, semi-employed and underemployed on a series of short-term contracts for his former law firm and several other businesses in the city. He called himself a consultant and sometimes bragged about his independence, but what he really wanted was a real job with a steady paycheck. He'd been looking for full-time work since the day he left his old post.

Fiona suffered from the opposite problem. Even in the world of overworked professionals, her workload was astonishing. Her firm had pioneered the concept of dormitories in the office so people could spare themselves the trouble of going home. In fact, Fiona had no apartment of her own; she lived in the law firm dorm in a constant state of ultratime. She was Jessica's age but she looked ten years older; her skin was pale, almost translucent, and her cheeks were swollen; she could lose thirty pounds and still be overweight.

As Jessica joined them, Zeke was discussing his new computer system. "Once it's running I'll have the best set up around," he bragged. "Even Fiona can't do what I'll be able to do."

"How long before you start?" Jessica asked.

"When I get paid on my next contract. I almost have enough for the new Panther."

"Panther?"

"The latest in network security. I saw on *Enemy Within* that a new wave of cyber-terrorists are breaking into systems and running riot."

"How long have you been waiting?"

"About three months for Panther," he replied. "But I'm patient. It took even longer for Alcatraz.

"Alcatraz?" Jessica was getting a bad feeling about Zeke's computer system.

"Alcatraz was the best until it wasn't the best anymore. I saved for it for a long time, and the week before I bought in, *Giga-Terror* reported a new vulnerability. I dodged that bullet! Now I'm saving for Panther."

"How long have you been waiting to start your new system?"

"Not quite a year," Zeke replied. "But it's worth it. You've got to stay ahead of these terrorists!"

Jessica shifted conversation towards Fiona and her office, which never waited for anything. She learned that this birthday party was Fiona's first night off in months, and that she'd moved a cot behind her desk so she could lie down during dizzy spells. Suddenly Jessica had a flash. "Why don't you give some of your work to Zeke?" she exclaimed.

Both of her friends looked at her blankly.

She clarified. "Zeke doesn't have enough work and you have too much. Can't you give some of your work to him? You could hire him on a contract basis or add him as a staff attorney. Your firm obviously has too much to do."

"It doesn't work that way," Fiona stated. "I can't give my assignments to somebody else, and I certainly can't bring my friends into the office as staff attorneys."

"Okay forget about Zeke," Jessica conceded. She didn't have Zeke in mind anyway, but the larger point. "Some people in this world have too much work and some don't have enough. Can't we put them together and create a happy medium?" Jessica felt like she was onto something and she was fishing for input.

"I can handle it," Fiona snapped. "I'm not afraid of a little work."

"You would have more time off," Jessica insisted.

"What for?" rebutted Fiona. "Besides, additional help costs money. Where would it come from?"

That sounded to Jessica like an excuse. No doubt the firm could find the money, although spreading it wider would probably mean a smaller share for each. People would trade more time for less money. To get there, the overemployed – people like Fiona – would need to see the underemployed – people like Zeke – as a relief shift, not a threat.

Two friends carrying a birthday cake dimmed the lights and called everyone together. The cake was a yard across and frosted with a photographic likeness of Gloria wearing a halo of flame-proof glow wands. They all sang *Happy Birthday* and someone yelled, "Make a wish!"

Gloria closed her eyes, puckered in concentration and everyone cheered as she switched off the glow wands.

"Just in time for *Paradise Square!*" somebody cried. The group shifted towards the television. The couch already faced the screen and additional chairs were rushed from other rooms; the cake was forgotten in the rush. Zeke and Fiona seated themselves on pillows on the floor and looked hungrily at the opening scene.

Jessica stood by herself in the back of the darkened room. She had come for friends and conversation, not to watch television. She wasn't curious to find out if Gloria looked like Helen on *Paradise Square,* and she cared less about the fictional lives on television than the friends who had literally turned their backs on her. She found her jacket and edged slowly toward the door. With all eyes focused on the screen, nobody saw her leave.

Chapter Fifteen

Happenstance Jackson was coming to town. The man himself, not a holographic image or archive tape, the actual Hap Jackson was traveling to New Angeles on business, and he was working out of the building that housed the Family Safety Division. Staff were notified that additional security would be in place and that Jackson would address the Division in person on his very first day.

A full week had passed since the first wave of reorganization and Hap's presentation of challenges ahead, but the remaining staff had responded heroically. Amazing feats of endurance led to the swift completion of impossible tasks, and the short-term indicators all looked good. Malcolm himself was proud of what he'd accomplished, solving problems of metallurgy without metallurgists and even finding extra minutes for personal research.

Entry screening expanded from a quick scan to a full frisk, while additional officers walked the corridors and patrolled the lobby. Garcia said he'd received additional training and practiced new drills.

"As if you need extra work," Malcolm remarked.

"I like it," Garcia replied. "It's good experience and I earn merit points. I'm closing in on a promotion and a raise."

One morning security was so tight Malcolm needed fully half an hour to make it through. Soon after he reached his desk Garcia poked his head in. "I think he's here."

Malcolm kept working, and around noon the announcement came. Hap Jackson had arrived. He wanted to meet the Division staff in Singleton auditorium, the building's largest room, in just fifteen minutes.

People literally ran down the corridors and lines formed at elevators. Malcolm didn't run, but luckily his office wasn't far from Singleton. He got a good seat in the middle of the auditorium; minutes later, no seats were left and people stood along the walls.

The room buzzed with excitement. Music played and spotlights zigzagged on the stage. Jackson's personal ushers tossed packets of jelly beans and Tentek T-shirts into the crowd. They sold raffle tickets to a Titans game for just one Globo, with a new drawing every other minute. The man sitting beside Malcolm bought a ticket, lost on the first try, then bought two tickets for the following round; he kept buying more and more tickets as the excitement mounted and winners kept walking down the aisles to collect their prizes amidst wild cheers.

With the room packed far beyond capacity and the thrill at its zenith, the Division Secretary called the crowd to order. He was a very tall, older man with silver hair. "Greetings, all!" he cried to wild applause. "Are you ready?"

"Yes!" the crowd shouted in response.

The Secretary tugged his ear as if he couldn't quite hear. "What?" he said. "*Are you ready?*"

"*Yes!*"

"And what should we do first – the end or the beginning?"

"*The beginning!*"

"What?" Tugging his ear.

"*The beginning!*"

"Then let's get started. We begin with the foundation, the pledge of allegiance. Let us pledge with all our hearts, so the heart that leads us will know what we can do."

He lifted his hand to his chest and led the crowd in the sincerest, loudest and most heartfelt pledge Malcolm had ever heard. *I pledge allegiance to the Tentek Corporation of America. I will serve loyally and work hard for our great goals: a safer, more productive, more prosperous world for all.* People recited the words as if they were speaking directly to Jackson himself, with special emphasis on "working hard" for the great corporate goals.

Then the introductions really got going. The Division Secretary introduced the Vice President of Production, who introduced the Vice President of Sales, who introduced the Vice President of Development. Each person had kind words to say about the next person, the staff, and of course Jackson himself. Along the way, Malcolm learned that the "Division family" had added three new babies in the past month and that four of the "family's children" had graduated from college. Two staff members had been promoted to higher positions within the Division and three had retired after long years of service. The audience cheered each accomplishment and individuals were invited to stand. A woman who'd had her baby just the day before teetered as she stood but she raised her hands in triumph.

The last Division Vice President introduced the Division President. The end was near, and everyone knew it. After the President there was only one person left to introduce. The President drew the audience still farther forward in their seats with a glowing preamble. He told of the illustrious Jackson family and the meteoric rise of its gifted son. He described how Hap Jackson rocketed through Harvard Business School to the Jackson Conglomerate and finally became Chief Executive of Tentek Corporation. "Not deterred by the expectations of success, not weighed down by the burden of being a Jackson, this little boy overcame the crusty traditions of hereditary wealth to become his own man. His strength is a model to us all. It is my privilege to introduce to you, the man himself, Mr. Happenstance Jackson!"

The crowd leapt to its feet. The spotlights danced and turned rainbow colors. Jackson magically appeared on the edge of the stage, wearing a suit of midnight black and a scarf of burgundy wine. In a stride familiar from the daily pledge he walked to the podium and raised his arms.

The audience erupted with whistles, cheers and deafening applause. Jackson seemed taller in person, towering above the Division executives lined behind him on the stage. He turned to shake each hand and clapped the Division President on the shoulder. The audience cheer took a precise shape, the familiar chant of "*Hap Jack! Hap Jack!*" in rising crescendo.

Malcolm stood on his tiptoes like everyone else, craning his neck for every inch of a better view. Jackson was always exciting but in person he was electric.

Jackson motioned his arms downwards to settle the crowd. Slowly people halted the chant and wound down the applause. The music quieted and the spotlights converged on the podium, which stood out like a pinnacle of sunshine. When he had the audience under control, Jackson announced that despite all obstacles the Division was in the midst of a record-breaking quarter. The cheers were instant and Jackson made no effort to slow them down. He raised his hands high overhead like a touchdown had been scored. The crowd responded with another round of "*Hap Jack!*"

When the chanting subsided, Jackson explained that everything was going according to plan and that many things were going better than planned. "And *you* deserve full credit for that," he thundered. "You are the heart and soul of the proudest Division of the proudest company on the face of the Earth! There isn't a home or office on this planet that doesn't use Tentek products and there is only you to thank for it. Ladies and gentlemen, give yourselves a hand."

The staff went wild. People cheered and stamped and clapped as if the Messiah had come. Malcolm applauded until his hands stung.

Next Jackson brought the address to more mundane topics. He'd heard that the nursery was getting worn and that new furnishings were needed. The incubator for newborns was on its last legs. He authorized refurnishing plans and invited the Division to form a staff committee to govern the project. He asked the mother of yesterday's baby to chair the committee, and promised her child the finest daycare money could buy.

Finally he turned to the matter of staff compensation, a source of occasional tension in the Division. "As you know, last year this Division performed below expectations and nobody got raises. This year it is doing well." He paused while the audience tensed in anticipation. "We have determined, however, that we must be certain of our position before we undertake increased financial commitments at the staff level. We must be sure the shareholders receive adequate dividends and that accounts are fully in balance. Especially in our ultra-competitive environment, this is in the long-term best interest of the company.

"In the future, I promise that each and every one of you is entitled to the expectation of a raise. Count on it. The expectation of a raise. Let's keep pulling until we are out of this rut. I will keep you apprised of our – and your – financial status. Let us keep our collective best interest foremost in our minds. God bless you all."

The audience erupted in thunderous ovation as he quit the stage, and kept clapping until he returned for another bow. Some folks rushed the stage to touch his feet but security kept them away, and a new round of "*Hap Jack!*" rose for his final exit. As people filed out, Malcolm asked the man next to him how he felt about the salary hold.

"Tentek first," he replied. "None of us eat unless the corporation does. You can't play on a team if you think only of yourself." To Malcolm he sounded like a talking version of the corporate greeting on his computer screen every morning, but he seemed entirely happy and sincere.

Malcolm sailed through the rest of his day. He finished the installation plan for the radiator fins with the triple purpose: cooling the steam, capturing the distilled water and reusing the excess thermal energy. He was proud of his accomplishment and knew that he'd resolved a central challenge. Still floating, he walked down the hall to find Kira to ask if she had heard from "upstairs" about approaching desalination from a different direction.

"No way," she replied. "I wrote a memo. I explained your idea and volunteered your service. The denial couldn't have been more clear."

"Maybe later," he ventured.

She looked at him like he'd suggested rocks for breakfast. "You think it's a good idea and I think it's a good idea. But company leadership doesn't think it's a good idea – and they know best. I'm certain they gave it full consideration and I'm certain of their answer." She saw his disappointment and offered consolation. "You'll do better next time."

He decided that if the idea was going nowhere, it was best to play it safe. "Thanks. I'm sure you're right. This morning's speech was incredible. Isn't Jackson amazing?"

"He sure is. It's inspiring just to know he's in the building for a while. I heard we could paint the walls in the nursery if we wanted to."

* * * * *

Jessica dozed at her desk, her jacket pulled over her head. She was exhausted. She'd read every statute and ordinance in Indonesia, and half the treaties governing trade in the Pacific rim, searching for a legal basis for Brother to win its lawsuit against the Indonesian start-up.

Finally she'd found one. The start-up had failed to obtain a license permitting testing of certain electrical components used in the adapter units. The license requirement hadn't been enforced in decades but it was still on the books. Brother held a license from its previous socket manufacturing operation, and it could claim that the start-up's skirting of the licensure requirement conferred an unfair trade advantage.

Jessica remembered when a discovery like that felt like striking gold. She would spend the entire night writing a triumphant new brief. Now the discovery left her disgusted. She paced the hallways in frustration, then fell asleep at her desk.

She didn't want to help the company that was going to win anyway. Microtech and Dawkins didn't flourish because they were best, but because they had accumulated the most power. They were coasting on past success and they could coast indefinitely, crushing legitimate opposition.

These companies made a mockery of capitalism, she realized. In theory, everyone in the market got what they wanted. Sellers and buyers were *both* winners: if they weren't both happy then they went separate ways. But nobody ever walked away from Microtech. Competing ideas were obliterated and consumers were muzzled into compliance, baffled by advertising and driven by artificial need. Jessica didn't doubt that people chose freely, but their freedom was guided by forces beyond their control. A person at a table with five foods would freely choose the food they liked best – but the person with power was the one who set the table.

She was still suspicious about Tentek's compliance in the Indonesian price wars. Sure it had an interest, but was it so close to Microtech's that it would replicate its strategy, right down to the price?

She felt herself on the brink of a discovery, but still she didn't really know. She needed more information. She needed more facts to ponder and examples to explore. Earlier in the day she'd daydreamed about finding a way to draft Tentek into Brother's lawsuit – she had some questions she'd love to ask. But for now she was only daydreaming; when she woke up she would need to write her brief. Her job was to help Brother win in Indonesia.

* * * * *

The order came from nowhere. A message flashed across all three of Malcolm's screens. He'd been reassigned from the desalination project. All of his files on *Many Drops* were transferred out of his account and his communications links within the team were severed. He'd solved the central problem of energy redirection and this was his reward. Severance.

He didn't know what had happened or how the team would proceed without him, but apparently that was no longer his problem. He wasn't so indispensable after all. He was reassigned to the Odor Eater and told that the organism that deodorized garbage was once again dying in transit.

He vidlinked Kira to ask what was going on. The system informed him that she was too busy to take links from his extension; it did not invite him to leave a message.

His new supervisor on the Odor Eater linked to his desk. "We are delighted to have your creative energy on the team," said a young woman dressed in blue, with blue hair ribbons and blue fingernails. "As you know, this problem has been haunting us. We are eager to see it go away."

Malcolm managed to say something courteous without betraying his real feelings about seeing things go away. The Odor Eater wasn't the only thing dying. He was. Reassignment killed the only thing that made work worthwhile, and it might kill his private project too. *Many Drops* required research into drinkable water; he needed that cover for his personal research. But was the reassignment a response to his outside work? There was no way to know.

He couldn't do anything anyway. He just controlled himself and settled down to review the too-familiar files on the Odor Eater. Surely something obvious was wrong, but he didn't have the heart to look for it. As the day faded and it seemed responsible to leave, he called Jessica to ask if she could meet him on the way home. They found each other at a *Cafeteria L'Express* halfway between their apartments.

Malcolm arrived first and bought two cups of coffee. He pushed one towards Jessica as she took off her coat and sat down. They shared their news of the day.

Jessica summed it up: "That's two people and two lousy days. The good news: we're batting one hundred percent."

Malcolm wasn't amused. "I was finally doing something worthwhile. Even *Many Drops* was worthwhile, even if it was glorified tea. My own organic research was irreplaceable."

"It's not irreplaceable. Tomorrow you'll get back to work replacing it. You'll find a way. I'm sure you will."

Malcolm felt like Jessica was being dense; he needed an ally, not a cheerleader. This wasn't just a setback or inconvenience; *Many Drops* provided access he needed to the Tentek archives and cover for unrelated research. It provided opportunity to attend meetings at which the subject was saltwater desalination and how to get it done. "Garbage bugs won't do the trick."

She still didn't accept his conclusions. "What can I do to help?"

"You can't."

"Don't be so quick. I work for the government. I have access to vast archives and consultants willing to perform all sorts of favors." She refused to give up and didn't care who might be listening.

Malcolm wasn't impressed. "You're a lawyer. You don't have files on water desalination or biological engineering."

"I'm a lawyer in a *trade* office," she responded. "I have access to records relating to patents and trademarks. If anybody ever invented anything similar and applied for a patent, I might be able to find it. You could look at their designs."

For an instant Malcolm perked up. That was something he hadn't considered, and a flash of desire crossed his eyes. He was hungry for answers, maybe hungry enough to break the rules.

But the hope vanished almost as soon as it arrived. This wasn't simply a question of looking something up. It was a matter of sifting through entire libraries, hunting for clues and discovering relationships. Malcolm never knew what he was looking for until he found it, and even then he had to maneuver it into place. He had to do it himself. Unless Jessica could provide unlimited access to all her archives, he couldn't make much progress. Even then he would have to keep pace with his new assignments at Tentek, whatever they turned out to be. It wouldn't work.

Finally Jessica gave up too. She was a lawyer, not a technician, and she was offering access to files she probably couldn't deliver anyway. It was little more than a gesture. "Then how can I help?" she repeated, but only the words were the same. Last time the offer was tactical; this time it was consolation.

"You can't."

They sat for a long time in silence. The life of the *L'Express* whirled around them, televisions flashing and images flickering in every direction. The people beside them left and were replaced by two others, who also left before Malcolm and Jessica spoke again. Malcolm finished his muffin and started picking up each remaining crumb with his fingers. Jessica ordered another cup of coffee and waited for it to cool before starting to sip. She was cutting into David's time.

At last she said, "It will take a lot longer now."

"It will take forever."

"No," she insisted, an edge creeping into her voice. "It will just take longer. You'll discover a way to desalinate seawater organically, or you'll persuade Tentek to do it. It's not a race. It's okay to take more time." She swirled the white powder that had settled to the bottom of her cup.

Malcolm stared at her emptily.

Jessica changed the subject. "Did I ever tell you about my father?" She'd been thinking of him a lot recently. The Indonesia case brought him up

"What does he have to do with this?"

"My father was an independent businessman," she continued, "or at least he wanted to be. He had all the right skills and made some pretty smart decisions. He worked in a big firm until he developed a plan for his own business. Then he made his move."

"Go on."

"People in our neighborhood didn't have a place to get their hair cut. They could travel one direction for a barber shop or the opposite direction for an overpriced beauty salon, but nothing was convenient or nearby. My father thought he could open a barber shop in our apartment building.

"Hair cutting isn't that special a skill and barber shops don't require much equipment or inventory. Dad didn't expect to get rich or famous running a barber shop, but he figured he could earn a living and be his own boss. The commute was pretty good, too."

"What happened?"

"He couldn't get a loan. He needed a little capital to get started but nobody would lend it to him – not at any interest rate, not for any length of time. Our neighborhood bank said they didn't give small loans. They said it cost more to administer a large number of small loans than a small number of large ones. The next two banks had kind words for his business plan but said he didn't meet their criteria."

"What were the criteria?"

"Already having so much money you don't need a loan." Jessica was still bitter. "They didn't phrase it like that, but that's what it amounted to."

"And the rest of the banks?"

"There were no other banks."

Malcolm could see where this was leading. "Then what?"

"It sounds so clear when I tell the story, but it took a long time to figure all that out. My father sweated for months and burned all our savings trying to make it work. Mom worked double shifts to pay for food and rent, but she needed help. They fought a lot at that time. I couldn't understand the arguments, but I heard the shouting.

"We knew he was finished when a beauty franchise moved in across the street. The banks said it was a coincidence but my father never believed them. He thought somebody had tipped the franchise off to the opportunity in this neighborhood.

"Dad took a job in another big firm. He always considered that his insurance, figured that if his plan failed he could get another job like his old one. But it turned out to be harder than he thought. He searched for months. Eventually he settled for a position that used just a fraction of his skills and paid a fraction of what he was worth. I remember that too, but I didn't appreciate its importance. Every morning my father – who lived for independence – punched a time clock and spent the day doing other people's bidding in a cubicle.

"When our accounts turned positive my father experimented with different little projects, exploring options and new ideas. Nothing worked. The closest he came was electronic publishing. My parents had artistic friends – people who wrote poetry or created artwork. Most of them had scut jobs and they were always looking for publishers or display space.

"Dad thought that with no more money than he could raise from his friends, he could create a space on Eugene devoted to their work. Dad would run a business and his friends could publish their work. Everyone would win."

"So what went wrong?"

"Eugene turns out to be highly bottlenecked. A small number of businesses control key transaction points – satellite linkages, cable networks and the like. They charge exorbitant fees to use their services.

"Eugene is also closely regulated. All kinds of permissions are needed to create pathways in and out of the public domain; other permissions are needed to register your address. Every transaction is carefully controlled. Dad couldn't even charge users a fee without depositing it in an escrow account until the statutes of limitations for all possible claims against the fee had expired – usually seven to twelve years. In the meantime, no income."

"Nobody can do business like that."

"Certainly not a start-up. He had to give up Eugene too."

"What happened next?"

"There was no next. He got depressed. He started acting weird. I was fourteen by that time and I remember it pretty well. One day he pulled out his toenails with a pair of pliers. He got blood all over the bathroom. He said he wanted to see if it was possible." She gulped the rest of her coffee.

"The next week he packed up his workroom. We'd always paid for an extra room so he had space for his projects, and he'd accumulated a lot of junk. He piled all his stuff on a big table in the middle of the room. He had huge boxes of paper documents and other boxes filled with magnetic disks, buzzers and clippers he got cheap during his barbershop venture – all kinds of scraps from his undertakings. He wrapped it all in a tarp that barely fit on the table, and the table could barely hold the load. One leg had always been wobbly.

"I asked him what he was doing, and called his attention to that wobbly leg. He said it was an experiment. He was going to make a really big change. Then he got a pulley and a rope and he asked me to leave. So I did." She picked up her empty coffee cup and strained futilely for the few drops left at the bottom.

"The coroner reconstructed it like this. He said my dad tied the rope around his neck and ran it through the pulley, then he tied the other end to the bundle. When he kicked the wobbly leg all the junk fell down, hoisting him into the air by his neck."

Malcolm looked up in horror. "He hanged himself in reverse."

"With all the evidence of his failings," Jessica confirmed, "all his dreams for a better life." A commuter rushing down the tight rows of countertops nearly knocked her out of her seat, but she ignored him and wiped up the juice he left on her shoulder.

"Underneath the pile we found two envelopes. The first envelope contained an accounting. There was no explanation, no goodbye. Just a ledger. My father was very methodical and bookish – in some ways like you. He calculated how much he would have earned if he had stayed in normal jobs his whole working life. From that amount, he subtracted one person's ordinary expenses – food, clothing, commuter fees and the like. He was very careful. He added interest and deducted a reasonable rate of inflation. Circled at the end was his estimate of his value to the family."

Malcolm interrupted. "His *dollar* value."

"Whatever," Jessica talked right past him. She'd been through this many times before.

"What was in the other envelope?"

"A life insurance policy for exactly that amount."

Malcolm's head jerked up. Now he understood why Jessica wasn't impressed by his setback in the water research. But she wasn't finished.

"We never got paid. Dad didn't read the fine print. Suicide was expressly exempted by the insurance contract."

Malcolm's misfortune was small in comparison. Jessica knew it, and now Malcolm knew it too. "So you refuse to give up."

"So now I'm a lawyer."

Chapter Sixteen

Malcolm found a way. Jessica was right, and he found a way. Opportunities presented themselves as soon as he started on the Odor Eater the next morning. The Odor Eater was already a project of organic design; it gave him every right to open files about the creation and manufacture of the underlying bacterium. He had all the cover he needed to explore archives crucial to his own ideas. The Odor Eater might be even better than *Many Drops*.

His schedule was better too. He'd been working full throttle on *Many Drops*, convinced of the importance of his own contributions and committed to staying central to the mission. Now he resolved to scale back. He could easily stretch two days of work on the Odor Eater so it filled three. The stakes were low and nobody would know the difference; the balance of time he could fill with his own ideas until Tentek started adding more assignments. He thought maybe he'd have even more freedom because he might be less monitored on lesser projects – but he knew that was just guessing. He had to just plow ahead.

In the middle of the day Jessica linked him at his office. He wanted to thank her and admit that she was right, but she started too quickly. "I need a favor," she said.

"Anything." He was grateful for a chance to reverse the roles. "What is it?"

"Phil invited me to a fundraising dinner for the Von Hirsch campaign. He wants to 'reward' me for the breakthrough in the Indonesian case. He says Von Hirsch wants to thank me personally."

"That's great. What's the problem?"

"The problem is I don't want to go. This whole Indonesian thing makes me sick." She put a hand to her throat. "He wants me to go shopping."

"What?" Malcolm didn't see the connection.

"He doubts if I have 'suitable' clothing. He suggested I leave work early to buy something new."

"Did he give you money for it?"

"Of course not."

"Then you don't have to go shopping." He took control. "Skip the dress. Leave work early. Go graciously and have a good time because it's probably something new."

"It will be new," she agreed. "And the food will probably be good."

"I'll take care of David."

Jessica looked up in astonishment. That was the favor she'd called to ask.

He joked, "I don't know what I'm doing, though. I don't know what he eats and I flunked First Aid."

"Don't worry. He'll show you what to do. Really, he's on autopilot. I just pay the bills and take the credit."

A few hours later a limousine from the Von Hirsch campaign picked Jessica up outside her apartment. Phil was already on board. Jessica had never been in a limousine before, and the luxury amazed her. The seat recognized her height and weight, and automatically adjusted to the contours of her back. The theme song of the Von Hirsch campaign played while the autobar offered her a drink. The child in Jessica wanted to play with all the gadgets but she was self-conscious in front of Phil.

Phil looked like a different man in his black, tailed tuxedo. Gold buttons ran down his cuffs and his lapel, giving him an elegant, cultivated look from a different century. The buttons appeared to signify something – like military stripes – but Jessica was too embarrassed to ask. She suspected his outfit was rented for the occasion but she found no comfort in the thought; she already felt inadequate even in her best dress. He told her how much a single ticket to tonight's event cost. More than she earned in a month.

The limousine drove straight from Jessica's neighborhood to an affluent district of grand mansions and designer homes. A guard waved them through a checkpoint with a barred gate. On the other side the road was smoother, and lined with flowers. Long stretches of verdant landscape separated one home from the next, with the largest houses set farthest back from the road. Through the trees Jessica glimpsed fabulous palaces and miniature skyscrapers of metal and glass. She could only guess what life was like in these homes, with hints gleaned from the movies or the carefully presented biographies of the rich and famous. The people who lived here were as different from her as she was from the residents of Kaiserville.

Soon the limousine turned down a driveway that wound past trees laden with fruit and sculptures of Greek gods in marble. They pulled up to a stone mansion draped in ivy; the limousine doors opened automatically and a luxurious voice wished them well. Phil looped his arm through Jessica's and escorted her to the entrance. She didn't complain; the protocol was quite beyond her.

Inside was opulence beyond her wildest fantasies. Crystal chandeliers glowed overhead, tapestries draped the walls, and in the corner a willow tree leaned over a brook that trickled through a channel in the marble floor. A butler took their coats and led them downstream to the ballroom.

Phil again took Jessica's arm as they entered a room filled with music and laughter. An immense window looked over the ocean, a full moon sparkling across the waves. A full orchestra played in the center of the room, the conductor whirling and gesturing to the music.

But the ultimate glory belonged to the people. Women danced in shimmering gowns, their hair sculpted into tall towers studded with jewels. Men paraded in tuxedos of every color, carrying staffs of walnut and bronze. Like any party, the people gave it life; and life here danced on a plane Jessica had never even imagined. The fanciest scenes in the most extravagant movies paled beside this spectacular reality. Even the grandest buildings in public life – the old museums and courthouses, or the atriums of modern shopping malls – couldn't compete with the splendor of a party in full swing.

Directly before them stood a woman wearing a mountain of fur. Ermine draped from her shoulders to her heels while foxtails swung like tentacles from her waist and coiled pythonlike around her neck. At the pinnacle, ostrich feathers reached upwards from an ermine cap. Jessica almost laughed at the spectacle: the woman looked like a bear eating a parakeet.

Phil didn't seem to notice the woman in fur. He stood beside her, scanning the crowd, eyes darting among faces, seeking opportunities. Without saying a word, he dropped Jessica's arm and took off. In a moment he was lost in the swarm. Jessica stood by herself.

She shuffled toward a fireplace in a nearby wall and sat on an empty couch. A great English wolfhound curled by the warmth of the fire. A man whose shoes sparkled neon at every stride offered her hors d'oeuvres, pointing to items on a tray and naming them in languages Jessica didn't understand. She selected one at random, a golden triangle topped with saffron.

Wow. That was delicious. Hot, moist and tantalizingly spiced, the juices ran down her fingers and the mix of flavors ran a shiver down her spine. She used to think the food at her favorite restaurants was excellent, but that bit showed her that it didn't even rate. She licked her fingers and reminded herself to make the best of the evening. She rose from the couch to find a companion, maybe even dance a little. Before she left, she reached down to pat the wolfhound but her hand passed clear through. It was a hologram.

She meandered through the crowds, admiring some wardrobes and scoffing at others; she approached the first person she saw standing alone, a middle-aged woman in a long ruby gown. As she stepped closer, the gown changed color from ruby to aquamarine, then emerald; at first Jessica thought she was confused then she realized the fabric changed hue with the viewing angle. Jessica stepped in front of the rainbow woman and stated simply, "Good evening."

"Good evening," the woman said, and walked away.

Jessica was stunned. The woman hadn't been rude or supercilious; she was perfectly courteous but perfectly uninterested. She treated Jessica like a merchant selling something she didn't want.

She devoured more hors d'oeuvres and looked for another person alone. "Good evening," she said to a young man in a black tuxedo with a striking magenta sash across one shoulder. She followed up with her name and connection to the Von Hirsch campaign, to prove she belonged.

"I'm very pleased to meet you," said the young man as he walked away.

Again she was stunned. *My dress isn't that ugly!* Jessica thought as she watched the man find a different companion and strike up a conversation. He had treated her with respect but indifference; he couldn't even be bothered to be rude. A waiter navigated past him on feet of sparks. "I hope you catch fire," she said aloud.

Suddenly, the window overlooking the ocean faded to black, then returned as a window overlooking mountains. Instantly Jessica realized it wasn't a window at all, but another visual trick. She thought the mansion was perfectly situated over the ocean but now it could be anywhere. For all she knew, the ballroom looked out to the highway or a nearby house.

In front of the viewscreen Phil waltzed with a woman more than twice his age. Jessica tried to catch his attention but failed; he didn't see her or he was avoiding her. Phil danced well and Jessica suspected he had taken lessons. As she watched him she realized he had a winning strategy: competition would be keener among the youth than among the elderly: the young lions were positioning themselves in the corridors of power and couldn't waste time with the likes of Jessica. She needed to find someone who didn't figure in the political calculus, either as an aspiring youth or a grand old powerhouse.

Two hors d'oeuvres later she spotted an elderly gentleman sitting alone. He seemed bored by the whole affair and waved away a young waiter who sparkled past with a tray of drinks. He looked better in his simple business suit than many men in sartorial fantasies. Jessica introduced herself.

"And what do you do?" he asked.

Jessica blushed and considered lying, then as delicately as possible explained that she worked in Von Hirsch's office.

"Wonderful!" he exclaimed, "a person who actually works for a living. I remember when work was actually honorable. Please sit down."

They chatted for a while, discussing the artwork on the walls and some recent headlines. Eventually she asked his connection to the Von Hirsch campaign.

"He's my nephew. My sister's son and a great little boy."

"Will he be a good Governor?"

"He'll do just fine."

Just fine? That wasn't the kind of endorsement she was expecting. "Will he do better than the other candidates?" The least she could do at this political event was seek political information.

"They'll do fine, too. It doesn't really matter who wins the race." He talked slowly, as if to a novice, but he seemed happy to explain.

"Actually, I thought the differences were exactly the point."

"Hah!" He exuded a relaxed, experienced cynicism. "All the candidates are having parties just like this one, and all of them dance for the people who pay. It doesn't matter who wins. The candidates dance, and the bureaucracies are as steady as the tide."

"But the campaigns address political issues and the candidates take opposing sides."

"Only on tiny issues that don't affect the greater scheme of things – like whether to build a particular weapon system or whether to outlaw an activity that only a few people do. On issues that matter their stances are almost indistinguishable. Nobody even asks them."

Jessica looked out the window overlooking the mountains. They were beautiful in the distance but she knew they weren't real. Presently the view shifted to a field of daisies; in the new scene it wasn't even nighttime.

"Why bother?"

"Because it's a democracy. The process is crucial. If we didn't have elections people would lose faith in the government, and that wouldn't suit anybody. Besides, it's great fun. Get yourself a drink."

A ripple of excitement passed through the room. Heads turned towards the main entrance and Jessica followed them until she saw what was happening – Carlos Carellos Santos, star of the new film *Topless* had entered the room. All eyes followed him as he walked across the dance floor to a man wearing a tuxedo and a top hat. Santos looked magnificent in a scarlet robe.

"Is that Carlos ..." Jessica started to ask.

"He isn't real."

"What?"

"He isn't real. He's a hologram. Celebrities lease their images for use in events like this, but they don't attend personally. Just you watch. When he finishes talking to Von Hirsch he'll leave. For an extra fee he would read a speech or propose a toast, but I doubt Peter paid that much.

Sure enough, when Santos finished talking to the man in the top hat he walked back the way he came. The crowd returned to normal and the orchestra started a new tune. Jessica regretted that she hadn't seen Carlos Corellos Santos in person, but at least she had learned which one was Peter Von Hirsch. It saved her from yet another embarrassing question.

"Does everyone know he's phony?" Jessica asked.

"Some do, some don't. But it doesn't matter if he's real. Either way it's an important event."

Jessica frowned.

The old man patted her shoulder and stood to excuse himself. "Remember," he said, "any of the candidates will do fine. As for myself, I'm voting for my nephew. Enjoy the party."

Jessica thanked him and wished him well. Before she could decide what to do next, Phil landed in the man's vacant seat. He was drunk.

"Did you see that?!" he garbled. "Carlos Santos was here! I told you this would be great. Wait until I tell my wife!"

Jessica nodded. She was thinking about the upcoming election. She had always voted and even brought David with her to the polling station. She considered it a civic duty. She thought elections were for people to voice their concerns, and that the opinions of the majority carried the day. If the old man were right then the whole process was a charade....

"Don't sit there all night," Phil was saying. "Go forth and mingle. But don't do anything stupid. Remember, you're my date."

"Right, Phil," she replied, and departed with – she hoped – a fraction of the dismissiveness others had used on her earlier. By now she knew what to do. Her next stop was Peter Von Hirsch.

She knew he would be difficult to catch so she staked him out carefully. Tracking his tall top hat, she watched him pilot around the room, shaking hands and making conversation with everyone he crossed. Twice she placed herself directly in his path, but both times he veered off in another direction. Once, for an instant, he was alone, but Jessica moved too slowly. A woman wearing a sapphire gown and diamond tiara engaged him before she could reach the spot.

She tried a different tactic. While Von Hirsch talked to an elderly woman in a silken shawl, Jessica walked up and stood as if she were part of the conversation. Ultimately, they would have to include her or disregard her conspicuously; if that happened, she would know she was wasting her time.

"The key is incentives," the woman was explaining. "People should be able to enjoy the success of their hard work."

Von Hirsch replied, "You're correct, of course. That's why I'm fighting for refined transpo seating fees. All the seats shouldn't cost the same. People who work harder and earn more should be able to buy a seat near the front."

The woman heartily agreed. She told a story of a man who offered twice the fare but still had to sit in the back of a transpo. Von Hirsch listened until she finished, then clapped her on the shoulder and turned away as if Jessica didn't even exist.

She grabbed his arm and pushed directly in front of him. "I'm Jessica Frey," she declared. "I worked on the Indonesian case."

He shook his head blankly, showing not the slightest flicker of recognition.

"It's the case with Brother Corporation and the electrical license."

He didn't try to leave but he still appeared not to understand.

"I work with Phil Barnes," she attempted.

He cocked his head slightly; something registered.

"Yes! Phil Barnes ... he works in my office." He looked around as if he expected Phil to materialize instantly, or perhaps he was planning his escape. "This isn't about work, is it? I'm rather busy."

Jessica was starting to feel foolish. "I'm the person who discovered how to give Brother the advantage in Indonesia. Phil thought that ...."

"Yes, yes," he interrupted. "There is some kind of case in Indonesia. Whatever it is, I'm sure Phil will handle it." He wheeled away, terminating Jessica's existence in an instant. Immediately he reached the next guest and greeted her warmly with an outstretched hand. "How nice of you to join us…"

The rest of the evening hardly mattered. Jessica enjoyed the food and drinks but made little conversation. She never got to dance. A few more celebrities wandered through, keeping to themselves or talking briefly to Von Hirsch, then leaving immediately. Nobody gave speeches or presentations. Politics were completely absent from the affair.

Long past midnight the crowd started to thin. Phil found Jessica resting on the couch by the holographic dog and told her it was impolitic to be last to leave. He clasped her arm – as much for stability as appearances – and together they walked slowly to the door. A limousine carried them home.

Chapter Seventeen

David's childhood dominated Jessica's apartment. His toys cluttered the floor and his artwork decorated the walls with exuberance and disarray. Malcolm wasn't sure what to do without Jessica, but he figured he could bungle along. He picked up a lion that David had made from clay, and asked him what it was.

"A lion," David replied.

Malcolm's technique needed improvement. "Did you make it in school?"

"I made it in art class."

"How?"

"I'll show you." David showed him a picture of a lion he had used as a model, then gave him a guided tour of his favorite art projects and the other items on display – a few books, simple decorations and photographs. Most of the photographs were of David growing up; one was the marriage of Jessica's parents, set like a throwback to a different era, with a black tuxedo and flowing white gown.

One photo set apart was a young woman standing alone in ocean surf, solitary and strong, hand on her hip. Malcolm picked it up for a closer look, attracted by its simplicity and power, then realized he was looking at Jessica. He studied it closely, overwhelmed by a feeling of history unfolding. A few years later the same woman, still alone, decided to have a child.

And that child had just cooked him dinner. He'd done a nice job, too. Apparently he'd selected meal cartridges before Malcolm arrived, and timed them for completion when he figured they'd be hungry. Obviously he had plenty of practice. "You're a regular Autochef," Malcolm remarked.

David didn't get the joke. He said, "Aren't you going to ask what I did in school today? Mom always asks me what I did in school today."

"Okay, what did you do in school today?"

"Same old stuff," David replied, then cracked up when he realized that answer was ridiculous. They talked a little about his day, and Malcolm learned that David went to Kid Kare for a few hours before and after the traditional school day, traveling both directions by transpo on his own. David said that school was fun, especially math, but that Kid Kare was more fun because they did art projects. Today he'd started to make a sculpture from papier-maché. "It's a lion. A boy lion. It's orange." He planned to finish it during the next few days.

"I'll bet it will be beautiful."

"Handsome," David replied. "Do you have kids?"

"Not one."

"More than one?"

Malcolm laughed but shook his head from side to side. "No kids at all."

"Why not?"

Malcolm wasn't sure what to say. "No particular reason."

"That's no reason. When I say that to mom she tells me to figure out what the reason is."

Malcolm smiled. David was an innately precise child, and he was being raised by a lawyer. He said, "Some things usually happen before kids, and for me those things haven't happened yet."

"But you're not opposed to kids. As a matter of principle, I mean."

"No, I'm not opposed. Not as a matter of principle."

That seemed to satisfy him.

After dinner they watched an educational program on television that David said they watched every day. Malcolm soon realized that the program was coordinated with the national school system and designed to supplement each day's lesson.

Today's show started with counting practice. David enthusiastically sang out the numbers from one to ten while numbers and pictures danced on screen. Slowly the exercises grew more difficult. David was asked to count backwards and forwards by twos and fives. His favorite image corresponded to the number twenty-five: two groups of ten chocolate Beta Bars followed by a group of five chocolate Beta Bars. After the counting exercise, the program broke for a commercial break that showed, among other things, the Ultra Super Beta Brothers eating chocolate Beta Bars.

After the break came arithmetic exercises. The television called out simple problems: "Two plus two!" and "Three plus four!" followed by problems of greater difficulty: "Ten minus six!" and "Twelve minus eight!"

David's task was to call back the answers, and the television evidently listened because a running score showed in the corner of the screen. From time to time, advice messages for parents rolled across the bottom of the display. Malcolm found a notebook and recorded the notices.

But he was doing more than recording notices. The visuals were appealing, the music was catchy, and David's spirit's lifted his own. He was having fun.

David barely distinguished between the programming and the advertisements; he was equally absorbed by both. He jumped with delight during an ad for a new movie, *Monkeys Over Manhattan*, about terrorists who released thousands of wild monkeys into New York City. Animal lovers prevented the authorities from killing the monkeys until they had proliferated beyond control. The ad showed monkeys tearing out cable jacks, pulling down satellite antennas, throwing garbage at pedestrians and swooping off with beloved pets. The terrorists laughed over the pandemonium while scientists sought a solution .... David leapt about the room like a monkey in Manhattan, then looked wishfully at Malcolm. He recorded that in the notebook too.

At the end of the program, the screen displayed the message, "Would you like a printout of your child's performance?" In the instant that Malcolm was unsure what to do, David shouted "Yes!" at the screen. The display replied, "Printout sent." Malcolm had no idea where to pick it up, but he was sure that both David and Jessica did. His note keeping was unnecessary after all.

David played videogames by himself while Malcolm cleaned up dinner, then David declared that it was time for bed. "Good night," he said.

"Good night," Malcolm replied. "I had a lot of fun."

"Will I see you in the morning?"

"I don't think so. I'll leave when your mom comes home."

David gave Malcolm a little hug on his leg and climbed peacefully into bed. A minute later he asked for a glass of water, which Malcolm happily brought him. Then he was quiet.

Jessica had instructed Malcolm that he could leave after David fell asleep, but he wanted to stay to make sure, and the next program on the education channel caught his attention. This time the catchy tunes and clever animation were about decontamination after a terrorist germ attack, but soon the images of skin lesions and bleeding made him feel queasy. He turned the television off before it eradicated the warm afterglow of the evening with David.

He wandered about the room, moving quietly so he wouldn't bother David. He cleaned up from dinner then returned to David's art projects and the photographs of him growing up. Malcolm couldn't have associated the boy in the next room with the infant in the photos, but intermediate shots showed the link. For an instant he had a strong sensation of a life unfolding before his eyes, a life with infinite possibilities. He wondered if either of his parents had a display like this in their living rooms. He doubted it.

He found the printer with the record of David's evening work. It listed his performance on the math drills and every advertisement that had played: it even included coupons for Beta Bars and *Monkeys Over Manhattan* because the audio input had detected the viewers' high levels of interest. Malcolm admired the system's accuracy and self-consciously dropped his own notes in the trash.

He put on his coat and checked to make sure that David was asleep. The little boy lay curled in bed, his breath deep and even, the very picture of youthful innocence. Malcolm watched him a while, worried about leaving him unprotected … but Jessica said it was okay and no doubt she'd checked every fire alarm and escape system in the building. He tucked the blankets gratuitously around David's shoulders, then headed out to Tentek. He didn't want to use Jessica's home computer and leave tracks back to this family, and the work he was planning exceeded the capacity of his lifelink.

Every time Malcolm entered the Tentek building he had a moment of doubt: *Will they let me in? Has my clearance been revoked? Are they lying in wait?* But his retinas scanned cleanly and the officers paid him little attention. He stopped at the statue of Hap Jackson and gazed up at the brave eyes, the daring chin. Jackson looked so confident, so sure. A fragment of the daily pledge popped to mind: *I will serve loyally and work hard for our great goals.* Malcolm knew he was testing the limits of loyalty and breaking some rules – but he was definitely working hard for great goals. Jackson should be pleased. If he wasn't, then damn him.

Malcolm went straight to his office and started where he'd ended last, with that interesting freshwater protist and some new leads on organic design he'd gotten from the Odor Eater. He started cross-referencing terms and reviewing the protist research to see if its genetic characteristics had been adapted for other purposes. He was well rested and in a wonderful mood. Ideas jumped as fast as he could navigate the database.

He had a hunch that the protist had flourished because it consumed the salt in seawater as a nutrient. Other freshwater species had died when the water turned brackish but this mutation proved life-saving. He was checking to see if earlier scientists had shared this intuition and what, if anything, had come of it.

A few hours later he had an answer. Tentek geneticists had worked on this protist while other technicians examined the acidity of the water that had killed so many other species. They had even given the organism a name, *Jakoba survivorus*, the first word indicating its place in the single-celled world and the second word reflecting its achievement.

The pieces came together in a straightforward way. Although they were all archived in different departments for different purposes and *survivorus* investigation had stopped, to Malcolm the connections were clear. He vidlinked Jessica to see if he could meet her for breakfast. He expected to leave a message but she'd just returned home and wasn't yet asleep. He said it was urgent.

* * * * *

It hardly seemed like he had left. Malcolm checked on David, still curled up asleep in his room, before he even took his coat off. The only change was Jessica sitting where David sat during his exercises, still dressed for a party. She pointed to a coffee pot and told him to help himself. He skipped the coffee and sat down.

"They have it," he declared. His tone was electric.

"What do you mean?"

"Tentek has Kahn's water."

Jessica looked at him quizzically. "Tentek has *your* water that was stolen? Or Kahn's water from a different source? I thought his spring was destroyed."

"I don't know. I don't care. It doesn't matter. They have the stuff. Tentek has an organism that desalinates seawater, exactly like Kahn's. It lives in water, consumes salt and excretes chlorine. The combination takes the salt out of seawater and purifies the freshwater left behind. No matter how the water starts, the final product is safe to drink." He said it as conclusively as the score of yesterday's ballgame.

Jessica wasn't convinced. "If Tentek had something like that, we'd all know it. It would be on the market in minutes, and people would pay fortunes for it. A product like that would be revolutionary. Your *Many Drops* project would be useless."

"I know. I don't understand." He stood up and helped himself to coffee in the kitchen, then walked around the apartment.

"Suppose you're right." She humored him. "Suppose Tentek actually has this organism. Where would it be right now?"

"There are two possibilities. First, it might have been flushed down a toilet after experimentation was complete. The genetic code would be databased but the organism would be destroyed if it wasn't being used. Live samples are a pain."

"And second?"

"If we still have it, it's probably in the specimen laboratory."

"You need to check."

"I can't."

"Security, right?"

"Right. The laboratories and files are off limits to me. I don't work in the life sciences and my involvement ends with design. I see results from people who build prototypes but I never see the thing itself. Just records."

She leaned back in the couch and examined him searchingly. "You'll need to stop by the lab and have a look."

"It's off limits." He sipped his coffee.

"You need to break in then."

Malcolm's coffee tried to go down the wrong way. He sat up fast, choking and gasping, coffee running down his chin. *You don't just break into the specimen laboratory!* As a teenager he'd done his share of pranks, but he knew better than to attempt a fortress like that. The process was closed to him.

Jessica's old anger came back. She was tired of always being on the outside, and she wanted some answers. A world of decisions were being made around her. Governors were being picked, news media were deciding what stories to broadcast and gigantic multinational conglomerates were deciding when to attack puny start-up competitors. She had no idea where decisions were made, on what grounds or by whom. "The world needs this water, and it needs you to get it for them."

She stood up and strode to the center of the room, spun around with her hand on her hip. In her posture, Malcolm didn't see a single mother struggling with work and child care. He saw the young woman barefoot in the surf, with capability beyond the horizon.

She stepped towards him, eyes afire. "If you get it, I'll sell it for you."

It didn't seem obvious until after she said it. Jessica hadn't signed a no-compete agreement; she owed Tentek no obligations. Malcolm stood up and walked towards her, focused in a way he hadn't been before. "Counterterrorism knows I had a sample. Internal Affairs knows I've been wandering off track. My apartment's been burglarized and I wasn't careful with my electronic tracks." He spread his arms. "Could I get in more trouble?"

"You can't go back."

"They'll fire me eventually. I'll never find another job."

"You could go to jail."

"Where the inmates don't like bioterrorists." That much he understood.

"Time is not on your side."

"What is?"

"Me. Knowledge. Access to water that could save the world and make you rich."

"'Access' might be an overstatement." But the mood had shifted and they both knew it. Only the indifference of the system had kept them safe this far. It wouldn't last.

The rest of the night was devoted to strategy.

PART THREE

CHOICE

Chapter Eighteen

Malcolm napped an hour on Jessica's couch then walked to work with a sense of renewal. His stride was crisp and clean, muscles imperfectly tuned but still athletic; the season was warming and a faint sweat broke out beneath his clothes, inspiring him to walk faster until he was nearly jogging. More than ever, he felt hope and he felt alive. It was thrilling.— *What's that?*

He ducked as a transpo zipped past swinging a huge axe. "Too tired to chop your own?" the advertisement asked, then told him that Brother made a video fireplace that "looks and smells like real wood burning."

He struggled to reconstruct his thoughts. It was so hard to think. He craved advice and security even as he made decisions that put him alone and at risk. Jessica was behind him, of course, but he wanted more. He wanted friends to tell him that he was doing the right thing – or at least something they could understand. If he failed, he wanted friends to say, "Good for you for trying." He expected Internal Affairs would say something different.

He didn't even go to his desk. He checked the directory in the building lobby, right under the nose of Hap Jackson in bronze, and determined the location of the specimen lab. He went there first.

The specimen lab was a bustle of activity. Malcolm's work happened at his desk and he could finish a hard stretch of ultratime without leaving his chair, but here work happened on the move. People dashed from room to room, pushing carts filled with phials, tubes and electronic equipment. He didn't doubt that every move had purpose but it looked like anarchy. The lab wasn't built for visitors so there wasn't even a receptionist. Eventually a young woman in a white lab coat noticed him.

"Can I help you with something?"

"I'm curious to see a project I've been working on."

"What for?" Designers had no reason to visit the lab, and they rarely did. "Would you like to see a printout of recent results?"

"No, thanks. I want to see the thing itself."

She looked at him in confusion. She seemed willing to help but didn't understand what he was looking for.

Struggling to sound personal and confidential, he explained that he had worked at Tentek for a long time but he never got to see the fruit of his labor. He specifically named the Odor Eater. "It's a silly little thing, but I wonder if I could watch the next time it came out for testing. It's my creation and I want to see it in action."

She cocked her head understandingly and smiled. "I saw a movie about that once. *Untasted fruit.* Have you seen it?"

"I will now." He lied.

She checked the logs to see when the Odor Eater was next scheduled for performance. "I'm sorry. The Odor Eater has been sent back for revision and no testing is scheduled until modifications are made. I don't know how long it will take."

Malcolm knew that, of course, since he was responsible for making those revisions, but he'd learned enough. "Can you keep me posted?"

"You bet."

Malcolm went straight to his desk and straight to work. The Odor Eater was dying in transit and the faster the lab received modifications the sooner he could watch the tests.

An hour later Garcia stopped by on his rounds. He saw Malcolm working feverishly and turned to leave, but Malcolm motioned him in deeper. "Garcia, may I ask you a question?"

He stepped fully into the room and swung the door half shut behind him – closed enough for privacy but not enough to look like they were hiding something. Garcia mixed the training of a security guard with the instincts of a competitor raised in communities where conflicts were fierce and stakes were high. He nodded for Malcolm to continue.

Malcolm wondered how much Garcia knew. Was he involved in the interrogations by Internal Affairs? Did he probe for information during these amiable visits? There was no way to know. All Malcolm knew for sure was that he liked Garcia, trusted him, and most importantly, needed him.

He didn't waste any time. "Garcia, what kind of security is in the specimen laboratory?" He understood that simply asking these questions put not only Garcia but probably his entire family at risk.

Garcia said nothing so Malcolm filled the silence. Briefly he explained that he needed to examine a specimen inside the laboratory. He swore that it had nothing to do with industrial sabotage or spying for a competitor, just that Tentek had begun a series of experiments then foolishly left them unfinished. He had tried through normal channels to convince Tentek to complete the project or even discuss the mistake, but Tentek was too indifferent or too bureaucratic to understand. The only solution was for Malcolm to go into the specimen lab and bring it out.

The explanation was a little thin but it was all he dared. "Can you help?" he asked. "The product being developed could help a lot of people."

Garcia stood still for a long time. He was thinking, and Malcolm gave him time to do it. He sat quietly at his desk while Garcia leaned against the wall, obscured from the corridor by the half-closed door. "The specimen lab isn't part of my ordinary sweep," he said at last.

"I may be able to pay you for the extra work."

"You will not pay me. We must be very clear about that. Maybe I can help you, as you have helped me. If I am able to help you, then maybe you can thank me another time. But I am not providing a service and I will not accept a fee."

Malcolm nodded.

Garcia stayed in the corner by the door. "Security around the specimen lab is considerable," he said. "First, it's in the center of the building. There are no walls to the outdoors and obviously no windows. All ventilation occurs through ducts smaller than a human being and internally barred. Second, as I am sure you have noticed, there are video cameras throughout the building. There are no blind spots. The scene from each camera is observed at least once every minute by officers specially trained to observe suspicious behavior, and the images are recorded."

"When are they played back?"

"They are played back in the event anything unusual occurs."

Malcolm was starting to realize how foolish this project had become.

"You probably also know that the specimen lab is a maze of small rooms, each with its own purpose and its own security. If the experiment is not active, then you probably need access to Central Storage." He looked to Malcolm for confirmation.

Malcolm didn't know any of this, but it made sense to him too. "Go on."

"Central Storage has only one door. It is heavily guarded and monitored during daytime hours. People can enter only after retina scans and proof of business. Staff is rotated regularly so improper relationships do not form."

He looked Malcolm in the eye to convey irony, then continued. "Between the hours of midnight and six in the morning, no entry is permitted to Central Storage. It's usually quiet at that time. Tentek decided that a full staff cohort was wasteful but light staffing was too risky. So they just seal the area. Anybody running experiments overnight needs to plan in advance. The door is closed, locked and alarmed."

"Is that all?"

"No. Inside Central Storage are light sensors at the entry and exit of every aisle. The light beams cannot be seen but if they are interrupted when the door is closed, an alarm will sound."

"And is that all?"

"That's all I know about. As I said, it's not on my sweep."

* * * * *

In her office, Jessica was having problems of her own. She was tired from the long night and she absolutely did not want to see Phil. He had lied to her about the importance of the Indonesian case to Von Hirsch, and she suspected he had an agenda of his own. Nonetheless, deadlines were approaching and they had to discuss the case. Both of them acted as if the previous evening hadn't happened, but both were irritable.

"Brother doesn't want to limit liability to the new corporation," he began.

Jessica knew that bad news was about to follow.

"Liability for the wrongdoing should attach to the individuals themselves. Brother is seeking payment from the people who created the corporation as well as the corporation itself."

"That makes no sense," Jessica replied. "The people didn't act individually. They formed a corporation, which entered business as a collective entity."

"Pierce the corporate veil. Go after the individuals."

She stood up and pulled a book from the shelf, a well-known treatise of corporations that explained – probably in chapter one – how the corporate structure protected individual investors. "Maybe the Corporation broke some licensing rules, but those individuals had nothing to do with it. Wanna bet that they weren't even in the room when the violation occurred?"

"They ordered it. If they didn't order it, they approved it. If they didn't approve it, they created the structure and authority that permitted it. Responsibility starts at the top. Go get them."

"I might as well 'go get' Hap Jackson," she replied bitterly. "Tentek lowered its prices too. That was the final blow that drove the new company under. Maybe it was collusion. Let's join Tentek as a party and fine Jackson himself. Want to?"

Phil was unamused. "No, I don't. What I want is for you to move on this case, before deadline, and to go after those people in Indonesia."

"There's no legal basis for such a motion."

"I'm sure their lawyers will take that position."

"I need a good faith reason."

"Then find one." He stormed out of her office, and slammed the door behind him.

* * * * *

Garcia stopped by Malcolm's office later that afternoon, surprising him because visits at that hour weren't part of his ordinary rounds. He held in his hand a silver disk about the size of a bottle top.

"This is a VIP retina," Garcia declared, "When people come to the building who need significant, unassigned right of entry, we give them one of these. This one is expired, but when they are operational they are used to open doors and obtain access that regular staff gain via retina scan. It's easier to create a universal retina than to input personal retina patterns and customize parameters for each visit and each visitor. We just give VIPs one of these, and let them come and go as they please."

He returned the disk to his pocket and continued. "Access begins when we hand it to them and ends 24 hours later. Lots of VIP's are around these days because Jackson is here. They don't always return their retinas because they're too busy ... that's why the access terminates automatically after a fixed time. Twenty-four hours is usually plenty, and it's better to renew a VIP who needs more time than to cancel one who's still using it.

"I wish it were cleaner, but VIPs are busy and hard to control. We must accommodate their patterns. Even when they do return the retina, it remains operational until it is manually cancelled or 24 hours pass." He looked at Malcolm to see if he was getting it yet, but Malcolm still didn't understand.

"If a VIP retina is returned to me, I will pass it immediately to you. You will have the remaining time to use as you please." He said this like it was a simple fact, not an astonishing act of insubordination. "But there are terms. First, I do this as a favor for a friend. I don't want to know what you intend to do with this and I don't want you to tell me."

Malcolm nodded.

"Second, if you get caught with the retina I give you, I will say you stole it. Do you understand?"

"I understand."

"Third, I might know when the 24 hours started and therefore when they will end, but I might not. Probably you will not know when your unit will cease to function, or where you will be at that time. Do you understand?"

Malcolm must have looked as scared as he felt because Garcia kept pausing for him to digest the information. "I understand," he said. He hoped he did.

"Lastly, I don't know when I will come into possession of a VIP retina. Maybe tonight. Maybe not until the end of the year. You will need to be ready when it happens."

"I understand."

"The VIP retina's primary function is to open doors, and it will open the door to Central Storage. It will not disarm the light beams. That's a separate system. Also, the door closes and locks immediately after entry. The same retina will let you out if you leave within ten minutes. If you do not leave during that window, you will be locked in and must request secondary authorization to exit. Nobody lingers in Central Storage.

"The opening will be recorded but it will not be played back if nothing unusual occurs. It will register in the security booth as an authorized VIP entry and the guards will think nothing of it. No alarm will sound."

Malcolm waited for him to continue, then realized he had finished. "Thank you," he said. He felt humbled by Garcia's precise briefing, and by the trust and risk that stood behind it. "I thank you for more than just myself–"

But Garcia raised a hand to silence him. He didn't want to know. Without a backwards glance, he left the room to resume his duties.

Malcolm stayed at work until midnight that night, walking around regularly to get a feel for nighttime security. He watched the guards roving the corridors and studied the video cameras with dismay. He had never appreciated how many there were. Now they seemed to be everywhere, omnipresent observers of everything. These were not the tiny pinprick cameras Tentek had developed for covert surveillance; these were bulky conspicuous cameras that told people they were being watched.

The next day he came in late and stayed until 3 a.m., even later than he stayed on ultratime. He was deliberately drifting through the entire clock, planning to become increasingly nocturnal so he could watch the nighttime security in operation. He considered and ruled out visiting Central Storage during the day – posing as a VIP or trying to lose himself in the bustle. He would need to visit Central Storage in the dead of night, when the bustle was quiet and the facility was empty.

At some point he was assigned additional work on other routine projects, and at some point he solved the problem of the Odor Eater. It involved repackaging more than organic design, but he knew that the viability of the packaging would need to be tested as soon as that department finished the details. He expected a call soon.

In the meanwhile, he took breaks to walk the halls, studying how many guards were in the booths and how often foot patrols walked their rounds, and he made sure to smile as they passed so they got used to seeing him. He wanted to be become known as a wanderer so his movements wouldn't seem strange when he stayed late and walked to unusual places. During all of this, he watched the cameras at the end of every corridor, but there was nothing to learn by watching. The cameras were tireless, expressionless and dull – but they were everywhere, looking out over everything.

He became impressed by how many officers there were, and how much he hadn't noticed before he started looking. He realized now that Jackson had his own security staff, who walked the halls wearing the same Tentek uniform but with a different button on the lapel. Malcolm could tell when Jackson entered and exited the building by the behavior of those guards.

Late on the second day he went to visit Garcia in the Division security booth. He had occasionally looked inside as he walked past but he had never before entered. The booth was filled with electronic equipment – long consoles of buttons and dials, and rows of video monitors mounted overhead. He wasn't ordinarily permitted inside, but Garcia waved him in.

Malcolm had thought hard about the cameras but couldn't make any headway. At first he thought he could ignore them – he worked for Tentek and nothing was wrong with him being inside the building. But he had no business in the vicinity of Central Storage, especially when it was closed for the night. That was the kind of image that would probably generate additional scrutiny. He went to the video center to learn what he could.

His cover was an upcoming basketball tournament. He brought a notebook filled with statistics and the tournament elimination ladder. He started by asking Garcia who he was betting for, then included other officers in the conversation, who were surprisingly talkative. Malcolm tested some theories about who was the best center and whether a team with better rebounding could beat a team with better shooting. All the while he watched the security operation and kept his pen moving in his notebook – though not recording sports statistics as he tried to make it appear.

Four officers watched the video screens with unblinking attention. They showed no interest in the conversation and their eyes never strayed from the screens. Malcolm counted a six-by-ten array of video screens – sixty in all – and noted that the image on each screen changed at fixed intervals. He recalled that Garcia said each camera was observed at least once a minute, and he reasoned that the images must rotate through the Division in sequence, leaving some cameras unwatched at any given time – though available for playback in the event of unusual occurrences.

In the corner of each screen was the number of the camera being displayed at that time. That was the key. Malcolm copied the camera numbers as swiftly and completely as he could. He didn't think or distract himself with analysis. That could come later. He just wrote down numbers, and every now and again recorded the exact time. All the while he kept up conversation with the guards, though from time to time they turned full attention to their real duties, which left Malcolm free to devote full attention to his notes.

When conversation grew thin he excused himself. Garcia ushered him out with a joke about Malcolm's performance in the previous basketball pool, and his hopes that he would do better next time. If he guessed Malcolm's purpose, he didn't let on.

Malcolm returned immediately to his office and deciphered his notes. Working on scratch paper rather than his computer he created a matrix with the monitor number on one axis and the camera number on the other. The lowest camera number he had recorded was 1 and the highest was 335, and most numbers in between were captured somewhere on the scrap. He assumed there were 335 cameras displayed on 60 monitors. He counted how many times the camera changed in several one minute time gaps, and concluded that images shifted every ten seconds. What did that mean?

It took him half an hour of calculating to discover an algorithm that satisfied the constraints. He spent another half hour trying to find other algorithms and determined there were none. So. He took a break then reviewed what he had learned.

The cameras moved sequentially around the Division. If he started at a fixed location at a fixed time, he could move contiguously through the Division, always in view of a camera that was not being watched. He would still be recorded but nobody would bother to play it back unless something unusual occurred. He could walk in plain view of the video cameras without being seen. He had found a way to beat the system.

Chapter Nineteen

The next morning the computer in Malcolm's office greeted him with an ad just for him: "Next week is your mom's birthday," advised a giant bookstore called The Cave. "Last year at this time you bought her a book. This year, is she still your mother?" The advertisement advised that shipping was free for advance birthday sales, but fees would soon revert to normal and express delivery cost more. "Act fast!"

The ad was right about timing and right that he'd forgotten his mother's birthday. He went ahead and linked to The Cave's inventory. He might as well take care of this right now; he figured The Cave would advise him what to buy.

Before he reached the next step Gary came storming into the office, slamming the door shut behind him. Malcolm had never seen him so unhappy.

"My wife lost her job. They fired her."

Malcolm rose from his chair in alarm, but he didn't know what to say. He looked on blankly.

"She called from the street outside her office. They kicked her out like a dog. She's crying." As if on cue, an infant's wails burst from the hall, urgent, like someone had poked it with a stick. The whine testing continued. "She worked there for ten years."

"What happened?"

"Restructuring, reorganizing ... all the rest of it. They said her position had disappeared and they didn't need her anymore. Office security guards grabbed her and escorted her outside. They said her personal belongings would be boxed and sent home, and that the company would pay her an additional two weeks. The guards said the policy was severance instead of notice." Another burst of crying came from down the hall, quieter this time but more personal, as if the baby were not poked but hungry.

Gary said, "Now she's on the street and I'm mixing whines for terrorists."

"You need to go to her."

"I can't. I'm on deadline." He looked pained.

"Can I cover for you?"

Gary thought hard about this. He wanted to go to his wife but he was obviously torn: two out-of-work parents would be a disaster. Then he decided. He stepped over to Malcolm's computer and started punching keys. In a moment, files from the whine team started to appear. Gary pointed to a few files and described the situation. "You can solve these problems with half your brain. It won't take long but finish before noon." He turned to walk out, then called over his shoulder, "Thanks."

Malcolm went straight to work. He'd been down this path many times before. Tentek kept its material well organized and everyone always worked as if someone else might take over. Malcolm was routinely pulled into projects on short notice and asked to help meet a deadline, and he knew the drill. The sound of crying down the hall no longer seemed a distraction; now it was fitting background for the problems on his screen. He even generated a few whines of his own – though he was careful to keep the volume down.

Then the sound of real crying sounded across the hall, an adult, not a child, and not a soundtrack being manipulated. This was authentic. Malcolm walked to the door to see what was happening, and saw two Tentek security guards pulling a woman out of her office.

"Look, it's not our fault," one officer said. "We don't make these decisions. HQ decides what personnel are needed. We just deliver the news."

"But I need more time!" Another sob escaped her.

"Time we can't do. Some people who get time use it to make trouble."

"But I won't." They were nearly down the hall by now. "I promise."

"I believe you. But some people do." They turned the corner out of sight, and soon even their voices faded away. Just like that, another life drifted downstream. Malcolm stood staring down the empty hallway a minute more; he knew that the nearby offices were all occupied, but nobody else looked out.

A memory emerged from deep in his mind. Some combination of the crying and whining and the woman disappearing triggered a memory from his childhood. He coaxed it out until finally it was clear in his mind, a moment when he was younger than David was now, maybe half his age. He was sure of the timing because it happened in an apartment his family left when he was four.

In this memory he was crying. He was crying for his mother.

He remembered that she'd been leaving the apartment. He wanted her to stay but she was walking out anyway. He remembered clinging to her leg, pulling her back as hard as he could. He remembered being lifted at every step, banging his head on a table but still hanging on. He was crying and screaming, *"Mommy! Stay!"* but she wasn't listening, just lifting him up and bumping him down in stride. Lifting up, and bumping down. She pried him off when she reached the door, then pushed it shut in his face.

He realized now that she'd been going to work. It was an ordinary day.

He remembered pulling on the door to follow her but it was too heavy or maybe locked. He pulled and pulled, failing to reach her, crying for what seemed like an eternity. Then through his own crying he heard a sound that terrified him, a funny echo on the other side of the door. It rose and fell, muffled by the door, like his own screaming coming back to him or maybe, he imagined, a monster come to punish him because he didn't listen when his mother told him to let go. He listened to it until he was sure it was real, then ran away, hid in the bathroom and kept crying by himself.

The memory was powerful, unmistakable. He remembered everything about the space – the apartment with blue wallpaper and the bathroom with the stool so he could reach the sink. He remembered huddling between the toilet and the sink, dreading those muffled cries, sobbing until the memory trickled off. No doubt something had happened next – perhaps the babysitter had rescued him, or he'd cried until he fell asleep. He couldn't remember how it ended.

Now he figured out something new, something that only the intervening years and his adult perspective could explain. The sound on the other side of the door had probably been his mother. She'd probably been crying too. Thirty years later he imagined her leaning on the other side of the door, sobbing on her own. Thirty years later he realized that she, too, wanted to stay.

The computer was right. Her birthday was next week. He set aside the whine machine and linked her at her office. He just wanted to hear her voice.

She picked up right away. He saw her looking tired, in an office piled high with work. "I got the letter," she said. "I guess I'm still next of kin. Do you want to see it?"

"No thanks, mom. I know what it says."

"My birthday isn't until next week."

"I just wanted to call now. I was thinking of you."

"That's nice."

"Listen, do you remember one time when …"

She interrupted. "Yes, I remember. Last year you sent me a book for my birthday."

"No, before then." He struggled to begin.

She helped. "Is there anything new? Are you dating?"

Anything new? What wasn't new?! But he didn't want to talk about Sayeh Kahn or desalination or Internal Affairs. He really didn't know what to say. Truly, he was just thinking of her and wanted to talk. He lacked the will to pull this forward. "I'm dating a little. What's new with you?"

"Same old stuff. I'm glad you called."

"Have a happy birthday next week. I'll probably buy you a book."

"A book would be nice. Goodbye."

"Goodbye." Malcolm switched off and got back to the whine machine. The conversation he wanted was decades too late.

* * * * *

Jessica linked Bobeck's home and listened to it ring. She'd tried an hour earlier, and an hour before that, and she knew what it meant. Finally the message intervened. "The extension you dialed is not in service. Please check the extension and dial again."

The family had moved. She searched for them on Eugene and found only displacement – related to Kahn's water, no doubt. She hoped they'd been absorbed by family and friends. Hopefully, Bobeck would call her, perhaps for money. She wanted to offer cash and a stake in the business.

Her business plan involved word-of-mouth advertising, bottles sold from a truck and hasty exits. Formal markets and the legal distribution she understood – including their limitations – but knowledge of informal markets and personal networks were missing. She expected that young Bobeck of Kaiserville would prove useful. If she could find him.

Her real work continued in the basement of her building. The material she needed on corporations – reasons to pierce the veil and attack the individuals – was so old it was in books. Of course, they'd been digitized and she could read them at her desk, but many were in the basement library. Somehow the older technology felt better for research like this, and the books felt satisfying in her hands. She reached high to pull them off the shelf and turned pages, looking for a legitimate basis, some fraud or wrongdoing for which the entrepreneurs were personally responsible. The room was quiet, and too dark for easy reading.

She didn't find anything useful. The individuals had been conscientious and careful, starting a business in ultimate good faith. Soon she was just turning pages, going through the motions of research, barely registering the words, not even keeping notes. She found a scrap of paper and wrote, "Is anybody out there?" She signed her name and date, and left it between pages of a random book, a message in a bottle for future generations.

Jessica's mother had always accused her of being rash. She opened the photo of her mother she kept in her lifelink and admitted for the thousandth time that in some ways her mother was right. Sometimes she was a little hasty. Her mother had counseled against her "rush to pregnancy," but supported her once the decision was made.

She worried that she'd gotten Malcolm into trouble. It was enough for him to seek a desalinator in his spare time. Suppose Tentek had such an organism in its basement – who cared? Let Tentek sort it out after

Malcolm developed a design. Had she pushed him to this length just to satisfy her own curiosity?

She watched the clock ticking towards deadline. Surely, she could push some contentions into legal form. The Indonesian entrepreneurs could find counsel to rebut and the courts could sort it out. It didn't matter if she lost in the end. She could think of it as her own contribution to the livelihood of corporate counsel halfway across the world.

But that's not what she went to law school for – to keep the world safe for corporate counsel. Her foot tapped uneasily on the floor as she turned pages and watched the clock.

* * * * *

Early in the evening, a young woman wearing a bikini and a sunhat vidlinked Malcolm from the beach. She looked vaguely familiar but he couldn't quite place her, and he definitely wasn't expecting any links from the beach. "I'm Donna from Central Storage," she said.

Malcolm must have looked confused because she flipped a switch and suddenly appeared as she did when they met a few days ago, wearing a white lab coat and sitting in front of data screens. "Sorry, I keep my linkscreen set for Tahiti. Lots of us do it to keep our spirits up." She went on to explain that the Odor Eater had been modified and was scheduled for testing in an hour. "You're in luck. It's in lab 121 West, which has a viewport. If you meet me there, I'll let you in."

That was good, but not really what Malcolm wanted. He needed to see Central Storage, not the Odor Eater.

He pushed his luck: "If I come sooner can I watch you set it up?"

She hesitated before answering. "Come quickly and we'll see what we can do."

Fortunately, Malcolm had already met Gary's deadline on the whine machine. He was keeping up with his own obligations and figured another walk to the specimen lab wouldn't hurt. With his eye on the cameras and smiles for the guards he made it there in less than five minutes. When he arrived he asked Donna, "Is the Odor Eater in Central Storage?"

"Probably. It's easiest to wait at the lab. It's just around the corner."

"Aw c'mon," he sounded like David, but Donna quickly relented, still willing to humor what she perceived to be a designer's peculiar fancy. She pulled out her lifelink and started transmitting messages of coordination, then told him to follow her through a labyrinth of twists and turns and eventually to officers in a control room in front of two huge doors. The officers greeted her by name and waved both of them past.

The doors to Central Storage were tall and sheer, with massive hinges and no visible latch or knob. A single red light glowed on the wall alongside. Outside, awaiting entry was a forklift towing tanks of fluid like a train.

A young man spotted the two of them, and walked over. Donna introduced Malcolm to Josh, then excused herself.

Josh was all business. "Things move fast around here. You can join me but you need to stay out of the way. I'm only going to tell you things once."

Malcolm nodded agreement. "I know how you feel."

At that moment, a solid clunk resounded within the doors and the indicator light changed from red to green. The doors opened slowly outward. A blast of cold air rushed out.

Immediately the forklift started heading inwards; the people all followed but came to rest a moment later, stopping inside another room, like an airlock, with another set of doors ahead of them. The first doors started to close as soon as they had fully opened, and eventually the same solid clunk told Malcolm that they had come all the way home. The group stood stationary in a small empty room, everyone else relaxed and patient, Malcolm struggling to appear the same. For more than a minute nothing happened except the rush of warm air being pumped out and cold air pumped in. The chamber grew colder. Finally, the next set of doors started to open. A moment later they were all in Central Storage.

It was a vast space, brightly lit and cold, with a glazed concrete floor. Aisles with shelves extended in both directions. The aisle in front of the door was numbered zero; to the left extended odd numbered aisles; to the right, even. Josh walked quickly to the right and without explanation turned down aisle twelve. Malcolm followed close behind. He didn't see any light sensors at the opening to the aisle, but he didn't doubt they were there.

Every few strides a letter was painted on the floor. The first letter was A, and the letters proceeded down the alphabet to Z, followed by AA on the other side of an intersecting aisle. Central Storage was a gigantic grid. Malcolm looked at Josh's lifelink and saw he was destined for hold 12DD/3. He knew they were in aisle twelve; he guessed they would stop at double D and that the

Odor Eater would be on the third shelf from the floor. He guessed correctly.

Josh pointed to the Odor Eater and said this was the third time he'd taken it out for testing. Meanwhile, he pressed buttons on a nearby control panel, a simple keypad with numbers and letters and a few command buttons. Now that his attention had been called to it, Malcolm saw that similar control panels were stationed all over, so a person never had to walk more than a few steps to reach one. Josh typed 12DD/3 into the keypad and pushed the button marked "lift."

Far overhead an electric crane whirred into life. It slid on tracks to berth 12DD/3 and lowered a chain to the floor. At the same time, the third shelf slid out from the others and lowered itself hydraulically to ground level. In a moment, Malcolm found himself face to face with the Odor Eater *feteovorecoccus*.

Entire barrels were filled with the organism, tubes entering and exiting to provide nutritional support. Several crates Malcolm recognized as earlier package designs established as failures but still kept on hand. Without saying a word, Josh disengaged some tubes and attached the heavy chain hanging from the crane onto structural supports on the Odor Eater shelf, then pressed one more button on the control panel. The crane lifted the entire shelf high into the air and started moving along its tracks back towards the door.

By the time Malcolm and Josh reached the door, some staff had already rolled a large cart to the spot where the crane made its deposit. Josh pushed the cart a few steps to the main door where the same forklift, now empty, was already waiting. When the whole crew that entered was fully assembled, the same clunk sounded and the doors started to open. A minute later they were through. Malcolm complimented Josh on his efficiency and followed him to lab 121 West. Josh introduced him to the lab technicians and returned to Central Storage for the next trip. Malcolm was ready now for the next phase.

The technicians didn't suggest that he use the viewport, and he certainly didn't mention it. They simply greeted him and started working around him. The motive for his visit was now so many steps removed that they didn't know or care what it was or who he was. They simply accepted him and treated him like a VIP visitor, a welcome break in routine. They discussed performance expectations and measures while setting up the experiment. Quickly and expertly they measured out fluids and connected complex networks of cables and hoses to fixtures on the wall.

In the back of the lab was a computer terminal. As soon as the tests started Malcolm faded back towards it. Nobody seemed to mind. The lab techs were busy and they assumed he knew what he was doing.

In fact, he did. He had correctly guessed that this terminal could access production files that his own computer could not. He typed *jakoba survivorus* into the machine and a long list came back. The *survivorus* had generated a great deal of activity, and now he saw that some of it required testing or was linked to product development. He saw that many experiments had begun but they were all designated "discontinued." He didn't see any evidence that *survivorus* still existed or where it was located. Every now and then he looked up and feigned interest in technicians spraying mock trashcans with Odor Eater samples.

To make sure he was using the program correctly, he searched for the Odor Eater. It came up quickly, along with status information right down to present use in 121 West. If Tentek had the *survivorus,* it should have come up the same way. As consolation he looked for its genetic code; if he couldn't find the thing itself, he could at least walk away with a blueprint that Tentek or someone else could replicate.

A lab technician looked back at him, said a few words to the others, and stepped purposefully toward the back of the lab. Malcolm's heart skipped a beat. For an instant he froze in terror, then as quickly and casually as possible he cleared his searches and returned the terminal to the start position – though he knew his activity could be reconstructed by anyone so inclined.

The technician held out an empty jar. "Smell it."

Malcolm worked to keep his hands steady as he took the jar, then gently smelled it. "Lemon," he replied. "Nice."

"Smell this one." The tech passed him a jar that looked identical.

Malcolm could smell the stench before it even got close to his nose. "No, thanks." He pushed it away.

"The second one is the organic waste," said the tech. "The first one was the deodorized result. The Odor Eater that turned the waste into the result had been in the container for a week. Our goal was five days. I think we've got it cracked."

"Congratulations!" Malcolm managed a smile. The technician returned to work, where the others were already starting to take the experiment apart.

Malcolm steadied himself. He was so close! But he wasn't there yet and he didn't have much longer. Quickly he reviewed everything he knew. Work had been done on the original protist, but the work had all been description and exploration – not modification of the underlying genetic design. They might never have coded the gene.

But if they hadn't coded the gene – and he saw no evidence that they had – then surely they must still have the original organism. One of those had to be true.

Suddenly he realized what he was doing wrong. The computer in use in this room would probably start in an active database. Discontinued lines of research would be archived somewhere else. He backed out and quickly found a directory of discontinued developments. The technicians were stacking the final items on the cart as he entered what needed to be his last search. A few short keystrokes brought the result: the protist *Jakoba survivorus* was alive and well in berth 23XX/1. He had it, just like that. He wanted to cheer and run back to Central Storage, ask Josh to pull it off the rack … but sadly it wasn't so simple. The same technician who brought him the odor sample now caught his attention and waved him towards the exit. Malcolm stood to leave, pausing only to thank them for their trouble and pretend, he hoped for the last time in his life, to care about the Odor Eater.

Chapter Twenty

There was no explanation. The next day Malcolm arrived late in the office, planning another late night to reconnoiter the specimen laboratory and practice the routes he expected to travel after midnight and in a hurry. But his computer didn't greet him with advertisements or even Tentek's daily maxim. All screens were brown with a simple message:

> *Tentek Corporation no longer requires your services. Please accompany your escorts to the exit. Human Resources will contact you shortly to answer questions. Thank you. Have a good day.*

He'd been fired.

He spun towards the door but it was empty; his escorts hadn't yet arrived. Sensing that this lucky window would soon close, he sprinted through his door and literally ran down the hall. He dared to glance back as he rounded the corner, and saw two guards in Tentek brown turning towards his office, scheduled to arrive mere heartbeats after the system showed that he'd opened his message.

But they were a heartbeat too late. They would reach an empty office. Quickly he calculated. They don't know I'm on the run yet; they'll think I woke up my computer and went for coffee or the bathroom – planning to read messages when I return. They'll probably wait a few minutes for me to come back.

After that, they'll get suspicious. They'll wonder why I logged on and walked out.

His calculations went no further. He was flying blind.

He walked quickly but casually to a different elevator and selected a floor at random. Exiting, he started walking like someone who belonged there, passing through long rows of offices with people at their desks and a few people whispering in the hallways. He meandered while he considered his options. How long could he get away with this? He knew that eventually he would pass patrols making their rounds. At first they wouldn't recognize him but then the alerts would go out. He couldn't hope to evade a thorough search, and he wasn't sure what he hoped to achieve anyway. He walked at random while he tried to work that out. One thing he knew for sure: he could leave only once. He needed to mean it.

More than anything else he wanted to know why he'd been fired. Was this routine reorganization and downsizing, or had he been targeted? Did they know what he'd done in Central Storage yesterday? Was he fired in retaliation, or simply fired? Tentek didn't even bother to explain; the indifference added insult to the injury. He just kept walking.

After a while he felt conspicuous, passing through places he'd passed before, still with no business and nothing to do. He stepped into the next available elevator, planning to stroll another floor, but his hand froze over the panel of buttons, overwhelmed by the need for decision. He stared in amazement at all the choices, dozens of buttons in orderly columns, unable to decide which button to press. They all looked the same. One button led to Internal Affairs, he knew, and another led to his own office; he had recently learned the location of the specimen lab and he already knew the floor for the cafeteria and the gym. But that was all. He could only account for a handful of choices staring him in the face. Which one should he choose? Were the other floors like his own, lines of cubbyholes with staff hunkered over computer screens? Which one was Human Resources? Was the decision to fire him made in this building, or halfway around the world? He didn't know, he didn't know. The buttons taunted him, mocked his ignorance with a graphic measure of how little he understood.

It occurred to him that standing in the elevator, all by himself, he was a sitting duck for surveillance. Elevators were easy to monitor and choke points for transportation; someone looking for him would begin by watching the elevators. With sudden frustration he punched a button at random in the middle of the array. One button glowed orange, number fifty-four. The elevator rose and his head started to clear, but before he reached the fifty-fourth floor he realized he'd made a mistake and he pressed a different button. The fifty-fourth floor was probably offices. With this last elevator ride, he decided to aim for the cafeteria and lose himself in the crowd. It was an innocent place to spend time and easy to explain if he were noticed.

He reached the cafeteria floor and stepped off with others. On the way to the cafeteria he saw Garcia, walking purposefully down the hall, probably on his daily rounds. Immediately Malcolm wondered if Garcia had learned about the firing, and whether he could let himself be seen. The questions barely registered before Garcia looked up and caught his eye. If Malcolm turned to run now, it would look like flight. He had come this far with Garcia, there was no point in turning away now

Garcia looked worried too. "Can we go to your office?"

"No." Malcolm offered no explanation, but the question suggested that his escorts hadn't yet sounded an alarm.

"I have it." Garcia tapped his pocket. "I have a VIP retina."

It took Malcolm a long time even to remember what he was talking about. Finally his eyes opened wide and Garcia saw that he understood.

They stood together for a long, quiet moment, saying nothing, not moving at all, getting used to the idea. Two people walked past carrying coffee and chatting about the weather. Garcia and Malcolm stood silently and watched them go, then Garcia reached into his pocket and held out his hand as if for a handshake. It seemed almost childish, a scene from the movies, but Malcolm recognized the gesture. This time it was real and the stakes were impossibly high. Malcolm took his hand, and felt Garcia slip him a small metallic object. When he had a good grip he pulled his hand away; they moved casually on, each in their own direction with nothing visible to distinguish the event. A full minute passed before Malcolm dared to drop in his pocket a thin metal disk that changed everything.

Heart pounding, Malcolm meandered the cafeteria, acting like he was deciding what food to order or what drink to pour. He wandered the tables as if he were seeking a place to sit, and visited the bathroom more than once. He watched people serve themselves doughnuts and watched a line form at the coffee dispenser. He wondered if he could spend his whole day like this – wandering the building, staying out of view, protected by anonymity and motion. He walked the perimeter and checked every door, but all exits were locked and alarmed. Signs advised him to use the elevator, that the stairways would open in case of fire. The only security guard in view seemed oblivious to everything, but that could change at any time. Malcolm started to feel like a fish in a barrel.

He realized now that he'd left his lifelink in his office when he hurried out. At first he felt helpless without this fundamental tool, but soon he realized that it was actually lucky. Anybody tracking his lifelink would be led to his office and learn simply that he wasn't there, which surely they already knew. But forgetting something so important would tell the authorities that he hadn't left in an organized manner.

Eventually he felt a need to move on. Staying in one place made him feel like bait in a trap.

He considered buying some food. It would bolster the most natural explanation of why he had come, and prepare him for a long day of cat and mouse. He felt the cash he'd started keeping in his pocket but didn't get his usual surge of security; nothing would be stranger than a Tentek employee paying with cash in the Tentek cafeteria. Better to use his account and see if it was still active; they would learn his location but he would get a clue about the status of their investigation. A trade. He decided to buy supplies while he could.

He pulled a few bagels off the rack and chose the shortest line, still keeping an eye on people around him. Nobody looked familiar to him, and he didn't seem familiar to anyone else. The officer on duty chatted with customers.

The cashier didn't look at him or acknowledge him in any way. "For here or to go?" She was already reaching for a bag.

Malcolm leaned his eye towards the retina scan, fearfully, like it might blind him. The machine chirped to inform him that two Globos had been deducted from his account. He wasn't shut out yet. The cashier pushed his bag over the counter and started on the next person in line.

Malcolm took his bag and made a beeline for the exit, stopping just shy of the elevator foyer because people were already waiting for an elevator going his direction. He didn't even need to press the button; he stood with his face against the wall, back to the elevator, listening for the chime that would tell him it arrived. A glance into the cafeteria showed him that the officer was no longer chatting but scanning the room intensely, like he was looking for something.

The elevator chimed. Malcolm turned around to see four security officers race out and surge towards the cafeteria. He slipped behind them as they rushed ahead, and stepped onto the elevator with a group of strangers as the door closed. He pressed the button for the gym, and had the good fortune of riding the elevator with a woman wearing a large hat. Nobody exited on the gym floor with him.

Like most Tentek employees, Malcolm paid a monthly fee to use the gym and, like most Tentek employees, he rarely did. But the fee separated users from non-users so he needed a retina scan for entry. Malcolm knew enough not to reveal himself in that way. He lingered in the hallway, leaning face-first against the wall as if he were stretching, until someone came to use the gym. She scanned her retina and opened the door; he slipped in behind her like he belonged.

Inside was an enormous open space filled with fitness machines of every description. Wallscreens broadcast news and sporting events, mirrors kept the space bright, and everything smelled of antiseptic. A few people scattered around, stretching or using exercise machines. A stack of towels stood by the door; Malcolm grabbed a few.

He surveyed the room while dabbing his face with a towel and identified a machine with a cowl that closed over the user; he stepped inside and pulled the cowl over top. He wasn't truly hidden, but he couldn't be identified without opening it. The inside of the cowl proved to be a projection screen, and the program greeted him with questions: his weight, his age, and what scenery he would prefer. He lied about his personal details and selected

Sylvan Wilderness for his scene. It sounded quieter and less distracting than *Final Lap* or *Hit and Miss*. He was rewarded with images of snowy fields and frozen lakes, and the foot pads started to move in a way he realized was supposed to imitate cross-country skiing. Piano music filled the background; an owl hooted. He could stay here for a while.

He struggled to relax. He tried not to think about his next job or his no-compete clause, Sayeh Kahn or the fate of young Bobeck. His whole life now was the passage of time. He needed to stay out of sight for the day, and hope that the VIP retina would still work at night. Nothing else mattered. He needed to relax. He pedaled slowly, conserving energy, and tried to enjoy the scenery; it was beautiful.

Suddenly an announcement took over his view. The sylvan wilderness disappeared and his own face appeared on the screen. A deep voice announced that the corporation was searching for employee Malcolm Moore. "If you see him, please advise him that we are looking for him. If he does not comply, please contact Internal Affairs. Thank you for your time and attention."

So much for anonymity.

A trio of guards entered the gym. One stood by the door and two more walked around, peering behind equipment and interviewing two people stretching in the middle of the room. Malcolm looked for an escape but the officer stood by the only exit.

Trying to look like he had merely finished his workout, he opened the cowl and jogged towards the locker room, wiping his face with a towel along the way. Could he stay in the locker room while they searched the gym? Malcolm doubted they would be so careless; he noticed that one officer was male and the other was female, surely no coincidence in a gym with two locker rooms. Entering the locker room he checked behind the door, wondering if the kind of slip he used to board the elevator would work again – stepping out as the officer stepped in -- but the configuration was all wrong and another guard stood by the exit. Quickly he realized that toilet stalls would all be checked and so would the sauna. He was running out of time.

He ripped off all his clothes as the male officer entered the locker room. By the time the officer reached his shower stall, Malcolm had a head full of lather and a face covered in shaving cream.

"I'm looking for Malcolm Moore," said the officer, pulling aside the curtain.

Malcolm feigned surprise. "Who?" He turned away for understandable privacy.

"Never mind." The officer shut the curtain and moved on.

Malcolm didn't congratulate himself at all. He didn't feel smart and he didn't feel like a master of cunning and stealth. He felt lucky. Management wanted him, and knew he hadn't left the building. It was still morning and they'd only started to search; he needed to stay out of sight until after midnight. He couldn't last like this all day. He needed someplace to hide.

* * * * *

Garcia's supervisor rounded up his team and called them in for questioning. He asked if any of them had seen Malcolm during the morning. Garcia was third in the line-up and he thought hard while the officers ahead of him all answered "No."

He decided it was best to tell the truth. "Yes," he said when his turn came. He stood still while people behind him all denied contact. The supervisor dismissed the rest of the team but asked Garcia to stay.

"What time did you see him?"

"Approximately nine in the morning."

"Where were you?"

"In the elevator foyer near the cafeteria."

"What were you doing there?"

"It's part of my sweep."

The team leader nodded in acknowledgment. The whole team knew Garcia's sweep, and 9 a.m. was right on schedule. "Did you talk to him?"

"I said good morning. We greeted each other and moved along. The alert hadn't issued at that time." He gambled that the fact of conversation was knowable, probably even recorded, but not the details.

Garcia didn't mention that an hour earlier he'd noticed an obviously important person standing by a limousine in the executive garage while his assistants loaded his luggage. Garcia had taken a few steps off his path to politely remind the man to return his VIP retina, if he had one.

He'd never spoken to an executive like that before and it was none of his business. Even if the man hadn't returned the retina, it could sit in his pocket or luggage until it expired. But Garcia succeeded at appearing to know what he was doing. The VIP reached into his pocket and handed him the small metal object, then stepped into the limousine. None of the assistants paid any attention. Garcia used the VIP's retina, rather than his own, to exit the garage. It worked.

Now it occurred to him that the mere act of requesting the retina was probably a felony. Actually using it, even to test on the garage door that Garcia was fully authorized to open, was probably a second felony. Delivering it to Malcolm was a third and even more colossal felony.

Lying about it was probably also a felony. Even if it wasn't a felony, it was enough to cost him his job.

But Garcia stayed true to his course. He didn't do it because he owed Malcolm a favor. He did it because they talked about the Red Sox every morning. In this entire building Malcolm was the only member of the professional staff who treated him like a human being. Garcia was more to him than a door lock or a bookshelf, a piece of equipment that kept Tentek running smoothly. He was a person. Security personnel were never invited to department staff meetings, even though the agendas often affected them too. Malcolm usually told Garcia what happened in the meeting, simply because he was curious.

Now Garcia helped his friend simply because he'd been asked. That's what people do for each other.

His supervisor seemed to be reading his mind. "You were friends." He stated it like a fact not an accusation.

"We were friendly," Garcia replied. They'd never actually been to a ballgame together.

"Do you know what he could be up to? Maybe vandalism, maybe theft? You know how some people act when they lose their jobs."

"I don't know."

The supervisor probed still farther. "His personality profile indicates loyal acceptance and exit without incident. This is the first time he ever bought bagels in the morning. Do you know what he's up to?"

"I don't know. Maybe he just needed time to blow off steam."

"Maybe. Or maybe not."

* * * * *

In the back of the men's locker room in the Tentek gymnasium was a closet. Malcolm missed it during his first, hurried hunt for a hiding place. The door was flush to the wall, and the seams and handle were artfully concealed in the wallpaper. But in the back of the room, beside the sauna, was a closet.

The door was locked, of course, and he was discouraged until he realized the solution was sitting in his pocket. VIP retinas were designed for access to high places but Garcia said they worked everywhere. This was a chance to see if high-level executives had the right to enter a locker room linen closet.

Malcolm held the small disk in front of the retina scanner, which efficiently identified the object, found the pattern and checked it against its database. The door popped open. VIPs were allowed here too.

Malcolm entered the closet and pulled the door shut behind him. The space was larger than Malcolm's office, and filled with Tentek towels along with buckets, hampers and cleaning equipment bearing the pink logo of Snappy Kleen. The personal property of Snappy Kleen staff filled one shelf at the far end. He turned over an empty bucket and sat down, letting out a long breath and feeling safe for the first time since he sprinted from his office.

If the VIP's activities were being tracked, he realized, then the VIP had just done something very peculiar. If Malcolm were found in here he could not innocently claim to have been showering or working out. He had defeated a lock, was in possession of stolen security material and hiding in a closet. He would be in trouble.

Now is the time to doubt, he told himself. It wasn't too late to abort. He could drop the retina down a disposal chute and walk out the front door. Management would notice his exit and never wonder why it took an extra hour. The unscheduled entry to this linen closet would go unsolved, if it were ever detected. He could quit now and forget the whole thing.

Nobody else would ever know about his odd request to Garcia. His trip to Central Storage would just be a designer's idiosyncrasy, known only to himself and a few lab technicians who barely paid any attention. His weeks of research would be a waste of only his own time, going nowhere but hurting nobody in the process. He could act like it never happened. The quest would be over but so would the risk.

He checked his watch. It was barely ten in the morning and he needed to stay until at least midnight. During that time he would start on one of two very different lives. One life had him discovering a revolutionary microorganism and delivering it to the people of the world; the other life had him rotting in a prison cell serving time for untold counts of falsification and burglary.

Or else, of course, he could quit now and return to the life of product design. Tentek might not be aggressive about his no-compete clause. If he got a job at an irrelevant firm and worked on products of an entirely different nature, Tentek might let him be. Product design was interesting enough, and his health was good. He had no real complaints. He could continue on his previous, straightforward path in life. Someday Tentek might even release the *survivorus* on its own. *Now was the time to doubt.*

But he had no doubts. His hands were steady and his mind was clear. He searched hard for regrets or indecision, and came up empty. He was simply executing a decision he'd made some time ago. He was in the middle of the stream, not entering it.

He thought of Garcia, the risk he'd taken and the faith he had. For just an instant he wavered: his own capture might blaze a path to Garcia. Then he thought of the millions, no billions, of people like Garcia who would benefit from the organism locked in a room just a few floors away. He had to find it. He would sit here until midnight, take a nap if he chose or eat bagels in the dark. Now it was time to wait.

* * * * *

Phil stormed into Jessica's office looking ready to kill. "*You missed the deadline!*" he accused. "*You did it on purpose.*"

Jessica had nothing to say.

"You mouth off about good faith reasons and put it into practice like this? In defense of a trifling, bankrupt adaptor plug company on the other side of the planet? *Even if you were right, you shouldn't care enough to be this stupid.*"

Phil paused for breath but Jessica still had nothing to offer in her own defense.

"Get out," he concluded. "Just get out. I don't want to sce you anymore. I'll send inquiries up the chain of command, see how bad the damage is, and if you'll ever come back. Right now, just get out."

Jessica shut off her computer and put on her coat. She took her favorite picture of David off the desk in case she never came back. Then she walked out. Slowly, with only her briefcase and a heavy heart, she walked alone towards the exit.

David was in school and she had nothing to do. Usually extra time was a treat, an opportunity to chip away at endless lists of projects and chores. But not this time. She had no goal and no destination, just more time than she needed to regret her decision.

Phil was right, of course: why *did* she care about that Indonesian start-up company? It mattered to the handful of principals, of course, but nobody else. She could have dreamed up some frivolous motion and submitted it by deadline. She'd been foolish. Now she was paying for it. So would David. Malcolm might pay for it too, depending how far he'd slipped down the path she'd mapped. *What was she thinking?*

Her lifelink chimed with an unidentified caller. She hoped it wasn't Phil: any decision made this fast would be an angry one. She took the call.

It was Malcolm calling from an unknown location, his face a dark ghost on a low-resolution transmission. "Where are you?" Jessica asked in alarm.

"Never mind," he said, talking fast. "I can't talk long and I need you to do some things. Tonight is the night. Pick me up at Tentek at one in the morning. Cruise the block and look for me.

"As soon as you can I need you to go to my apartment. Open the door, log onto my system and make some calls. It doesn't matter what you do – just make it look like someone is in the apartment. Do enough to fool remote surveillance. Got it?"

She tried to intervene. "Malcolm do you have to --?" She wanted to talk, needed to tell him what happened, invite him to reconsider.

But he cut her off. "Yes, I have to. It's happening. I got lucky to find this link and make this transmission but I need to get off before it's traced. Goodbye. I'll see you at one." He recited some codes she would need to access his apartment, and disconnected.

There was no going back. She walked off the rollway the whole distance to his apartment, entered with ease and fired up his systems. Then she sat down on his couch. There was nothing else to do until David got out of school, and he'd be delighted to be picked up early. For the time being she would just stay in Malcolm's apartment, maybe take a nap or help herself to a snack. Now it was time to wait.

Chapter Twenty-One

At half past midnight the locker room was dark and empty. Malcolm turned off the light in the closet and opened the door just a crack to assess the outside. Satisfied, he stepped out completely and nearly panicked when all the lights flashed on – then realized that motion detectors had simply detected his presence and done the courtesy of turning on the lights.

Behind him the closet door closed and locked. He decided to test anew the VIP retina. Better to find out now than at Central Storage whether the retina still worked or if his captivity had been wasted. The door clicked open. So far so good.

The gymnasium too was dark and empty, but the lights turned on as he entered. He walked carefully to the exit, alert if the space were not as empty as it appeared, but nothing moved. At this hour the gym truly was abandoned. He pressed a button to open the door, hoping that the motion detectors were not centrally monitored and that computers didn't notice someone exiting a room that nobody had entered.

He'd considered disguising himself before he left the closet. There were enough Snappy Kleen clothes to rough out a uniform and some oil he could use to change his hair. But he decided that the uniform would make him conspicuously out of place without a Snappy Kleen crew – and with no idea where he should be, what he should be doing or even what language to speak.

He also left his hair ungreased so he wouldn't appear deliberately deceptive if he were caught – but he found an old baseball cap neglected in a corner. When he saw that it was the Red Sox it was settled. Now he pulled it low over his eyes as he stepped out of the gym and pressed the button for the elevator. He faced the wall in an athletic stretch that was barely plausible in this location but couldn't be used anywhere else.

In his original plan he assumed that he could walk freely within the building. He needed to be careful not to be noticed by the cameras – but until he made his final move into Central Storage he was doing nothing wrong walking the hallways, greeting anybody he happened to pass. Now things were different. He needed to be completely invisible to everybody at all times.

Sneaking around made him nervous but the truly crushing part was his ignorance. He didn't know if Tentek authorities were still looking for him. He didn't know if Jessica had attempted his ruse or whether it had worked. He didn't know if he was a much-wanted suspect of corporate espionage in possession of a VIP's stolen retina, or if he was merely a disgruntled employee still malingering long after he should have left.

The hallways were unusually quiet this evening. Malcolm didn't pass a single person on foot, and even the

Snappy Kleen crews seemed to be missing. The only signs of life were a few poor souls in their offices, hunkered down over their computer terminals when millennia of evolution told them to go to sleep.

His entry process needed to start at the security booth where it all began. His original plan was to verify the sequence of the cameras to be sure it hadn't changed, then start his stopwatch at a known point in the sequence. Timing was everything. The zero point would ground all of his movements.

When he made that plan he was allowed to walk straight up to the security booth and monitor the screens from the hallway, or perhaps talk about basketball until he had seen enough. That wasn't possible now.

As the booth came into view he forced a plan. The booth's wall was plexiglass so he could see everything happening inside – four officers on swivel stools monitoring the viewscreens while two other officers arranged their equipment. But try as he might he couldn't see the numbers on the screens. They were too small to read at this distance. He leaned furtively against a wall while he considered his options.

Just then a Snappy Kleen crew came around the corner. One man vacuumed while another emptied trashcans into a cart. The first man ran his vacuum outside the door while the second entered the booth for trash. The officers who'd been arranging equipment scowled at the invasion, marked a status board and hurried down the hall on patrol.

Malcolm seized the opportunity. The officers watching the monitors were fully absorbed and paying no attention to anything else, deliberately ignoring the movement of the cleaning crew. Gambling that the custodians hadn't been included in the alerts or were too busy to pay attention, he stepped up to the booth and looked straight inside.

The numbers were clear and the grid familiar. He scrutinized the monitors for camera number one, whose location would orient him in the rotation, but it wasn't being viewed at the moment. He waited patiently until the views shifted, but again camera one wasn't being viewed. He just stood still, feeling more and more conspicuous, watching Snappy Kleen at work, waiting for the next rotation – which still didn't reveal camera one. By now all the trashcans had been emptied and the vacuum man was continuing down the hall. He couldn't stay much longer. He had no other ideas.

The next rotation solved the problem. Camera one appeared on screen seventeen. He wanted to cheer and flee but he needed to watch one more rotation to confirm that the sequence hadn't changed.

To his alarm, a pair of guards came into view walking towards the booth, probably the shift replaced by the pair who left. They hadn't noticed him yet, mixed in the bustle of the Snappy Kleen crew. He dared to stay just a few seconds more, sidling down the hall in the direction of Snappy Kleen, then sidling back when the views shifted. There it was. In the next rotation camera one appeared on screen twenty-four.

He set his stopwatch to zero and started walking in the direction of Central Storage. Thankfully, the incoming officers thought nothing of the single man who walked right past them, wearing a baseball cap, nose buried in numbered papers.

Quickly he calculated his position on the matrix. The sequence didn't seem to have changed: screen seventeen was supposed to be followed by screen twenty-four. If his calculations were correct, then he was presently being monitored but in one minute and twenty seconds this stretch of corridor would go off screen. He would begin then. Until then, he would wait.

He walked casually down the hall, hat low, ambling slowly at a midnight pace, trusting that his face couldn't be recognized in a video monitor without zooming or special attention. He examined the wall paper and the patterns cast by the overhead lights, seeking every opportunity to face the wall, his memory inadvertently flashing back to his father on the jailhouse floor.

A co-worker strode past, not at a midnight amble but like someone rushing to meet deadline; Malcolm didn't greet him and the man didn't seem to notice. Malcolm paused aimlessly at an intersection, controlling his breathing, counting down. He looked at his watch and tried to stay patient. Nobody else was in view and he knew that in five seconds he would go off screen.

Five seconds passed. If his calculations were correct, he had just disappeared. He reset his stopwatch to 00:00 and stepped forward into the rest of his life.

First he reversed his course. He stepped back down the corridor opposite the direction he'd been going when he was last in view. He walked quickly, needing to reach the next intersection before twenty seconds – two rotations – had passed, but not so quickly that anyone he met would pay attention. At the next intersection he turned right and slowed down. He'd practiced this maneuver many times and knew exactly how long each segment took; it was as important not to get ahead of schedule as not to fall behind.

He turned left at the next intersection towards a stairway that was kept unlocked, bypassing the nearby elevator which would come on its own schedule and not necessarily during the ten-second window when neither the corridor nor the stairwell was watched.

At just the right moment he stepped into the stairwell and surged forward in a sprint, rocketing down four levels in twenty seconds in a move he had never practiced because it would surely attract attention and maybe even break his neck. He jumped steps three and four at a time, hand skimming down the banister and grabbing it tight to swing him around corners at the landings. At the fourth landing he waited twenty seconds, caught his breath, then descended ten levels in sixty seconds exactly. Heart pounding in his chest, he was now on the level of Central Storage.

He still had a long way to go. He walked the short corridors and sprinted the long ones, checking his watch at every intersection. He still hadn't seen any live guards.

He turned a corner – nearly halfway there – and almost bumped into a guard patrolling in the opposite direction.

"Working late?" said the officer.

Malcolm suppressed his natural courtesy, pulled down on his hat and grumbled, "Yeah." He'd seen ruder things and so had the officer, who left this cranky employee to his own business.

Malcolm exhaled softly and walked to the end of the corridor, grateful he hadn't passed the guard at a dead sprint. He reminded himself of Garcia's rules: *If nothing unusual occurs, the tapes won't be played back.*

Suddenly the lights flickered and Malcolm felt a jolt under his feet. *What was that?* He froze to think, examining his surroundings with all his senses. The weatherwatch had predicted thunderstorms this evening, and it could have been a lightning strike. If something unusual happened outside, the guards might manually scan cameras to investigate; when the cameras returned to sequence Malcolm would have no idea where he stood. He would look pretty peculiar running and walking down the empty corridors of the specimen laboratory.

But there was nothing he could do. He couldn't back up more easily than he could move ahead. He picked up his pace to recover lost time and prepared for two corridors of sprint ahead. By the time he reached the corner a cool breeze on his neck told him what happened: the jolt had been the air conditioning turning on. He was near the equipment room.

Two more sprints brought him to the entrance to Central Storage, the control booth closed and dark. *At least somebody gets some sleep,* Malcolm thought. But the red light on the wall told him that the massive doors were securely locked. He pulled out the VIP retina.

And then what? He didn't see the retina scanner. He hunted all around the door and the control booth and couldn't find where to display his VIP retina. Here in his hand was this rare and valuable tool – and he didn't know how to use it.

The memory of his visit with Donna didn't help. Guards who knew her had carelessly waved her through.

Now he wondered if the scanner was *inside* the control booth, and whether people being scanned needed to step inside to prove their bonafides.

His designer's instincts told him that couldn't be true. Even if the primary scanner were inside the booth, he couldn't imagine a significant door being built with no scanner by the latch. He ran a few steps to the red light that indicated the door was locked, though he still didn't see a scanner. He held his VIP retina up before the light, moving it gently, trusting that somewhere in this zone a scanner would find it. Time was wasting.

A clunk inside the door told him he was right. He still didn't see the scanner but it saw his VIP retina, and that's all that mattered. The clunk freed the doors and slowly they swung outwards, accompanied by a blast of cold air, a massive presence plainly visible to anybody watching the cameras. Somewhere, Malcolm knew, something had surely registered an entry. Hopefully it hadn't been a human being; if it was, he was counting on routines working in his favor. Hopefully that person just figured that the unscheduled entry was someone else's business, and they were busy enough with their own.

All Malcolm knew was that the doors stood wide open for him to step inside, and a moment later he stood alone in the closing sally port. The front doors latched with a resounding thud and again the air started to change, the temperature lowering in a sudden rush as the mechanisms drove forward automatically. Malcolm just stood with nothing to do but hope that the internal doors would finally open.

With nothing in view but empty wall and bare doors, he imagined the interior doors opening to a squadron of armed guards; he looked behind him to plan an escape but the exterior doors were impenetrable. Guards, he realized, would probably come from the exterior doors anyway. If he'd been discovered, Tentek would leave him in this refrigerator as long as it needed to plan its response.

Finally a click sounded and the inner doors started to move, swinging heavily inwards, large enough to admit giant equipment and heavy enough to bear the load; they had budged just the first step when Malcolm slipped through sideways and continued on his way.

Garcia had explained that he must exit within ten minutes or the same retina wouldn't authorize a second opening. The reality was more complicated. Malcolm had calculated that he needed to exit the prototype room after seven minutes and twenty seconds to be in a sustained blind spot. After that, the doorway would be monitored by video screens in the central security booth where the swinging doors would call instant attention to the late, unscheduled entry. Anyone curious to see who caused it needed only to look, and perhaps zoom in for as much detail as they wanted.

The next blind spot occurred after nine minutes and forty seconds, but it didn't last long enough for the doors to operate and Malcolm to escape around the corner to the next camera zone. Malcolm planned to be at the door and ready to exit by the seventh minute.

Garcia said the light beams were activated when the doors were closed; he also said the beams monitored the entrance to every aisle. If he were right, then the light beams wouldn't be a problem. Malcolm turned to the control board and dialed for the crane.

Up overhead the crane whirred to life and started for the door, then lowered the chain to make a pickup. Malcolm entered 23XX/1 into the keyboard, expecting the crane to hoist him up, over the light sensors, and deposit him at the shelf containing the *survivorus*.

The control screen said: "Entry invalid."

Malcolm's heart sank. Why? Was *survivorus* off limits? Or was it generally impossible to pick up products that had failed or been discontinued? Maybe he could get close. He entered 23UU/1 into the keyboard, estimating that the crane would drop him in the aisle just a few feet from where he needed to be.

"Entry invalid," it replied.

The clock was ticking and Malcolm worried that the invalid entries would trigger attention. He entered 23MM/1. He had to get into the correct aisle or he would need to cross the light sensors, and he had to get close enough to keep things moving.

The crane hummed into motion. Malcolm grabbed hold of the chain above his head and coiled a few links around his feet. In a moment he was airborne. Both hands held the chain but he still managed to check his watch. Half a minute had elapsed.

The crane moved slowly, interminably leftward along the odd numbered aisles. Malcolm had an uninterrupted, bird's-eye view of Central Storage. It was vast. Long shelves of products and prototypes stretched in both directions. He took a moment to be grateful he was comfortable at heights as he swung gently back and forth at the height of a three-story building. Then the crane turned down aisle 23, past the A's and B's, creeping with mechanical equanimity to the double letters, then lowering the chain at last when it reached the letter MM. Malcolm jumped the last few feet and dashed further down the aisle. If the crane reset automatically he might not have time to call it again.

When he reached the *survivorus* nothing inspired awe and he had no time for amazement. It was just a large translucent tank filled with fluid, tubes connecting it to fixtures to exchange nutrition, oxygen and waste. The protist was clearly labeled in Tentek style but no additional information or documentation described what it was, how it worked, or how to care for it; that information, no doubt, was in the database.

Then he ran into a problem he hadn't foreseen, a problem so simple, so elementary he would never forgive himself for not expecting it in advance.

The lid was screwed shut. He had no way to open it.

He'd always imagined himself filling a specimen jar and the crane carrying him triumphantly to the door for his speedy getaway – it all seemed so easy in his mind. But here he was – without a jar, without a tool. Nearly three minutes had elapsed and he was staring straight at the object of his search. He couldn't reach it and couldn't carry it home if he did. His mind burned with the memory of a container in the Snappy Kleen closet that would have served him perfectly.

He had to find a solution, fast. Equipment moved around Central Storage all the time; there must be a way to get this done. He hunted for options. Around the corner, past berth ZZ and in the aisle that divided ZZ from AAA on the other side, he noticed some repairs underway. A stroke of luck. Surely the workstation included a screwdriver.

But it wasn't so easy. Light sensors guarded the end of the aisle.

He suppressed his fear and forced himself to think: there must be a way to reach the workstation. Then he realized that he could crawl through the bottom shelf at ZZ – it contained a single, relatively small piece of equipment – to reach the intersecting aisle. He would cut the corner behind the light sensors aimed at the intersection.

The planning was easier than getting it done. The equipment in ZZ1 was relatively small but connected to the shelf with a network of tubes and wires that tangled him and blocked his path. When he reached the aisle a few strides brought him to the workstation but it was well cleaned with no tools in sight. The first of three drawers was filled with electrical equipment – wires, routers, switches and the like. Useless. The second drawer was well organized with gloves and masks, protective equipment for people using the workstation. Equally useless. The third drawer was filled with wrenches, arranged in size order, clearly organized but irrelevant for an ordinary household screw.

His main focus was the screwdriver but he kept a lookout for a jar, or even a soda bottle that a careless worker had left behind. Nothing met his needs, not on the desktop and certainly not in the bottom drawer filled with wrenches.

He started pushing around the bottom drawer, searching desperately for a screwdriver, coming up empty, until at last he hit upon a small box. Inside was a full set of diverse screwdrivers, a goldmine. He jammed the whole thing in his pocket and crawled back through the shelf at the bottom of berth ZZ. Two and a half more minutes had clapsed. It was no longer possible to make the blind spot in the seventh minute.

Opening the lid to *survivorus* proved to be simple, a phillips head screwdriver did the trick. Malcolm then removed his shoes and took off his socks, thick, absorbent and eager to fill themselves with fluid. He plunged them into the tank, not worried about contamination, then shoved them still dripping into his pockets. The water was relatively cool, and it soaked immediately down the leg of his pants.

He dashed back to the crane, still waiting, and ordered it to the door. Nearly eight minutes had elapsed. He grabbed the chains as they started to lift.

Slowly, slowly the crane winched up its load. Slowly it shifted into gear and slowly, mechanically, indifferently it wound its way up the alphabet. Eight minutes and twenty maddening seconds had elapsed by the time it passed out of the double letters and crossed to Z. Malcolm struggled to remember how long it took to make the first trip. He hadn't timed it. It didn't matter anyway; he would find out soon enough if there was enough time left. Nine minutes had elapsed before the crane reached the front of aisle 23 and turned towards the door. Just forty seconds remained.

Malcolm watched his stopwatch. It all boiled down to this, an entire life lived in just a few seconds, and a crane that couldn't care less. It ground slowly towards the door, stopped in front and started to lower the chain.

Malcolm jumped long before it was safe. He tumbled to the ground and limped to the red light by the door on a twisted ankle. Supporting himself against the wall he held the VIP retina in front of the light and hoped for a click. He was dizzy from the fall.

The click came. The doors started to open. Malcolm slipped through immediately then waited what seemed like forever for the doors to finish opening and grind shut again. The air exchanged and the outer doors finally opened midway through the tenth minute. He pushed through the first sliver of egress and accelerated hard down the corridor, favoring his uncertain ankle, then he turned the corner and looked at his watch the instant time expired.

He slowed to a walk and struggled to catch his breath, with plenty of time to reach the next intersection. He touched the wall to relieve the strain on his ankle and, for the first time, marvel at what he had accomplished: he was walking the Tentek corridors with a pocketful of water that could take the salt out of seawater and improve life around the world.

He just had to get it out.

Fortunately it wasn't far from Central Storage to the front door. Timing was merciful and by the time he neared the lobby his gait was almost normal. He didn't pass another guard or even civilian co-worker, and the security staff hovering around the exit paid no attention to just another Tentek employee walking haggardly out of the building in the middle of the night, hat pulled low over sleepy eyes and one leg of his pants looking like he'd had some kind of accident.

He stepped outside to the streets and walked only a minute before Jessica pulled over in a blue minivan. "Hey, good looking, want a lift?"

PART FOUR

POWER

Chapter Twenty-Two

All Malcolm wanted to do was examine the water. Did it work like the gift from Sayeh Kahn? Had he collected enough? Had it survived? Basic questions, easy to answer – but first they had to get away. The Tentek headquarters literally towered over them.

Malcolm hadn't expected to see a child inside, but of course David was in the back seat, bright and alert, looking like he'd been invited on a surprise and told he could skip school the next day. As soon as the door closed he asked the question that should have been on Malcolm's mind: "Where are we going?"

Malcolm didn't know what to say; he hadn't thought about that part.

"To the ocean," Jessica said.

"Why now?" David asked.

Malcolm and Jessica looked at each other, smiled at first then started to laugh. Why would they leave for a beach vacation without warning in the middle of the night? David was right to be confused, and he definitely didn't see why they were laughing. "What's so funny?" he asked.

Malcolm and Jessica kept laughing while David kept asking, until finally his frustration got their full attention. "Why now?" He was almost screaming.

"Something came up," said Jessica.

He calmed down. "Something good?"

Now his mother grew serious. She stopped laughing and let out a long sigh. "We're going to find out."

She turned to Malcolm. "I got fired."

"So did I."

He smiled as if to make it into a joke, but the humor didn't fly at all. Jessica clenched the wheel; she looked like she was about to cry.

David stayed quiet and stared out the windows as they put some miles between themselves and Tentek. Slowly the downtown of architectural wonders and tree-lined parks gave way to an urban sprawl of squat apartments and uniform storefronts. Flashy advertisements that spiraled and sparked gave way to conventional billboards and tired slogans. As they neared the highway Malcolm asked to stop at a convenience store.

"What for?" Jessica asked.

"For water."

By the on-ramp was a Casa Fiesta, the same chain they'd used in Kaiserville. A line of men leaned against a counter with yellow betting slips, loitering beneath television monitors with scores from around the world. Malcolm bought a pound of salt and two gallons of drinking water. He paid with cash, and bought David a Beta Bar with the change.

Back in the car he jammed his socks, still soaking, into one of the gallon jugs, then shook in some salt. David watched with interest, asking nothing but obviously perplexed.

"Want a taste?" Malcolm asked.

"Yech!"

Malcolm took a small sip. "Yech!" he agreed. "Too salty and too much sock." He rinsed it down with some freshwater from the other jug. David laughed, then turned his attention back out the window. Jessica might have understood – though probably not the socks – but she kept to herself.

The sprawl of New Angeles went on and on, an infinity of billboards and concrete. Eventually David curled up in the back seat and fell asleep. Malcolm and Jessica rode silently through mile after identical mile of urban wasteland.

Jessica's lifelink chimed in the silence. "You brought your link?" Malcolm asked in alarm.

"Why not?" She glanced his way as she pulled it from her pocket.

"Its location can be tracked."

"I didn't realize."

"I never mentioned it. My link is still in the office." He skipped the details of how that came to pass.

"Should I answer the call?"

"Might as well. Better to put it behind us."

Jessica connected the link without the video. She didn't want the caller to see where she was, and she needed to keep her eyes on the road anyway. Talking without video was a little suspicious, but not as suspicious as fleeing a crime scene. "This is Jessica Frey," she announced.

"Jessica Frey, I'm pleased to meet you! This is Mitch at U.S. Carpet One. Our records show that you have Singleton Select carpet in your home and a six-year-old boy. Pretty messy, huh? When's the last time you had your carpet cleaned?"

Jessica looked at the lifelink in disgust. "No thanks."

"But wait!--" She disconnected and stranded Mitch's plea halfway down from a satellite. She rolled down the window and threw the link outside, watched in the mirror as it smashed under the wheels of the vehicle behind them. "Bulls eye."

Malcolm was unamused. "Why'd you do that?"

"Did you want to keep it with us?"

"No."

"Did you want to bring it back to the apartment?"

"I guess not."

She grinned. "Well now we don't have it anymore."

The noise woke David up a little bit, confused and uncertain; Malcolm reassured him and he went back to sleep, curled up in a tight little ball. More miles drifted past. The moon hovered overhead, nearly full by now. The Microtech brand name was gone, replaced by *Brother*, and the moon was not gold but blue, like a disk of daylight in the nighttime sky.

Jessica said, "I packed you some clothes. Your toothbrush too." She spoke cautiously, as if maybe she'd reached too deep into his privacy, but Malcolm was barely listening. "You had no phone messages."

Miles later he broke his silence. "Do you have a knife?"

"What for? I brought a spoon to spread peanut butter."

"I need a knife, a sharp one. Stop at a store."

"Is it urgent? We haven't gone very far."

"Yes."

"But you won't tell me why."

"After."

The next exit had another Casa Fiesta. Malcolm reached for her hand, and squeezed before he went inside. "This may take a while." He strode across the parking lot.

Jessica watched him enter the store and buy something, then exit and use a key on the men's room. She reclined her chair and closed her eyes, taking advantage of the break. She was dozing by the time he knocked to unlock the door. His hands and face were damp, and he smelled of soap.

"It was Brij's idea," he said.

She shook her head like he wasn't making sense.

"Remember her tattoo from OmniSpan? She said OmniSpan used tattoos because implants were too easy to swap."

A look of horror spread across her face. She reached for his hand.

Into the glove compartment he placed a small knife, the price tag still on the handle, and pointed to a trailer outside. "My implant's on the back of that truck."

Jessica squeezed his hand tight, and held it until she needed both hands to maneuver onto the highway.

He held up a package from the Casa Fiesta. "I bought some pain killers. Do you mind if I sleep?"

As gray dawn washed over the sky the city started to thin. At times the land they traveled had no clear use at all, just empty scrub dotted with billboards. Every few miles brought an interchange and a shopping mall bustling with activity, then more miles of scrub. Jessica had long since left the major highways and was navigating smaller roads, sometimes mountainous, often twisting.

By the time the sun cleared the horizon they'd left the urban areas far behind. A sky of glorious blue arced across the heavens, layered by high wisps of white. David woke up for real while they drove through an enormous farm. Neat green rows grew in rich brown soil as far as the eye could see. "Look at that!" were his first words of the day.

A machine twice the size of a commuter bus rolled between the rows, belching black exhaust and a violet haze into the sky. The wheels fit precisely on the stripes of soil, but clearly it was doing something to the plants in between. Malcolm and Jessica could only guess what.

David spent the next hour pointing out such machines as they crawled sporadically across the landscape. One was so close to the highway they could see the ringed planet of Tentek Corporation on the door. *I guess we make those things*, Malcolm thought. Not once in the entire expanse of farmland did they ever see a human being.

All at once they exited the croplands and entered a forest. The transition was instantaneous: one moment they were surrounded by short leafy plants and the next moment by trees. A billboard explained the difference: *Brother Incorporated welcomes you to our forest plantation: the framework of a sturdy America.* Underneath was a new slogan that introduced the conglomerate to the people: *Big Brother is looking out for you.*

The trees were arranged in exact rows, just like the smaller crops in the previous plantation. Every few miles they entered a zone with trees of a different age – saplings barely taller than a man, followed by timber with trunks a man couldn't reach around. Once they crossed an entire range of tree stumps dotting the earth like razor stubble, no foliage anywhere in sight.

David said he was hungry and wanted breakfast. Jessica looked to Malcolm. It was time to make some decisions. He said he didn't want to stop driving and fished through his pockets for the Beta Bar he bought David earlier. He passed it back with a smile, expecting kudos from both David and his mom.

"I don't want it," David said.

"I thought you liked Beta Bars."

"I don't."

"Aren't the Beta Brothers your favorite?"

"The Beta Brothers are dumb. The stories never make sense."

Even in his hazy state Malcolm registered the change. Had David been thinking about this since the visit to Kaiserville? "What do you mean?"

"Look, the Beta Brothers have super powers, right?" David was a little testy. "But they just make up the powers whenever they want. They don't even explain what's happening. The Betas just win and that's the end. Last time I watched, one of the Beta Brothers actually rescued *himself*. It's dumb."

Malcolm needed a moment to digest this outburst. "Do your friends think so too?" Maybe David was simply outgrowing the Beta Brothers stage.

"My friends think the Betas are great," David replied. "My friends are dumb."

Malcolm's vague pride vaporized at this bit of news, but at least he'd distracted David from his complaints. Malcolm took a turn driving while Jessica pulled out sandwiches she'd prepared in advance and bottles of juice Malcolm recognized from his own refrigerator. As breakfast was served, they exited the trees and entered a different crop. This district looked like the farmland from the morning, with gentle hills and long rows of green vegetation. Again they saw the giant machines roving among the rows. David pointed out the Tentek logo on the door of one machine, and signs in the field as well. Malcolm realized blearily: *Tentek doesn't just make the machines. It owns the farm.*

Jessica took the wheel again as they left the farms and entered an immense wasteland. This region looked like it had been mined to the bottom in previous generations. Heaps of tailings and slag lined the road, and the decaying carcasses of obsolete equipment dotted the landscape. Vegetation was sparse and sickly, the land jagged and lifeless, almost lunar. David said it looked like a giant junkyard. For the first time he got fidgety and started to complain. They skirted along the brink of the desolation, accompanied only by billboards and the occasional shopping center, far smaller than the malls the day before.

At the top of one rise, in the distance, the ocean spread out before them. Malcolm saw now that Jessica was heading in that direction and, as they neared, urban life returned. Houses sprung up and shopping was easy. Traffic increased as more people busily went in their own directions.

Suddenly Jessica slammed the brakes.

"What is it?" Malcolm asked.

"Did you see that hotel?"

"Yes."

"What's it called?"

"Blue Moon Inn." The sign was battered but the large black letters were clearly legible, and growing clearer as Jessica turned around to drive back.

"Don't you see?"

His look made it obvious he did not.

"It isn't part of a chain. It isn't a Sheraton or a Holiday Spa. That hotel might be owned by an actual person. Let's go see."

The Blue Moon Inn looked like it had once been a large family home. It had a spacious front porch and a roof of blue shingles. Blue shutters adorned every window, though several of them hung at odd angles. The walls were built of real wood painted white.

In the entrance foyer hung a mobile dangling with images of the moon and stars. The sun hung prominently in the center, surrounded by Saturn with its distinctive ring and the moon wearing a great big smile. Cows, pigs and a medley of barnyard animals floated among the planets. The mobile spun merrily in the breeze as they entered, tiny bells tinkling their arrival while a grandfather clock ticked solemnly in the corner.

An old man with a cane shuffled out to greet them. He stepped gingerly over a threshold and took his position behind the counter. Like the building, he looked like an artifact from a different era. "Are you lost?" he asked.

Jessica answered, "I think we're right where we want to be. Do you own this place?"

"Lock, stock and barrel. It's been in the family for generations."

"How much will it cost to stay a few days?"

The price quoted was far below the fee for a Holiday Spa, but it looked like they were the only guests. The man actually seemed surprised they were considering a stay. He fumbled under the counter for the registration book. "How many rooms?"

"Just one," Jessica replied, "with two beds." To Malcolm she added, "We might as well start economizing. One for me and David. One for you."

Malcolm wasn't even listening. He had pulled out the water bottle filled with socks; he shook it gently and held it up to the light. Apart from the socks and floating flecks of lint, it looked like an ordinary bottle filled with water. He removed the lid and took a long sip.

"How does it taste?" Jessica asked.

His smile was relaxed and refreshed. "Like water."

Chapter Twenty-Three

"That's a start," the old man said. "But we can do better for lunch."

Soon they saw just how true it was. He brought tomatoes and cucumbers from the garden, and set them beside fresh cheese and a spicy herb bread baked, he said, by a woman down the street. Before their eyes he turned lemons into lemonade. "Would you like a sock in yours?" he asked Malcolm with a coy grin. "I have some unwashed laundry if you'd like."

They sat together for what seemed like a family meal, talking and relaxing with windows open wide. The old man's name was Mansel, and he told the story of each vegetable on the plate, starting with the tomatoes. David spotted a rabbit out the window and launched from his chair for a closer look. Mansel said he knew that rabbit well. "I just haven't gotten to that little monster's part of the story."

After lunch, Malcolm wanted nothing more than a flat place to lie down; his legs were heavy and his arms were lead. Gravity, it seemed, had never been so strong.

Jessica said it was too soon to rest. "We need some exercise. How's your leg?"

"It feels like someone stuck it with a knife."

To Mansel she said, "How far to the beach?"

He looked them up and down. "The pretty way or the fast way?"

"The pretty way," Jessica replied.

He described the route to a private cove and soon Jessica had them loading into the van. David groused about getting back in the car but Jessica said he could sit in the front seat, unbuckled in Malcolm's lap. Malcolm didn't get a vote but soon he found himself doing something entirely new – sitting unbuckled in the front of a van, windows down, wind blowing into his eyes, a six-year-old celebrating in his lap.

"Wahoooo!" David yelled. "Wheeee!" Malcolm let him stick his head way out the window, holding tight to his bottom so he wouldn't fall. They rounded corners and skitted across gravel as they descended quickly towards the coast. David shouted to nobody in particular, "Look at me! Look at me!"

The sky was infinite and blue. Seagulls raced in wild arcs, screaming and cawing with desire. The air filled with the scent of salt and ocean, and soon they pulled into a parking lot by a beach. "Time to get to work," Jessica said.

When she opened the back of the van, Malcolm saw what she meant. The cargo bay was stacked with five gallon jerry jugs waiting to be filled, along with funnels, buckets and other things that Malcolm hadn't thought about but suddenly seemed obvious.

She reached for a green bag in a corner. Out came a towel and bathing suit for David. "Go for it," she said.

His whole face burst into a smile. He starting ripping off clothes with no thought of privacy, then jammed his legs into the bathing suit and raced for the beach. Jessica took off her shoes, grabbed two jerry jugs and started after him. Malcolm followed with two jugs of his own.

Malcolm couldn't remember the last time he felt sand underfoot. He curled his toes into the texture, feeling the warmth on top and coolness underneath, the mix of soft and hard. Jessica and David were already in the water. He rolled up his pants and stepped in slowly, checking the temperature, watching the sand bury his feet.

Jessica held David's hand in the surf; when he spotted Malcolm he ran over, dragging her behind, and grabbed Malcolm's hand with his own. Now they each held one of the boy's hands, lifting him as he jumped high over the waves, splashing down and standing up for the next. "Look out! Here comes a huge one!" he called before waves that barely reached the grown-up's knees.

After a while, they made a group activity of filling the jerry jugs, then left David to jump while they lugged them back to the van. Malcolm reached for two more but Jessica stopped him.

"I'm the mule," she said. "Your job is math."

He looked at her without understanding.

She passed him a box filled with measuring instruments and purity testers he recognized from the pharmacy. "Do you have a watch?"

He looked at his wrist. He hadn't reset his stopwatch since Central Storage. Fourteen hours and twenty-one minutes had passed since he found camera one and disappeared from the corridors of Tentek Corporation. He zeroed it now.

"Figure out how long it takes to go from that ..." She pointed to the ocean. "To this." She tapped a bottle of drinking water from the store.

While he deciphered her meaning she picked up another pair of jerry jugs and turned towards the ocean. "You do quality. I'm on quantity." When she reached the surf, she filled the jugs and splashed with David, her black hair sailing in the breeze.

Malcolm rearranged jugs to make a workspace, then unpacked his portable laboratory. He measured out some *survivorus* water, mixed it into the four jerry jugs of seawater and recorded the exact time. He'd finished long before Jessica returned, but he chose to watch and wait rather than make another trip. The world seemed perfect while David and Jessica played in the waves.

On her next trip back Jessica shared the master plan. "When all the jugs are filled and ready – maybe tomorrow." She gestured towards his watch and the record books. "We'll make our move."

She put in his hand an empty liter bottle with a stylish label. "*Kahn's Original Miracle Water*," it said. In smaller print it explained what the water did and how to use it, emphasizing the importance of not using every drop. "*Refill the bottle before it's empty, and soon the Miracle Water is as good as new.*"

"Tomorrow we'll buy more bottles and maybe a bigger truck. Those bottles are standard sizes, and the labels can be printed anywhere. I figure we start by charging a Globo a bottle, which is what people pay for regular water anyway. There's no extra price to try something new.

"It costs about ten cents to make each labeled bottle. Once we calculate how many fit in the van and how many we can sell in a day, we'll know our margins."

Malcolm shook his head in amazement. "That's my math."

"We spend our nights filling and labeling, and our days making sales." She picked up another pair of jugs. "We need to move fast. We need to sell enough water to hire a lawyer when they come after us."

"By then it's too late," Malcolm declared. "After the first day of sales, *survivorus* will be out. They'll never get it all back."

"That's the plan. But when they come after us, we need lawyers to keep us out of jail and publicists to make us look like heroes. Robin Hood broke the law but everybody liked him."

Soon Malcolm had measured bottles in an organized array, and created a chart for tracking results. Most of his single gallon of *survivorus* water was now mixed among small experimental containers and the four full jerry jugs. Meanwhile, Jessica ferried back new jugs of seawater that he lined up in the back. As the *survivorus* multiplied he would spread it through the seawater jugs until the whole load was fit to drink. Maybe later today, maybe tomorrow. Right now, there was nothing to do but wait.

Wait, and play in the waves. His leg hurt, but not enough to stop him.

* * * * *

Back at the Blue Moon Inn, they showered as if fresh water ran like the sea and dressed in clothing Jessica had packed for them all. Mansel fed them dinner, then showed them to a large room with two beds. He assumed that the double bed was for the adults and the single for David, and there was no need to set him straight. While Jessica told David to stop bouncing on the double bed, Malcolm set his bottles out on the floor. He planned to check them hourly – through the night, if necessary – to determine how much *survivorus* generated how much purity, and after how long.

David asked, "Can Malcolm read to me tonight instead?"

"Sure," Jessica replied.

"Happy to," Malcolm said.

Jessica passed Malcolm a book from the suitcase. "It's published by Publius, a component of Viacom."

"I don't get it."

"Beta Brothers are a Viacom production. You will."

As Jessica went downstairs, Malcolm found a comfortable spot to lie down on the double bed. David snuggled in beside him, sharing his pillow and pulling on the book. They fit neatly together under one blanket. "We'll take turns reading," David said. "I go first."

The book told the tale of European settlers coming to America. The opening page showed Chief Powhatan, resplendent in feathers, looking over a bay filled with sailing ships. "Yes," David read, "We can be friends. Welcome to my kingdom."

The next page, Malcolm's turn, showed Indian women explaining which berries to eat and Indian men showing where to hunt. The settlers ate with the Indians and shared hardships during storms. It was a friendly history, true enough, as far as Malcolm could tell. When the Beta Brothers appeared he learned what Jessica had in mind.

"The Beta Brothers?" Malcolm asked. "Did they live there too?"

"Mom says it's just a story. Keep reading."

The Beta Brothers helped the Indian men catch a giant elk, and turn its antlers into racks for their hats; they helped Indian women pound blackberries into Beta Bars. The last page included coupons for blackberry Beta Bars and an advertisement for antlered hat racks.

"Is this a school book?" Malcolm asked.

"You bet," David replied. "I read one every day."

Downstairs Mansel and Jessica were drinking tea. Malcolm indicated that David was finished, but Jessica's attention was on Mansel.

"This used to be a general store," he was saying. "But then the chain stores moved downtown. We couldn't compete. I don't know where they got their merchandise so cheap. They charged less for retail than we paid our wholesaler."

"Could you sell different things?" Jessica asked.

"We tried. We sold local cheese and fresh vegetables, and crafts made by people in the area. This table was made by Jimmy from the north side, and you've never seen anything so solid." He gave it a thump to prove the point.

"The chains couldn't match quality like this."

"No they couldn't, but you can't run a store on specialty items alone. We needed to sell regular food and housewares – crackers, soap and the like. People could get those things cheaper downtown, and it wasn't worth a trip out here for fresh cheese. They just bought packaged cheese at the chain stores. Once people got used to it, they couldn't hardly taste the difference.

"The kids were gone by then, so we rented out their rooms. We did okay for a while, but soon people stopped coming to the hotel too. People just drove downtown and asked for the Holiday Spa. It cost more, but it advertised on the highway and it had a fitness center. We couldn't do those things. Without guests at the hotel, the store lost the rest of its customers."

Mansel went on and on. His mind was keen and he was happy for the company. He explained that his wife had died some years ago and his old friends had scattered, looking for work. Profits that used to stay in town now left for the treasuries of corporations far away.

"They killed the town," Mansel spat. "They sucked the life out of us."

Jessica tried to soothe him, coaxing him back from despair.

"I'll try to sell the hotel before I die," Mansel said. "The kids don't want it. They hardly talk to me anymore. The hotel chains won't want it – it's too old and decrepit. There's no fitness center." He pronounced the words "fitness center" like they were a cancer. He was watching his life drain away.

An hour had passed since Malcolm last checked the *survivorus* water. He went to the van and found that the first loads from the afternoon were clean enough to drink. The pharmaceutical tester said so, and they passed the taste test too. Jessica joined him as he was unloading the van, pouring about a liter of *survivorus* mix into each jerry jug of straight seawater.

"The whole load will be drinkable by the middle of morning tomorrow," Malcolm said. "After breakfast."

"We'll buy liter bottles before breakfast, repackage, and hit the streets in the afternoon. When it's hot." She lifted and poured quickly, without spilling a drop.

As they finished the load, Jessica turned grave. "Do you think they know where we are?"

"They might not be paying attention yet. If anybody is, they know we've left. That might be all for now. You and I aren't personally connected to the system." He pointed to his thigh where the implant used to be. "We've been buying with cash. I think we're hard to find."

"Let's hope so."

"Let's hope so," he echoed. As they stepped back towards the hotel, their arms slipped naturally around each other's waists. They slowed the pace and leaned into each other as they walked, two warm bodies holding together in the evening chill until the stairway forced them apart. They took turns in the bathroom and climbed into their separate beds.

Malcolm awoke to the singing of birds and the first pink of dawn. David and Jessica were curled up together in the next bed, fast asleep. David's head was covered by blankets and tightly tucked, but his feet were hanging in the breeze.

Malcolm dressed and left a note, then walked quietly down the stairs, hoping he wouldn't awaken people when he started the van. A pair of small furry animals crossed his path as he drove out the driveway, then disappeared into the brush.

In town, the chain stores were all lined up in a row, familiar names with well worn slogans. He bought a hundred empty bottles from each of five different stores, paying from Jessica's horde of cash. At a print shop, he ordered five hundred and twenty labels – the extra for mistakes – to print while he waited.

Behind the counter, the television broadcast the popular news program, *You are the News,* hosted by the dashing Bob Holliday and the sleekly gorgeous Juanita Korematsu. As Malcolm watched, Bob laid a row of giftwrapped boxes out on the table.

"What have we here?" Juanita asked.

"It's Brother's new line of summertime toys," Bob explained. "How can you celebrate summertime without new toys?"

"Big Brother really is looking out for us."

Bob held up an odd-looking pair of goggles. "Here we have the Brother Super Tecno Nite Vizors. Based on technology developed in secret for the military, these goggles let you see anything day or night. Coming up next is the story of a five-year-old boy who used his Nite Vizors to stop a home intruder."

"He stopped an intruder! I can scarcely believe it!"

Malcolm was packing up and walking off as Bob shared his conclusion. "We couldn't say it if it wasn't true."

Chapter Twenty-Four

Malcolm returned too late to the Blue Moon Inn. The police car passed him in the opposite direction, lights flashing, as he approached the driveway. Even the siren had disappeared by the time he parked. At first he didn't make the connection but when he reached the building it kicked him in the face. The front door had been knocked off its hinges and lay flat across the entry foyer, covered by chips of paint and wood. The celestial mobile, torn from the ceiling, had been crushed underfoot. David clung to Mansel on the stairs.

"They hit her!" he cried. "They hit her and made her bleed." He curled himself into Mansel, burrowing inwards like he wanted to disappear. "She was bleeding."

Mansel nodded agreement. His eyes were bleak and his skin was pale. He looked like he'd seen something he didn't want to see.

David couldn't stop. "They kicked her. She was bleeding." His body went taut like a convulsion; he screamed as if it was still happening. "Make them stop! Make them stop! She's bleeding!"

Smears and footprints told more of the story. The window on the landing was broken, and a cold breeze cut down the stairs. Malcolm stepped gently up to David, and touched him on the shoulder. At first David winced and curled tighter into Mansel, then he recognized who it was. He pushed off Mansel and threw himself into Malcolm, squeezed him tight.

"Make them stop," he pleaded. "She's bleeding. Make them stop."

Malcolm could see that he was looking at one particular spot on the landing, a corner of the carpet saturated with red. A smear spread toward the door like someone had been dragged.

Malcolm carried David to a couch in the living room and just held him there, rocking and crying, rocking and crying. He tried to think. It was his father's story all over again. Jessica had probably been taken to the local police station, and she needed a lawyer. Only a stroke of fortune had Malcolm away when the squad arrived. He would need to move faster than he did with his father.

"I'm going to get your mother," he said. "Do you want to come with me, or stay here with Mansel."

"Come with you. And stay with Mansel. She's bleeding. Make them stop." It was okay that he didn't make sense.

Mansel stepped forward again. "Stay with me, David," he urged. "I need you to keep me company. Malcolm will go for your mother."

It took a while. They coaxed him gently and wrapped him in a blanket. Somehow Mansel produced a cup of hot chocolate and moved him into a chair. When Malcolm was clear to leave, he quietly asked Mansel not to clean their room, especially not the dishes on the floor. They were filled with *survivorus.*

Before he left he kissed David on the cheek. "Take good care of Mansel," he whispered. "I love you."

The officers were standing by the door when he turned to leave. Malcolm didn't know how long they'd been watching silently, or how much they'd seen, but he could tell they weren't regular police. Their uniforms were white and only one of them was armed. These were contractors for hire.

"Come nicely or come fighting," said the unarmed officer, stepping inside. He bent to a blood stain on the floor, smeared a dab with his finger and licked it clean. "Fighting won't help."

Malcolm looked back to the couch, where Mansel and David were curled up together, and David was watching everything. "Nicely," he said.

The officer escorted him to a sleek white sedan in the driveway, and opened the back door. "Empty your pockets."

Malcolm took out his wallet and the sizeable roll of cash left after the bottles. The officer examined the wallet, especially his identification, then put everything in a pouch around his waist.

"Can I have a receipt?"

"Don't worry about getting it back." He passed Malcolm a bottle of water and a pill. "Swallow this."

"What is it?"

"Tracer. You're not getting away on my watch."

Malcolm swallowed it.

The officer pointed to the open door. "Have a seat. Make yourself comfortable."

Malcolm sat alone in the rear of the sedan, the two officers in front beyond a plexiglass wall, monitoring him on video. As they pulled out of the driveway, Malcolm waved goodbye to the receding Blue Moon Inn. If David were watching from inside, he wanted everything to look okay.

* * * * *

Jessica sat by herself in a tiny cell. She didn't know how far she'd ridden or how long she'd been locked in the back of the cruiser, choking on blood and vomit. She felt the bumps in the road and heard muffled voices in the front seat; once when she lay stationary in a fetal lump, someone shined a flashlight in her eyes, then poked her with it. "She's still alive," the officer said.

They pulled her out of the car and forced her into a cell, dark and cold, with walls of concrete and a door of bars. One at a time she pressed every available item of clothing or linen against her nose to contain the bleeding. Eventually it stopped but the cell looked like a slaughterhouse. Her face was a dull, throbbing mask of pain. Her tongue probed a gap where a tooth had been.

Footsteps approached from down the corridor, and a man appeared in front of her cell. "So you're a lawyer," he said through the bars. "Interesting."

He was a small man in a dark suit. Jessica noticed how well it was tailored and wondered if he was important, or vain, or if everyone in his position dressed so well. But he was an ugly man with protruding eyebrows and a small, sharp nose. His face was fixed in a scowl, and his skin scarred by pox from an earlier age.

"I want an attorney," Jessica said.

"You are an attorney," the man replied. "Use yourself." He walked away, out of sight down the long corridor, his footsteps following him into silence. He had accomplished nothing on this visit, and Jessica wondered why he had come. Then the footsteps turned back.

When he reappeared in front of her cell, Jessica asked, "Why am I here? What have I done?"

"You know."

Yes, she thought to herself, *I suppose I do.* "I am entitled to a phone call."

"Yes, attorney, you are entitled to a phone call."

"I want it now."

"You are entitled to a phone call — " he stepped away, then back, "— in much the same way you are entitled to the air you breathe." He held up the bloody gag that nearly choked her when they silenced her screaming at the Blue Moon Inn. "Maybe we will grant you a phone call." Again he walked away down the hallway until even his footsteps disappeared. A door clanged open and shut.

Jessica was trapped. For the first time in her life she understood what it meant to be helpless. She had no control over any part of her life. She was trapped in an iron cage, covered with her own blood, at the mercy of a man with ethics quite different from her own.

And she didn't know anything. She didn't know what had happened to Malcolm, what had happened to her son. Had he been left behind, or been carried off himself? If so, to where? She couldn't find out. She understood that she was a target. But David was just a loose end in the bureaucracy of justice. Even worse than being a target, David was irrelevant.

She pulled as hard as she could on the bars of her cage, tugging back and forth with all her strength, and was denied even a rattle. She looked around for something to clang against the bars, but the cage was empty except for her own bloody linens.

She wrapped herself in a bloody fabric about the size of a towel, shivering because the blood, once warm, was now just wet. The cell was three paces wide and five paces deep – smaller than the closet in her apartment. She walked back and forth the length of her cage, counting the paces – five, ten, fifteen, twenty. She wondered how many lengths constituted a mile and tried to do the arithmetic, but she couldn't remember how many feet were in a mile. Malcolm would know; David might too. But that wouldn't help. Even her efforts at distraction led the wrong way.

After a while the ugly man came back. "Attorney!" he demanded. "To how many phone calls are you entitled?"

"At least one."

"One!" he snapped. "Exactly one. Before how long must you receive this phone call?"

She remembered the rule from law school, and recited it in the formal language of the academy. "I must be afforded a phone call within twelve hours of my arrest."

"Twelve hours," he declared smugly. "You will have your phone call within twelve hours of your arrest."

A lot could happen in twelve hours. She pushed in a different direction. "I'm thirsty," she said. "May I have some water? The constitution guarantees basic human necessities."

"Be patient. You're not even close to a constitutional level of thirst." Then with sudden enthusiasm he declared, "The constitution also affords you the right to know your charges. Would you like to know the charges you face?"

Jessica made no reply.

With obvious relish he continued. "The charges include but are not limited to exceeding authority, disobeying orders, obstructing justice and abuse of process. Would you like me to go on?"

"No, thank you. That won't be necessary."

"Other charges include but are not limited to treason, knowing assumption of unreasonable risk, and intellectual piracy. Would you like me to continue?"

"No, but I don't want to disappoint you."

The next list of offenses were petty in comparison. He accused her of making personal calls on the government vidlink, and of staying in a government building after hours on 145 separate occasions – a common practice among employees devotedly struggling to finish their work but, she now learned, a violation of government policy. As he listed the charges she noticed that none of them pertained to the burglary at Tentek. Maybe they hadn't discovered that yet – but she knew, of course, that the fruit of that burglary was at a hotel where she and Malcolm were the only guests.

She also realized with a shock that she was guilty. She had indeed disobeyed orders and accessed restricted data; she had certainly stayed late any number of times, and she didn't doubt that it could be proven from the office records of entry and exit. She was equally outraged by her own foolishness in breaking the rules as by the government's ability to search her personal life for technical violations of the criminal code, and to prosecute them.

When he finished reading the charges he pressed his face against the bars of Jessica's cell, his eyes alight with joy and expectation. "The minimum term you face is 35 years in prison. The maximum term is 315 years." His teeth were yellow and crooked.

"What about my son? What will happen to him?"

"You should have thought of him before you broke the law."

* * * * *

Malcolm's ride ended on a mountaintop, at a cedar-shingled lodge looking over the Pacific Crest. Snow-capped peaks lined the horizons, towering over pine trees and rock slides. The car pulled up against the edge, so close and so steep that Malcolm couldn't see the bottom. He moved to exit on the safe side, but that door stayed locked while the door on the edge sprung open.

Carefully, he stepped out onto a gravel driveway. A stone kicked here wouldn't stop for a thousand feet. He kept one hand on the car and watched his feet as he rounded the trunk, deliberately not looking over the edge, then took a deep breath of cold mountain air.

A kindly older woman came from the lodge carrying a blanket. She draped it over Malcolm's shoulders. "Don't want you catching cold," she said. "I'll make you some tea." The officers passed her the pouch of Malcolm's belongings. She took it and shooed them away. "Did they treat you well?"

"If I were hiring someone to make an arrest, they'd be at the top of my list."

"Heavens!" she replied. "You aren't under arrest. You're our guest."

"Then I'm free to leave?" The sedan drove away, leaving no other vehicles in the driveway.

"Come inside. It's cold out here. See the snow under that tree?"

She led him inside to a fireplace with soaring orange flames. Sparks flew and the logs cackled as he took a seat on the couch. "Tea or coffee?" his host asked. Malcolm seemed to be the only guest.

"Hot chocolate."

As soon as she left with the order, Malcolm headed for the door. He wrapped himself in the blanket and pushed it open. The doorman put a hand on his shoulder. "Not so fast."

His host reappeared. "Your hot chocolate is coming soon."

"I'll drink it while I walk."

"Not before you see him."

"Who?"

"Why, Hap Jackson, of course! He sent for you. He wants to see you on a matter of utmost urgency."

Hap Jackson?! Hap Jackson was behind all this, and he wanted to see Malcolm? He wouldn't have been more surprised if she had sprouted wings and soared to the sky. It involved the *survivorus*, of course, but surely Jackson had collected it already. What more could he want? "When will he be here?"

"Now that's a little problematic. Mr. Jackson is busy, you know. He planned to be here this evening but I understand he's running late. It can't be that long, though. He's scheduled for Tapei on Tuesday."

"So I should wait."

"So you get to wait. Enjoy!" She showed him to a concierge desk and left him in the hands of a capable young woman in a black strapless dress. She explained the resort's many attractions, ranging from hot tubs to ice climbing, in a tone suggesting that she, too, could be part of the package.

Malcolm thanked her but asked only to be shown his room. The hallway led across a catwalk so close to the windows it felt like a tightrope over a precipice. He held the banister and watched the mountains while he walked. "You're two miles over sea level," she said. "Those are glaciers."

His room contained a wardrobe for mountain climate and a bar stocked with drinks. It had a balcony of its own, looking over the tops of pine trees. Over the edge Malcolm could see the bottom of the valley, a stream of white water and rocks. As his guide turned to leave, he asked, "Can I have my wallet back?"

"You won't need it," she replied. "Dinner starts at six."

Over dinner of fresh trout and grilled leeks, Malcolm made a list. He found a paper cocktail napkin and borrowed a pen from the waiter to prepare for his interview. On the left of the napkin he wrote "HJ" and underlined it – a column for things Hap Jackson might possibly want from him, reasons why he might have arranged this meeting. To the right he wrote "Me," and underlined it crisply. What might he want from Hap Jackson?

He smiled as he wrote the first entry under himself: "The world." He was talking to someone who could deliver it, why not ask? Then he wiped the smile off his face and wrote "Jessica." That was what he really wanted. He wanted her out of jail. He wanted her safe, and he wanted it right away. No telling what was happening in the local jail while he dined out.

Under Jessica's name he wrote "David." Probably he came with her, but if Malcolm couldn't succeed on her behalf he didn't want David off the list. After a while he wrote "Bobeck." He seemed to be underground somewhere. Malcolm didn't want to incriminate him or lead the dogs in his direction, but Bobeck was someone else with a stake, and someone else he owed a favor. Garcia he didn't list. That was too dangerous.

Next he wrote "Promise to go public." Malcolm didn't care who sold the *survivorus*, so long as somebody did. If Tentek wanted to retain the rights and earn the fortune itself, that was fine by Malcolm. He just wanted *survivorus* in jerry jugs all around the world.

He waved off the waiter carrying wine and turned his attention to the other column. What could Hap Jackson possibly want from him? He expected this to be tricky but quickly he recognized the risk he posed to Hap Jackson and the Tentek Corporation. A few days of work and a few Globos of his own money threatened to derail Tentek's entire *Many Drops* investment – indeed, it nearly had. Directly underneath HJ he wrote *Survivorus.* Jackson wanted it back. Surely he already had the *survivorus* from the van and even the loose bottles in Malcolm's room at the Blue Moon Inn, but Jackson didn't know if that was all. Malcolm might have hidden more or distributed it already. Next he wrote "Information."

Again Malcolm declined wine, white or red, but he accepted more of the delicious trout. Many things he wished were different, but he couldn't complain about the food. Last on the list he wrote "Silence." Even without a sample Malcolm was dangerous. He could suggest organic research to competitors or embarrass Tentek with news of the treasure it was keeping off the market.

That was enough. Malcolm understood now why Jackson had arranged this indulgence. Malcolm felt like he had the advantage, and he looked forward to the interview. He didn't just want Jessica out of jail; he wanted her in charge of Tentek's new desalination division.

Early the next morning he went out for a walk. He grabbed a parka from his closet and a bottle of water from a rack by the lobby door. A young man stepped out behind him. "I'll be your guide," he said.

"I'm okay. I won't get lost."

"The trails can be dangerous."

"I'll be okay."

"Famous last words."

Malcolm couldn't get rid of him so he put him to work. "Which way to a short walk before breakfast?" The guide led him to a trail off the driveway, where an arrow pointed to the *Two Mile Highland Loop*. That sounded perfect.

The trail was chiseled into the mountainside, gray stones and reddish dirt. Not wide enough for two abreast, Malcolm's guide walked behind as they skidded down from the mountaintop lodge to the valley below. A wooden bridge crossed a narrow stream, probably the same one he saw from his balcony. He paused on the bridge to look up for the lodge.

Vultures turned circles over the building, their broad wings black against the sky, wingtips jagged like hands open to slap. The vultures made no sound. Unlike the greedy seagulls, they just turned silent circles in anticipation of a dying animal or bloody feast. Malcolm watched as if something might happen, then turned away in disgust.

From the stream the trail went up, zigzagging in switchbacks as it climbed the adjacent peak. Malcolm started to huff in the altitude and struggle in the rocky terrain. Once he lost his footing and skidded onto a knee, dislodging stones that careened down the slope. "Are you okay?" his guide inquired.

"Fine, thanks." He rested when they reached a bench, and drained half his water bottle. Tiny orange flowers grew in patches between the rocks.

The guide asked, "Do you see the ropes course?"

Now that his attention was called to it, Malcolm saw that ropes were set up for anyone who wanted to climb the granite cliff, and zipwires for them to glide back down. One zipwire led from a platform beside the bench to an outcropping far below. "Want to zip?" his guide asked.

"No thanks." Malcolm started walking, still uphill, higher and higher.

The next peak stood taller than the lodge. From the top, they looked backwards to the lodge or ahead to miles of jagged backcountry. They were higher than some clouds and higher than a hawk riding a current the length of the valley. One mountain in the distance stood taller than the rest, a pinnacle of glaciers gleaming blue and white in the morning sun. Malcolm leaned on a boulder by the edge while he caught his breath and finished his drinking water.

As if the summit weren't high enough, a wooden tower had been built on the top. The door was open, and a staircase led to a viewing platform. Malcolm climbed the stairs up to the strong breeze and limitless view of the observation deck, a square of wooden planks and folding chairs. Banisters bordered the square, and Malcolm tested them before he leaned. On the far side, a gap opened to a gangplank that reached over the valley like a diving board to oblivion. He kept one hand on the banister as he walked to the opening, then overcame millennia of instincts telling him not to step over the edge.

The plank was as broad as his shoulders, easy to balance on, flexible and strong. It rebounded under his cautious steps, creating an unstable feeling of lift. When he reached the end, breathless and thrilled, he looked out over a universe of white snow, blue sky and granite cliffs. Overhead were traces of cloud and a brilliant sun; below lay a chasm of scrub and rock; just looking over made him feel like he was falling, plummeting with scree a thousand feet to the bottom. When he couldn't stand it anymore he turned and walked back down the plank.

His guide was gone. Hap Jackson stood at the opening in the rail. He was smiling.

Chapter Twenty-Five

Jackson held up his hand for Malcolm to stop, and he did. In the middle of the plank in the middle of the sky. A fresh breeze pressed him sideways towards the edge; he leaned against it with little effort, but nearly went over the other side when the breeze died down.

"Stay where you are," Jackson said. He was a handsome man, with classic good looks from the movies. In person he looked older than he did on stage, but he also looked more human, more profound. His eyes were intelligent and intense; even without banners or an honor guard he was formidable. He stood as strong as a mountain, as cold as a glacier.

In his hand he held a rope tied to a latch in the rail. "See this trigger?" He displayed it like a fashion model. "Your gangplank is connected by pegs at my end. This trigger pulls them out."

Malcolm hadn't noticed the mechanism earlier, but he could see how it would work. On the rocks below, he noticed a skeleton, maybe a goat, picked clean by rodents and wind. "You wouldn't dare."

Jackson laughed. It was an honest chuckle, not cruel, as if a puppy had tipped over a laundry basket. "I've done harder things."

"You can't pull the trigger." Malcolm mobilized the list he'd made in advance. "You need me."

"Whatever for?"

"For the *survivorus*."

"I already have the *survivorus*. I have most of my own barrel, safe in Central Storage, and your van too. You didn't hide it very well."

"I've spread it around. You don't know where." Item two on his list was information.

Jackson grew steely. "Don't lie to me," he said. "You haven't spread it very far. Your van, your hotel, your apartment. That's all. Any *survivorus* I don't have, I'll locate soon." He looked down the length of the plank.

Last on Malcolm's list was secrecy. He'd been planning to trade for silence, but Jackson had in his hand a better way to guarantee that Malcolm would never talk. The vultures were just a few flaps away. His body would be identified by dental records twenty years from now, if anyone were still curious. With no more words, his list came to an end.

Jackson pulled up a folding wooden chair and sat down, still holding the trigger rope in one hand.

"What are you waiting for," Malcolm asked.

"For you to apologize."

"You're kidding."

"I'm not."

"Fine. I'm sorry. Can I go now?" Malcolm took a step down the plank.

"No. Not yet. You didn't mean it."

Jackson sounded ridiculous. Surely, that wasn't part of his master plan.

The Chief Executive of Tentek Corporation stretched his legs out before him like he had all the time in the world. "What do you call a police chief who stops all the crime in his district?" He spoke like a teacher to a slow-witted a schoolboy.

Malcolm didn't answer. He didn't see what Jackson was getting at.

"Unemployed." Jackson answered his own question. "What do you call a man who invents a pen that never runs out of ink?"

"What?" He could at least play the game.

"Bankrupt," Jackson said. "Not right away, of course. First he will supply everyone with a wonderful new pen. But only one. Far wiser is the man who invents a disposable."

Malcolm saw the point. "The *survivorus* reproduces itself," he said. "People only need to buy one bottle. Then they're on their own."

"Exactly."

"We knew that. It was fine by us. Our goal is *survivorus* everywhere, not a piece of every sale. *Survivorus* is a transformative commodity. One sale is enough for us. All we want is to set it free."

"That's what *you* want," he said. "But look at it from poor Tentek's point of view. We're happy the way things are. Why would we want a 'transformative' change?" He used Malcolm's own word against him. "What would happen to our farms if people grew their own food? What would happen to our grocery stores? Our restaurant services? Tentek wants *consumers,* not self-sufficiency."

Malcolm was silent. He was actually listening.

Jackson drove the argument home. "The water isn't the big sale anyway. Not *survivorus*, not *Many Drops* either. That's not where the profit is. Our goal is to sell the power lines and electrical generators feeding *Many Drops*. We want to lay the new plumbing that brings seawater to every home, a new line in addition to the freshwater plumbing that already exists. Those costs would be covered by government agencies, not individual consumers, and the government is far less sensitive to the cost. Which elected official would deny consumers access to home-based desalination? *Many Drops* creates entire new universes of demand, and the means to fulfill them.

"You can forget about the *survivorus*. Tentek won't make it. Federated won't sell it."

Comprehension raced across Malcolm's mind. His father was an inventory specialist. Sayeh Kahn had given him the water, and he immediately recognized the potential. He must have gone to his supervisors – like Malcolm went to Kira – but the threat was closer and Tentek's response was more urgent. His father hadn't lasted a week.

Jackson relaxed while Malcolm thought, stretching out his legs and watching the vultures that had shifted in their direction. He was relaxed but methodical, entirely in control.

After a moment he looked expectantly back at Malcolm, as if he were waiting for a question that never came. When Malcolm continued to disappoint him, he asked it himself: "Why do I tell you this? Why do I reveal our deepest strategies?"

He paused to see if Malcolm would reply. All he got was the flicker that he understood the question, so he went on. "Because once you understand our position, you will come to agree. Your resistance will diminish, not increase. You'll see that I am not cruel nor Tentek gluttonous. We're merely sensible. You can hope to convince me but can't change the nature of the marketplace. You can't win. You might even realize that you broke our rules and stole our property." He twisted the rope and his tone turned bitter. "I trusted you. Say you're sorry."

Malcolm sat down on the plank, one leg on either side. He wasn't going anywhere and he didn't need a stray breeze pushing him over the edge. His pants were torn where he'd stumbled earlier; dried blood stood out on his knee and the breeze chilled the bare skin, but he wasn't finished. "The cat is out of the bag," he said. "Last week it was Sayeh Kahn. This week it's me. Samples are still loose in Kaiserville and I haven't been careful with my own. *Jakoba survivorus* is out now, and it's not coming back. You don't need an apology. You need a strategy."

Now it was Jackson's turn for silence. Malcolm pressed his advantage, feeling new confidence with every word. "I can help. I understand *survivorus* better than anyone. I'll help you distribute the *survivorus.* I'll share our ideas to maximize profits and minimize future harm. Jessica will help. Let me off this plank.

"Do it before it's too late. Someone else will sell their *survivorus* sample. Amjat's neighbors will ask about the toxic spring. A reporter will figure it out, and the headlines will be humiliating. *Tentek Corporation Conceals Life-Saving Water.* You don't need that. I can help."

Jackson laughed again, but the joke was growing tired. "I'm afraid there's not much *survivorus* on the loose, and it's shrinking every day. There's a reward, you know." He tugged the rope until it was taut against the peg. "By the way, what newspaper will run that headline? A newspaper that we own, or one owned by Brother? Sure, we let a few small outlets run independently but they won't publish a story we want to suppress. They need our advertising revenue to stay afloat. No, I fear the *survivorus* story will die very soon." He looked over the edge.

"Or perhaps you would like to come off the gangplank. I can show police a video of you breaking into our storage facility and stealing our property. I might even show them the bottles intended for resale. The state builds buildings for people like you. They're called prisons. You'll never see the light of day." His voice was pure poison. "Is that what you want?"

"No."

In one hand Jackson held the rope; in his other, photos suddenly appeared, prints large enough for Malcolm to see clearly from his place on the plank. First, Jackson held up a photo of Jessica, a mug shot like she was being processed into the justice system. A tooth was missing; her nose was blackened and crooked. Her eyes were dim and her hair matted with blood.

Malcolm wanted to run down the board for a closer look but he was stuck where he was. He could no more approach the photos than swim the Pacific. Jackson moved Jessica's photo to the bottom of the stack and held up the next one. Bobeck. His hair had been shaved and dark circles lay under his eyes. Malcolm couldn't tell where he was, but this wasn't his first day in custody.

Before Malcolm could react, Jackson pulled out more – David, cowering behind the couch in the Blue Moon Inn; Mansel being loaded into the back of a squad car; the Inn engulfed in flames. Malcolm wanted to grab the photos from his hands, hug the photo of David and beg forgiveness. But he couldn't. He sat on the plank over the chasm, his soul as empty as the space beneath him.

The last photo was Amjat Jinn. He was reclining on a chair in a balcony Malcolm recognized from a lifetime ago. "He did it right," Jackson said. "You could learn from Mr. Jinn."

"How's David? Was he out before the fire?"

"Say you're sorry."

But Malcolm wasn't sorry. He had tried to help people, tried to apply his privilege and skill to something more meaningful than the Autochef. He was only sorry it had turned out this way. A few hours faster might have made the difference.

Jackson knew exactly what he was thinking. "Heroes have statues built in their honor. But they don't live to see them."

"I'm not doing it for the statue."

"Do it for yourself. Say you're sorry."

"No."

"Your friends are finished anyway."

Malcolm's heart cried out for Jessica. He couldn't help her. He couldn't help any of them. He wanted to see the picture of David. Was he hurt?

"What will you gain by this sacrifice?"

Malcolm leaned forward against the plank, touched his head to the board, pressed hard against the grain.

"Will Tentek release the *survivorus* as a tribute to your honor?"

Malcolm said nothing.

"Will it?"

Malcolm sat up and whispered. "No."

Jackson rose from his chair. "Will your sacrifice bring water to one person on this Earth?"

The answer was slow in coming. "No."

"Will it save your partner?"

"No."

"Will it help her son?"

"No."

The breeze rose again, strong enough that even clinging to the plank Malcolm felt the push towards the edge. Far below, a dried shrub tumbled down the hill.

"Perhaps your sacrifice will inspire others to take up the cause themselves. Perhaps others will hear of your honor and cry, "There is a man we must follow! Where does he lead?"

Malcolm rocked back and forth on the plank, felt it bounce back against him. The chant *Hap Jack! Hap Jack!* was ringing in his ears.

"Will people say that?" Jackson thundered. "Will they?"

"No." Malcolm had no choice.

"Why not?" Jackson's voice was a hammer.

"Because nobody will ever know."

"If I pulled the trigger, would anyone come here looking for you?

"No."

"Your friends?"

"No."

"Your family?"

"No."

"If you told people what you had done, would they believe you?"

"No."

Jackson leaned forward like a vulture over a kill. "Why not?"

"Because I'm nobody."

"Who?" Jackson was strident.

"Nobody."

"And what else?"

"Nothing."

Then Jackson changed his tone. "On the other hand," he said, "I appreciate people with intelligence and initiative. If you demonstrate the right kind of initiative you might be rewarded." His voice became soothing, conciliatory, a balm over fresh wounds.

Was it possible that Malcolm was *relieved* to be offered a bribe? He couldn't deny the joy of discovering that Jackson carried a carrot as well as a stick. Jackson spoke of an administrative position in the Tentek headquarters, a position with higher pay and less responsibility. "All you have to do is say you're sorry." Jackson sounded kind, beneficent; he had Malcolm's interests in mind. "Your friends are gone. Save yourself."

Malcolm stood up and turned his back on Hap Jackson. He walked to the end of the board and away from the safety of the observation deck, watching the clouds in the sky and the cliffs in the distance. He bounced on the end of the plank, feeling the spring, like a high diver considering his move, imagining the lift as he vaulted off the end, the spring as he soared into space.

Jackson was right. He was right about everything. He was right that Malcolm couldn't bring the *survivorus* to light. Right that he had stolen it. Right that all he could achieve was his own destruction and the last hope for his friends. The other choice was death or prison, and even that choice wasn't his own. Jackson could make it for him. Malcolm walked back down the plank, looking only at his feet, stopping one step away from the rail.

He straightened his head and looked Jackson in the eye. "I'm sorry," he said. He meant it from the bottom of his heart. "I'm sorry I stole your *survivorus.* I'm sorry I broke the rules. I'm sorry I caused you inconvenience." He saw the picture of David in the corner, and his eyes filled with tears. "I was wrong. Can you forgive me?"

Jackson smiled like hyena over a baby hen. "All is forgiven," he said. "It is my pleasure to forgive."

"I won't do it again."

"I know you won't." Jackson pulled out his lifelink and instructed Malcolm to arrange details with his secretary the following day. Malcolm would make a complete break with his part of the Tentek Corporation. His former co-workers would never see him again, and he would be assigned fresh to another division.

"Now raise your right hand," Jackson said. He lifted his own hand, and placed his other hand over his heart. Together, they recited the familiar words.

"*I pledge allegiance to the Tentek Corporation of America. I will serve loyally and work hard for our great goals: a safer, more productive, more prosperous world for all.*" The breeze carried their pledge to the horizons.

"Serve loyally," Jackson said. This time it wasn't part of the pledge; this time it was an order.

"I promise," Malcolm said. He felt like an insect.

"Welcome to Tentek Corporation. We're glad to have you back." Jackson didn't reach out to shake his hand or move to let him step onto the deck. With a final smile and knowing glance, he folded the photographs and vanished. He'd been a hologram. Even the rope and the trigger joint disappeared.

* * * * *

One month later, on his daily sweep of Tentek's regional headquarters, Garcia Mendez walked past the office where he used to say good morning to Malcolm Moore. The new occupant was surly and unpleasant; he disdained people who watched sports, preferring the movies. He brushed off Garcia's first attempts at conversation; eventually Garcia stopped trying.

Garcia never learned what had happened to Malcolm. He never heard why he was fired. He never learned what he used the VIP retina for, or whether it worked. Malcolm simply disappeared without a trace. The next day the custodial staff had packed his things and carted them off, then the technical staff reprogrammed his computer for a new user. Malcolm never even stopped in to say goodbye. A few days ago the department had held its monthly staff meeting, and as usual, the non-professional staff wasn't invited. In the old days, Malcolm visited after the meetings to explain what had happened, but with Malcolm gone there was no way to know.

Garcia started to wonder if he could find him. It would be great to see him, and interesting to learn how it all turned out. Surely, Malcolm could be located wherever he was. Tentek might even have a forwarding address. Maybe he could look it up, or find someone to ask ....

As he considered his options he walked past a television set where people were watching a baseball game. Bases were loaded in the bottom of the twelfth, and the fans were on their feet. The pitcher hurled a fastball and the batter whacked it deep to left field.

He got distracted and didn't finish his thought.

THE END